TO DREAM OF DREAMERS LOST

D1564465

DAVID NIALL WILSON

PART ONE

ONE

"You disappoint me, Antonio," Montrovant said, placing his empty brandy snifter on the polished wood of his desk. He sat back and steepled his fingers. Peering over the small temple he'd made of his hands, he added, "truly."

Bishop Antonio Santorini's face approached the hue of a ripe beet, and his huge frame shook with rage, but he kept his silence. He might hate the man who sat across from him more with every beat of his heart, but he feared him equally. Antonio wanted to reach a ripe old age and retire to a monastery...a pleasant dream. Montrovant didn't care about Antonio's dreams; Montrovant dealt in nightmares.

"I speak for the Church in this," Santorini grated

finally. "The bargain was not met—the alliance has been broken. Surely you can see our position."

"Has it now?" Montrovant's eyes gleamed wickedly. "I hope that you and I still consider ourselves allies, Antonio, truly I do."

"Of course," Santorini cut in quickly. "That is why I am here. You and I must forge a new alliance, and quickly. It is clearly the Order which has broken the trust. We must find a way to return what they have taken before Rome grows impatient with us both."

Montrovant laughed mirthlessly, reaching for the decanter on his desk and refilling both of their glasses. "You think I give a *damn* about Rome, Antonio? I do not. Your Church, and your Pope, can rot and fall to dust tomorrow and it is the same to me. You have known this from the start. Our alliance has nothing at all to do with faith. Those of my brotherhood may share your belief, but be certain of this, I believe only in the darkness, and in myself."

"There will come a time when you will regret that," Santorini replied, his voice little more than a whisper. "For all who walk the Earth, there is a judgment."

"When, and if, I am judged, my friend," Montrovant chuckled, "you will not exist, even in memory. Now, we have business to attend to, and I suggest that we get started. I have kept my end of the agreement. I have brought you proof. The vault is empty, as I suspect it has been all along, and the Order has vanished. I have provided a witness."

Montrovant's gaze slipped to the side, coming to rest on a sealed chest of the same dark polished mahogany as his desk. He stood, his tall, lean frame dramatic in a long, sweeping cloak and coal-black suit. The cross of the Templars was embroidered into the material, catching the light and glittering hypnotically. The Templars had been disbanded, officially, but Montrovant did not fear the wrath of kings, or God. He might have been a shadow, but somehow he made the simple act of standing seem elegant and fascinating. Santorini shook his head, trying to clear his momentary lapse of concentration, but all he achieved was to increase the pounding pressure of his headache.

Montrovant made his way across to the chest and stood with his hands pressed gently onto its surface. It was large, the length of a grown man and easily twice the width. The bishop could not remove the image of an elaborate sarcophagus from his mind.

The chest was bound in straps of polished metal, ornate but functional. No brass or copper here, but strong steel, and carefully worked. The sides of the case appeared seamless, but the bishop knew it had been opened at least once.

"Put your ear to the surface, my friend," Montrovant leered, his eyes flashing even more brightly. "You may hear something interesting."

Santorini's throat went dry, and he didn't attempt to reply. He kept his distance from the case. He also kept his distance from Montrovant. In all the years he'd been Rome's liaison with Montrovant's sect, he'd never felt such menace as he did in that instant. It passed quickly, but the memory lingered, cold and vast, and empty.

"Shall I let him out, Excellency?" Montrovant whispered, the sound carrying with unbelievable clarity though his lips barely moved. "Shall I introduce the two of you? A little first-hand experience? Perhaps you would like to chastise him for his failure, for the failure of the Order? He was not one of them, but he served them. No? A shame. It might prove an interesting diversion."

The man moved closer, holding Santorini's gaze with his own, a viper mesmerizing its victim before the strike. "You don't know, Antonio, how I thrive on diversion. I'm afraid I don't get out like I used to."

Suddenly control of his body returned, and the bishop backed away a step, gasping. Montrovant was laughing again, and the man's nearness was at last more than Santorini could handle.

"I will trust you in this," the bishop said quickly, nearly tripping over himself as he backed toward the door. "The Church has authorized me to bargain with you, and I will consider that bargain sealed. Find the relic, and return it to the Church, and we will provide whatever recompense you ask."

"I doubt that, Antonio, truly I do," Montrovant

said, still laughing harshly. "I doubt you could even comprehend my needs. Perhaps one day an opportunity for—sharing—will arise."

Santorini shuddered. Turning quickly, but keeping his gaze locked on Montrovant's tall, dark figure, he bolted for the door. He felt, somehow, that the danger of running into a wall or tripping from lack of attention would be a small matter compared to turning one's back on Montrovant. Some mistakes are eternal.

※

Montrovant stood watching as the portly, bumbling idiot of a bishop made his way out the door. Perhaps it had been indiscreet to push so hard, but the man was contemptible, and Montrovant was not one to withhold his contempt. He turned his attention slowly back to the case on the floor, his smile deepening and darkening at once. He rapped on the wood once, sharply, then returned to his desk to wait. The others would be arriving shortly, and he had his thoughts to collect. It was going to be an interesting night, and that alone made it all worthwhile.

※

Inside the case, the hunger ate at Abraham like acid, forcing its way through dry, empty veins and shriveling his will. How long since he'd felt fresh air on his skin? How long since he'd *moved*? Days? Weeks? What remained of his mind told him days, but the hunger screamed of eternity.

DAVID NIALL WILSON

He fumbled weakly with the wire that bound him, but it was futile. His full strength had been unable to free him; now the effort was nothing more than a focus for his mind, the only diversion left to him. Soon, he knew, he'd begin to try to gnaw at the wood of his prison, fighting toward the blood mindlessly.

He heard Montrovant knocking on the wood, sensed the other's presence, but there was nothing he could do. He called out, clawing at his captor's mind with talons formed of hatred and desperation, but there was no answering thought, nothing but an echoing laughter that reverberated through his mind.

He concentrated on the events leading to his capture, scanned the memories as if they were the faded pages of a book, or a holy scroll, searching for an answer that could free him. He had retreated through those memories so many times since his capture that they had blurred to a surreal haze, but he had no recourse. He was trapped as surely by those events as he had been by Montrovant's treachery.

The others had been long gone by the time Montrovant arrived. The Order had vanished into the dust of the road and the mist over the mountains. It was not only the Grail that had been taken. Abraham's promise had dissolved as well, the price of the service he'd offered and consummated. Now it had become the price of his imprisonment. The Order had gone, and his hunger remained.

Montrovant had slipped undetected into the mountain the very night of Abraham's betrayal. When the sun dipped and Abraham awakened to the darkness, he'd known instantly that something was different. The mountain and its labyrinth of passageways and vaults were usually filled with the scent of the brotherhood—the wonder of their blood, the magic of their auras, so full that Abraham would be dizzied by the sudden onslaught of it. This night he'd awakened to a void. They were gone, and the promise of sharing that wondrous blood, and the promise of the Grail, had been gone as well.

He'd made his way to the vault—knowing in his heart what he would find, but unwilling to sacrifice the last moment of hope remaining to him. The door to the vault had stood open, the cavern within had loomed, empty and barren. The Grail was gone. He'd never even seen it. None but those of the Order had seen it, in fact. Only legend had placed it in that vault. Still, there was an emptiness about the vault that spoke of loss beyond price. It was impossible to doubt that it had lain there, so close, and yet so completely out of his reach.

Then Montrovant had fallen on him, and he remembered little else. His captor was old, perhaps as old as those in the Order, and certainly more powerful than Abraham himself. His captivity was proof enough of that. He'd been taken like a child, bound and imprisoned without even the opportunity to fight for his freedom.

Now that freedom seemed an unlikely future. His best hope rested in swift destruction and in true death, with the judgment to follow. Montrovant was known for many things, legendary in his cruelty, but mercy had never been a trait ascribed to him. That the man would break Abraham's mind and spirit to get what he wanted was never in doubt.

All Abraham could do was wait. He had not partaken of the blood of the Order, and that might be the thing to save him. He would be far too valuable, had he done so, but the fact that they had betrayed him, leaving him behind to take the blame for their own breaking of faith with both the Montrovant and the Church, might see him through this. Even as his mind clutched at this flimsy hope, his heart rejected it with a sneer. His last memory would be hunger.

⁂

The first of the others began to arrive within an hour of Santorini's departure. Montrovant was ready for them, having forsaken his dark cloak and embroidered tunic for floor-length robes of velvet. He still wore the cross of the temple on his breast, but the ceremonial garb gave him the aspect of a priest, or royalty. The finery did not overpower him, but complemented the strength of his features, the beauty of his form and the strength of his presence. He might have been a prophet.

The others, while none had Montrovant's presence or dark energy, were an impressive lot. There was du Puy, long mustaches trailing down his cheeks, nearly resting on his shoulders, and hair to match—his eyes ice blue and ancient. There was Jeanne Le Duc, rebel son of a Duke who couldn't bear the thought of being cooped up with a castle and a crown, eyes dark with a hunger of his own. Though traveling on his own now, there was a bond between Le Duc and Montrovant that the rest would never understand.

They were all men with no solid roots, men with secrets and concerns of their own, but a heart that beat with a single rhythm. The Knights Templar had been a service to which few heard the true calling, but for which men would die. While the Templars had been disbanded, their spirit lived in this group. Montrovant's smile broadened as they trickled in.

Montrovant was the worst and best of the lot. None of the others knew a fraction of what there was to know about Montrovant, though Le Duc came close. They did not wish to know. It was enough that his leadership was strong and his will like iron. It was enough that he held the Church and Rome at bay on one side and the people on the other by the force of his presence. It was enough that he led, and they followed, and that the road was paved with blood and adventure. It was no matter, or concern, that he was a thing already dead. It was not spoken of. It was not acknowledged. It was a fact known to all. He was God's gift to them, and he was their strength.

As they came, they stopped beside the large wooden case within which Abraham clawed and shriveled. Each gazed on the casket-shaped prison with a mixture of reverence and awe. None showed fear. If they had feared such a thing as that case held, they would not have followed Montrovant. They treated their prisoner as a holy relic, with caution, and with concentration.

When the majority were in place, Montrovant rose, raising his hands for silence, and began to speak.

"We are faced with a dilemma, and a quest. Our present bargain with the Holy Father appears to be forfeit, though they will never act upon this. The caverns are barren, the Order has flown. We are left to sift through what remains and salvage what we can.

"This," he gestured at the case before him, "represents the only knowledge we may claim. This is the sole witness to the treachery of the Order. I bring him before you as witness and as a sign of the dedication we must all swear to the coming trials of our spirits."

Montrovant swept the room with his gaze, lighting for a quick moment on each man present, waiting for reactions to his words. There was little movement, but the light dancing in every eye was all the answer he needed. They would follow him to the very gates of Hell. If he told them that the hierarchy of the Templars had fallen to corruption, and it was their duty to purge it, they would follow him in that, as well. He and they were a single unit, a weapon of righteous vengeance. They lacked nothing, he lacked only faith. The irony was not lost on him.

They believed because he gave them strength. He believed in nothing but himself, and yet he fed off them in turn.

"We must follow. I don't know how, or where, but we must prepare ourselves for a journey that may end in nothing but death and suffering. We have a duty to the Church, a bond sealed in the blood of our brothers and the faith of our fathers. We have sworn to protect the Grail, and all other holy relics. The Grail has disappeared."

He didn't mention that he had never believed the damnable cup to be in those vaults. He didn't mention that the search for the Order of the Bitter Ash was as ancient as that Order itself, and that none before them had succeeded. He didn't mention that, when they completed their journey, it was not the Grail he sought, but the blood of those who held it. Montrovant had spent lifetimes seeking the Grail, and he had learned a great many truths along the way, as well as the reality behind quite a number of lies.

Du Puy stood, glancing around the room. He turned back regally to face Montrovant, eyes blazing.

"We will find this Order. Our arms are long. The eyes and ears of our keeps are without limits in the known world. No such group, with such a treasure to guard, could remain hidden for long."

Montrovant nodded.

"There is more," he said at last. "We must question this one, and then we must punish him. He is not of the Order, but he has served it. While it is for God to judge, it is for God's hands to punish, and though the Poor Knights of the Temple of Solomon walk in the shadows now, still we are those hands."

All heads nodded. Everybody leaned closer, every eye was locked on Montrovant's hands. He reached for the steel band that bound the center of the wooden case. He did not have a hammer, or a crowbar. He had no tool whatsoever, and yet none in the room doubted that the steel would give way. None was present who had not born witness to their leader's strength. The knights believed Montrovant possessed a faith beyond their ken, God's power manifest. At least, that is what they whispered to their hearts when the questions arose. Angel or demon, they followed him to death and beyond.

The first of the steel bands snapped easily, leaving only two circling the ends of the case. There was a sudden banging from within, a hysterical, scrabbling sound. Montrovant ignored it. He went first to one end of the case, then to the other, snapping the restraints as if they were paper.

"Behold our enemy," he hissed. He grasped the edge of the case, stepping back, and the lid came away in a sudden motion, revealing the man—creature—that lay inside.

Abraham shivered convulsively, wracked with hunger. He fought to surge toward those who gaped at him, fought to make his way to the blood that pounded through their veins, but his struggles were vain and pointless. The steel cords still bound him, and now Montrovant stepped forward to take those cords in his powerful hands, lifting Abraham as if he were a child.

Staring into his captive's wild, manic eyes, Montrovant's smile slipped to a sneer of contempt.

"You have made two grave mistakes, friend Abraham. You chose to serve the wrong masters, and you allowed me to catch you at it. Do you have anything to tell me, or shall I put you back in your little box—forever?"

Abraham twisted and squirmed, sobbing with his need, and with the shame of his captivity.

"I...I know nothing. They...left me behind. They...promised, but..."

Montrovant, his sneer becoming a snarl, shook the rope savagely. The cords bit into Abraham's weakened flesh, and he cried out in agony.

"I don't give a *damn* about their promises. I want to know where they've *gone*."

"I don't know," Abraham choked out. "I don't know. The night fell, and they were gone. I found the vault open and empty, just as it was when you took me. I don't know any more than you...please believe me. Please..."

Abraham swiveled his head, and his gaze locked onto du Puy's, the nearest source of warmth and blood. He began to gibber meaninglessly, his eyes rolling in on themselves, his lips drawing back to reveal the fangs beneath. Even though Montrovant held him as easily as before, this transformation from coherent man to slavering beast set du Puy back a pace. The tall knight muttered an oath under his breath.

Montrovant threw back his head and laughed uproariously.

"He will not harm you, my friend. He will harm none of God's children from this moment forth. Of that you may be certain. He may not be able to provide me with the information I require, but he can provide *entertainment*, and you have no idea how valuable that gift can be to one such as I."

Jeanne Le Duc stepped forward with a chilly smile, ignoring Abraham's writhing, twisting form. "My lord, we must act. This...child...he knows nothing. We must take the trail before the scent has vanished to the shadows."

"And so we shall," Montrovant replied, tossing Abraham contemptuously into the wooden case and turning from him without even deigning to glance downward. "We will leave at dawn. You must set your affairs in order and be ready to ride, all of you.

"Our honor, and our position with Mother Church are at stake. The Order must be rooted out, the treasures returned to the Church where we can guard them properly, and this failure put to rest."

There was no sound for a long moment when Montrovant had finished speaking, but every eye gleamed in anticipation. There was none among them comfortable within a castle's walls for long, and this promised to be a long and treacherous adventure indeed.

"Go," Montrovant said finally, dismissing them. "I will take care of this one, and I will meet you at the temple gates before dawn. Ride, and may God be by your side."

"And also at yours," they intoned as one, turning and heading for the door.

Montrovant watched them leave in silence. Behind him, Abraham flopped helplessly in the casket-like wooden case. He was face down, and his neck and back were bent at odd angles from the position into which he'd fallen.

Montrovant turned back to him.

"So, my friend, you are as weak in spirit as you are unwise in choosing your companions. I should have expected as much. How could you believe, after all the years they have hoarded their famous 'Grail blood,' that they would share it with such as you? You cannot even control your own hunger."

Abraham groaned, but he did not speak.

"I have a special treatment for what ails you. It is more than you deserve. What I should do is drain you dry myself, take what small strength you possess, and leave your dust to be spread by the feet of peasants. That would be fitting, and the memory of it would amuse me.

"Unfortunately, I am to be denied that pleasure. I need you to perform a service for me, a service that will prove invaluable to my upcoming quest. You will be my messenger to that bumbling fool Santorini. The message I wish to send cannot be carried by one of my own. They would not understand it."

With a supreme effort, Abraham lifted his head from the floor of the wooden case, twisting his face to the side. He spoke, slowly and barely coherently—an icy calmness seeping into his voice. Montrovant grinned widely, leaning closer to hear.

"You will never find them. They have left me, and they will elude you." He paused, collecting more of his ebbing strength, then continued. "You are a fool."

Montrovant stared at Abraham for a long moment, then threw back his head and laughed uproariously. He shook with mirth until he nearly collapsed back across the polished mahogany surface of his desk.

"Oh, truly, truly I have misjudged you," he choked. "You have more spirit than I would have dreamed.

"Know this, though," Montrovant regained control of himself, "you know nothing of my motives, or my dreams. I *will* find them, but not for the Church, and not for those who follow me, whatever they might believe. I will find them, and I will find the Grail. I have nothing but time, you see, and it is a worthy challenge.

"For now, the mantle of the Templars and the shelter of the Church suit me. Tomorrow? Who can say. The Templars have come and gone, and always I have been there. If I leave them, they may fade, but I will go on."

Montrovant grabbed the steel ropes again, pulling Abraham upright.

"Enough of this. It is nearly dawn, and I must be gone soon, as you must soon do me the service of which I spoke. Come."

He began walking, half-leading, half-dragging Abraham behind him like a dog on a leash. There was nothing Abraham could do but try to keep from falling and being dragged bodily. Montrovant never once looked back.

They made their way slowly to the upper levels of Montrovant's keep and finally exited through a huge wooden door onto the walls themselves.

Abraham felt a wave of giddiness wash through him as he looked down from the height, unable to use his arms for balance. He leaned as far from the precipitous drop as possible.

"There," Montrovant exclaimed, gesturing at the horizon. "There is your fate. You will be given a chance that you do not deserve, to live. It will be a grand battle for your soul, if you are a believer."

He searched Abraham's eyes, looking for some reaction. Shaking his head, satisfied, he turned toward the mountains in the distance again. "Well, then, without faith, it will purge you as well. A cleansing. A rebirth of strength and spirit.

"Of course, if you fail the test, and I expect that you shall, it will be a searing, blazing world of pain that will extinguish your sanity and leave you a pile of bitter ashes, making you a tribute to those you would have served."

Montrovant heaved his arm aloft suddenly, carrying his captive helplessly into the air and holding him as easily as he might a pint of ale.

"You will hang from this wall, and you will meet the sunrise. If you can find a way to free yourself while the ability to outrun our friend Death leaks through your sorry frame, then you can begin to rebuild your mind and soul. You will have the greatest of motivations and purposes, things you do not possess now. You will have revenge. You will have my face, my voice, to draw you onward.

"I do not believe we will ever meet again, but I

pray that we do. Some men crave women, others crave wine and song. I crave diversion."

He lowered Abraham over the side of the wall, letting the rope settle onto a huge metal spike that jutted out from the stone. Once his captive hung freely, Montrovant released the cord and stepped back.

Abraham swung like a pendulum, the steel cord biting into his skin as the pull of gravity dragged him earthward. He struggled uselessly against the pain that threatened to blank his mind. On the horizon, a reddish glow was rising to paint the morning clouds. It would be less than an hour before the sun crested those mountains.

"Die well, my friend." Montrovant intoned, backing away slowly. "If you should survive until that fool Santorini arrives, tell him where I have gone. Tell him what I have told you. His knights are gone. They were never his. His treasures are gone; they were always mine. Tell him he may care for my keep against my return, though I may not do so during his lifetime.

"If he comes too close, drain his useless carcass and use his strength to come after me. I would like that very much."

Then there was only silence. Abraham tried to control his thoughts, fought to gain purchase against the wall, but already the fingers of dawn were crawling over the horizon. He already felt the biting touch of the sun's rays. He began to scream,

DAVID NIALL WILSON

loud, ragged cries that split the silence of the morning air and echoed off across the plains.

Moments later, swathed in dark robes and a huge black hat, the cross of the Templars blazing on his back, Montrovant rode through the gates of the keep. For just a moment, on the crest of the first ridge beyond those gates, he reined in his horse, turning to watch, and to salute Abraham's tortured form. Then he turned again and was gone, flashing across the land.

Time, his eternal ally, was against him this once. The trail cooled with each passing second. He whipped his horse into a gallop, leaning forward and pressing into the animal's flesh. He could sense its fear, but he controlled it, pushing it beyond its limits, making for the gates of the temple.

Somewhere in the distance the blood of the ancients called out to him, and he answered that call. The screams echoing at his back seemed to wish him Godspeed.

TWO

Santorini's mount labored under a full load, but
the bishop hurried it along just the same. Santorini
knew Montrovant's hours, and he knew he had
precious few of them to reach the dark one before
it would become a matter of another day, rather
than another portion of an hour. Montrovant was
"unavailable" during the daylight hours, and
Santorini, for one, had no desire to test the limits
of this. Nor did he care to know why.

Images clouded his mind, some from the night
just past, others from shadows further back in time.
Bishop Santorini had known and feared
Montrovant for exactly the same number of days,
hours, minutes and seconds. The first moment the

dark one had been ushered into the same room with him, Santorini's heart had gone cold and dead inside. Montrovant's eyes had pinioned the bishop in place, rooting his feet so securely that he doubted a strong man could have dislodged him from that position at a full run.

Now it had grown worse. Though Santorini truly believed in God, and the Church, he also believed in evil. Montrovant was a strong evil, and Santorini himself was only a mediocre good. His heart was willing, but his flesh was as human as the next, unless that next was named Montrovant. The dark one had seen this in Santorini from the start, had known how to play against the bishop's insecurities. It was that quick glimpse of insight that had led Montrovant to request the bishop as the Church's emissary in his own dealings.

Montrovant's keep appeared on the horizon, the first hints of dawn's light creeping over the mountain tops. Santorini did not see the flapping, flailing shadow dangling against the structure's stone side until he'd come much closer, and even then it seemed nothing more than some odd banner that had broken free of its ties. He paid it no mind, concentrating his energy on the confrontation to come.

Montrovant would never allow Mother Church to dictate terms. The bishop knew that well enough. It was Santorini's unenviable task to try to convince his own superiors that they were in charge of this mess while pacifying Montrovant's ego. Seeing the red rays of sunlight working their way more forcefully over the horizon, Santorini dug his heels into the horse's side roughly. He had worked long and hard this night to get the permissions and signatures necessary for the re-forging of Montrovant's alliance. He had no intention of leaving the keep empty-handed.

As he rode up beneath the castle wall, he heard Abraham's lost, mindless screaming, saw in an instant the wildly gyrating form, the smoke rising, and though Bishop Santorini was not a genius for observation, the scene clarified for him in an instant.

Leaping from his mount, not even bothering to tie the animal up, he rushed up the stairs to the huge, ornate double doors and pounded. Then, mustering every ounce of courage his God could spare him, he turned the handle and pulled. The doors swung open easily, greased and mechanically perfect, as eerie in their smooth operation as Montrovant was in his unshakable control. Slipping inside, Santorini made straight for the stairs. Whoever was up there needed his help, and it was obvious that if Montrovant were in the keep he was not of a mind to assist his guest.

If he were lucky, the bishop mused, Montrovant was long gone, thought that would open an entirely new set of problems to debate. The Church Fathers were already unhappy with Santorini's dealings with the "knights." This would erode what confidence he'd given them in his ability to handle the situation.

He passed the door to the study, where he'd stood the night before, and a shiver of fear raced up his spine. His quick strides became a run, and he was making his way out onto the upper wall of the keep in moments. Long before he reached that wall, he heard the screams.

No human voice could have uttered the sound that assaulted him. No man had such pain, or such strength, within him. This knowledge nearly stopped the bishop in his tracks. If not a man, what? Montrovant?

Bishop Santorini tried to envision a creature, or a man, strong enough to leave the dark one in such a position. Then he tried to envision himself saving Montrovant from the wall, from the light of day. He tried, and he failed. If it was Montrovant hanging from that wall, he knew, he would turn, and he would walk away, eternal soul be damned. On the other hand, if it were an enemy of the dark one's, then perhaps he was about to find an ally.

Moving quickly so his cowardly heart could not fail him, muttering prayer after prayer under his breath and knowing that the pounding of his heart must be drowning out the words, he slipped to the edge of the wall and peered over.

The gaze that met his froze him as surely as a cloak of ice. Eyes, deep, hollow, both hideous and compelling at once, snagged his. Sound flowed incessantly over the thing's lips; though it had the aspect of a man, Santorini knew he faced a demon. No man could have withstood the depth of anguish in that expression. No man's skin would smoke where the morning sunlight hit it, and no man save Montrovant had ever held the bishop so easily with the power of his eyes alone.

The thing was trying to claw its way up the wall, trying to rip into the very stone of the keep itself with fingers covered only in a thin, shredded coating of flesh, but those hands were bound with what looked to be steel wire. More wire bound the creature's arms to its side, and it was from this binding that it hung.

Santorini saw that with an effort he could lean far enough over the wall to reach that wire, and he knew that, despite his portly, ungainly appearance, there was sufficient strength in him to lift that thing over the wall and to haul it out of the sunlight. He started to lean, actually dangled his arm over that wall, nearly into the grasping, claw-like hand that reached toward him. His mind was drifting, and a wave of nausea hit him hard, half from the dizzying height, from leaning out over the void below, and half from fear and loathing, from the stench of the creature's breath and the horrible power of its dying eyes. He cursed the guilt in his heart that would not let the thing burn.

He hung over that ledge, not leaning closer, not

retreating, suspended in time as surely as he was in
that position of precarious balance, and as he
watched the sun rose, oblivious to the drama below.

Suddenly a hideous screech rent the air, and the
creature's back burst into sudden flame. Without
thought, Santorini acted. He reached over the wall,
grabbed the wire rope, somehow evading the groping taloned hands, and he heaved upward. At first
it seemed he had misjudged, that it would be too
much for him, but then, suddenly, fired by his anger at Montrovant, and the rush of adrenaline
through his veins gifted him by his fear, his balance
shifted back, and the rope snapped up and over the
wall, flinging the creature past him and slamming
it into the stone behind.

The bonds still held him/it as it writhed in the
shadows, trying to put out the hideous flames and
only half-succeeding, but they could do nothing to
disguise the hunger, the madness washing across
the thing's features. Santorini stepped back, then
further, watching in morbid fascination. The flames
had receded, but the rays of the sunrise had not yet
slipped up over the edge of the wall.

It was one thing to grab the dangling wire and
yank the creature to the relative safety of the top
of the wall, but what faced the bishop now was a
more difficult task. How could he get near enough
to pull the writhing thing from the sunlight without being bitten, attacked, or overwhelmed?
Despite its captivity, Santorini did not doubt the

outcome if it got hold of him.

Moving cautiously forward, avoiding direct eye contact, the bishop spoke.

"I don't know everything there is to know about what has happened to you, but I know that if the sun is allowed to fall full upon you, it will be your death...or a second death..." The bishop hesitated for just a second, then plunged on. "I need to get you inside, to the shade, and you need to tell me what it is that you need to heal. If you attack me, you will not survive. There is no time for it. You must trust me."

There was a flicker of something—understanding?—in the thing's eyes, but it did not speak. Santorini took another step forward, and though those dark, smoldering eyes watched his every movement, holding him as hypnotically as a snake might a mouse, there was no motion to attack.

Santorini could see that this lack of aggression was costing the creature greatly, and in that moment the man behind the hideous features and the maddened eyes slipped through for an instant. Not the best of God's servants, the bishop was also not the least. He moved forward swiftly, took the steel cords in hand, and began to quickly, almost frantically, drag the prone man-thing's body toward the doorway to the interior of the keep.

As he moved, he prayed. It had been some time since Antonio had felt the spirit truly move him to prayer, but in that moment his faith, or the hope

of that faith, was renewed. The strength that drew
him onward did not feel as though it were his own.
He used the words that flowed easily from memory
and heart to shield him from the images that assaulted his mind. The creature spinning, breaking
free, rending him limb from limb, or worse yet,
Montrovant returning, coming suddenly up behind
him and asking just what he thought he was doing
removing a prisoner from the ramparts of a keep
that did not belong to him.

It didn't matter. His captive was bound
tightly…and though the thing had shown remarkable strength and ferocity while hanging on the
wall, it was growing very weak. As they moved to
the doorway it was necessary to pass through another patch of bright sunlight. The sudden assault
of the sunlight caused the thing to burst into flames
again, all over its body, and Antonio rushed it into
the shadows beyond the first door he came to, not
looking behind himself and nearly toppling them
both down the long, winding stairs.

By pressing into the wall frantically, the creature
was able to quench the flames, but the gibbering,
hopeless sounds continued. They were no longer
screams, but the depth of the pain they bespoke,
the anguish in the deadened sockets that had once
been eyes tore at Santorini's soul. He almost took
a step forward, so strong was that pull. Almost.

"Blood." the thing croaked. Antonio didn't really
hear it—could hardly distinguish the words from

the harsh, grating cough that was the creature's voice.

"What?" He stepped carefully closer, leaning as near as he dared. "What did you say?"

"Blood," Abraham repeated. "Bring me blood...please."

Santorini lurched back, staring. What was he doing? Here was this thing, this half man, half God knew what, lying in a heap, nearly burned to the death he should be embracing, and Antonio had stopped that from happening. Now it asked the impossible, asked for blood, and the bishop had made himself responsible.

Seeing the look of disgust, and terror, that flashed across Santorini's face, the creature that had been Abraham spoke again. "Animal," he croaked, "is fine. Please."

Antonio turned and ran. He did not look back, and if he could have done so without losing his balance and toppling down the steep stairs, he would have clasped his hands over his ears, closed his eyes tightly and screamed.

All the years, all the secret late-night talks with Montrovant, the innuendo and the threat—all of it fell to naught against the backdrop of final truth that lay on the floor above him. This creature was like the dark one, like Montrovant, and it fed on blood. Heart pounding, the Bishop raced into the yard and made for his horse, not stopping until he held the reins in his hand and his foot was firmly planted in the stirrup.

Then he saw the keep again, and he remembered who and what he was, and why he had come. He did not mount his horse. He stared up at the keep, at the walls far above, the hook on the wall where short moments before a man/creature had hung, burning in the sun. Then he turned, making his way to the stables, and began a long prayer for forgiveness that would not end until late that night when sleep overwhelmed him. There had to be animals, something. He prayed, as well, that it would not be a horse.

As it turned out, there were plenty of pigs in the sty and several of them were younger, not too hard to handle. It had been a few years since Antonio had slaughtered a pig, but such lessons of childhood are not easily lost. He had saved the blood, still warm, in the only thing he could find for the task, a feed bucket. The heady, cloying scent of the fresh blood nauseated him as he climbed, but he forced himself back up those stairs, to that thing, now scrabbling feebly on the floor, and he tipped the bucket, dribbling a small trickle of blood onto its lips.

The reaction was instantaneous and sudden. It lurched up, nearly spilling the bucket from his hands, mouth open wide and impossibly long, extending, stretching toward the blood. Antonio pulled back, steadying himself, then moved close again, holding the bucket further up and away and pouring the blood carefully, letting it fill the thing's mouth, waiting, then filling again.

The frantic motions stopped slowly as the thing guzzled the offered blood steadily. It was like watching a drunkard gulp a tankard of ale without taking a breath. The entire bucket was empty in only a bit more time than it would have taken him to pour it out on the floor, and suddenly the thing lifted its face to him...only it did not seem a thing any longer.

The young man had deep, earnest eyes, and the blood smearing his face no longer gave him the aspect of a slavering beast, but of a wounded, needy youth, sorely used. Santorini moved forward a bit, but hesitated. Finally, still impossibly weak, the boy said, "Take me to a place of darkness and leave me. When I awake, and the sun has left us, we will speak."

Antonio hesitated, still uncertain.

"Who are you?" he asked softly.

"My name is Abraham," the young man gasped.

Antonio made his decision in that moment. It was a sign, there was no other way for him to interpret it. Abraham, but in this case, it was not Isaac who'd been offered as sacrifice, but Abraham himself, and it was up to Antonio to see to it that the sacrifice was made where it mattered most, in the heart. A creature of the devil and blood this Abraham might be, but he was also a creature of

God. There was no way to deny that truth if one was to believe the Scripture, and the Christ, and to turn from him was a sin as surely as to turn from a dying child, or a woman in need.

The bishop grabbed the wires again, careful to remain behind the prone body of his still-bound captive, and dragged him down the stairwell toward the darker rooms below. There was a storage cellar just off the main hall, and the darkness there should be sufficient.

The crashing, violent descent must have been painful, but Abraham uttered not a sound. The young man's eyes were closed, his hair matted with pig's blood and his clothing in tatters. Antonio's breath was coming in heaving gasps, and it was all he could do to continue the exertion. He had no energy or inclination to make it a pleasant journey.

They reached the bottom in silence, and after only a brief hesitation to catch his breath, Antonio slid Abraham through the door to the cellar, not bothering to drag him to the bottom of the stairs, and turned to leave.

"Wait…" Abraham's words were clearer now, but still very weak. Antonio leaned as close as he dared, waiting.

"When you return," Abraham gasped, "bring more blood."

Antonio reeled back. It was too much.

"You must." Abraham fought to get the words out, his eyes closing as he fell toward a darkness the bishop could not even fathom. "You must, for your own protection."

Antonio did turn then, tearing his eyes from the young man's ravaged face and flinging himself through the doorway and out into the hall beyond. He slammed the door behind him, but even the finality of that portal closing did not abate his fear.

"Blood," he whispered. "For the love of all that is holy, I have become a thief, stealing blood."

He staggered into the courtyard and to his mount, wheeling it clumsily and nearly collapsing over the beast's neck as it cantered off toward Rome. He closed his eyes and clung to the reins, whispering over and over, "Dear God, I must be strong. I must bring him the blood." His mind seethed with images of punishment and redemption. He had to follow his heart, and his heart said not to let the thing die.

As he rode, he felt the horrible weight of Montrovant's dark eyes boring into his back, seeking his soul.

THREE

As strong an emotion as the memory and promise of terror can be, immediate danger is always more prominent in the mind. Bishop Santorini was back at Montrovant's keep long before darkness fell, stoking up a strong blaze in the fireplace in the sitting room. He could not bring himself to use the den, with its superior comfort, even though he was certain that the dark one had left. The sitting room seemed the least used of Montrovant's spaces...a place maintained for appearances, but avoided in reality...and that suited Antonio fine. The less the space stank of Montrovant and his knights, the more it appealed to the bishop at the moment.

In the corner was a basket from which the tops

of a half a dozen wine bottles poked. Each was filled with fresh cow's blood and stoppered carefully. He'd paid a pretty penny both for the blood itself, and for the anonymity of going through three separate intermediaries to isolate himself from the event. The notion of the Pope being notified that one of his bishops was supplying a *vampyr* with blood was not one that made him comfortable.

The words *There are many rooms in my Father's house* had deeper and darker meaning for one who had spent time in those rooms. There were those in the service of the Mother Church who marched to the beat of their own drums, some beating more deeply in the shadows than others. Shivering, he tossed another log on the fire.

The sun had been set for some time, and he knew he could put it off no longer. Taking one of the bottles in hand, not willing to open it until he was nearer his goal, he headed for the stairs and his fate. In his other hand he gripped a bottle of rich, deep, red wine.

He tucked the wine under his arm and reached for the door handle. He knew that Abraham was still bound, and that those bonds had been sufficient to bind the creature to the wall of the keep, but it did nothing to abate his fears. He meant to release it. He meant to make a bargain with a creature who must surely come from the depths of hell itself, and he meant to do it for the sole reason of keeping his own sorry reputation and life intact. He needed to find Montrovant, or the Order, and he needed to get back what had been stolen, or lost. If that meant chancing death, or worse, at the hands of this Abraham, then so be it.

He pressed the door wide, letting the dim light from the flickering fire down the hall seep into the interior darkness. At first he thought he was alone. Then he saw a leg extending from the darkness like a shadow and he let his eyes follow that leg, accustoming themselves to the lack of light slowly. A soft sound, the scuff of cloth on stone, nothing more. Antonio's heart was hammering, and he couldn't explain why...until the oddness of the silence struck him. No breathing.

He moved in quickly...worried now that it had all been for nothing, and that his captive was dead. He flung the door wider, stepped fully onto the landing, and it was then that he saw the eyes staring at him from the darkness. Resting low against the stone wall, shoulders leaning easily into the stone, hair a bit less wild than the last time they'd met.

"You have returned." Abraham's words were formed as a question, but something in his tone led Antonio to believe there had never been any doubt.

"I brought blood," the bishop stuttered, moving no closer.

Abraham nodded.

"First," Antonio added, "we must talk."

Realizing that the vampire was not going to be launching at him from the darkness, he moved a bit closer, squatting so his eyes could pierce the gloom and make out his captive's features.

"I have to know that you will listen. I have to find a way to believe that if I release you, you will not kill me, or worse."

"You saved me…" Abraham said slowly. "For that alone I would spare you. What is it that you want of me?"

The trembling in Antonio's shoulders did not cease immediately, but he found his voice again.

"I seek the one who left you on that wall. Montrovant, damn his black heart. He has put my life on the line. Alone, I have no chance of finding him, or, even if I did so, no expectation that I would end up any better than I am now."

"You want me to hunt Montrovant?" Abraham's eyes flashed briefly, then the laughter started. It began as a soft chuckle, building in strength and rising to such a volume that the sound filled the room, and still it did not stop.

Antonio backed off a step…eyes going wide. As the volume increased, he covered his ears, but he could not block that mocking, half-insane sound from his mind. With a cry, he spun on his heel and launched himself through the doorway once more, fleeing down the hallway toward the fire, the haunting sounds of Abraham's mirth floating after him.

Then, as suddenly as it had begun, the laughter

stopped, and in the silence, a single word.

"Yes."

Antonio stopped in his tracks, hands still pressed to his ears, wondering if he'd heard correctly. Then the word was repeated, removing all doubt.

"Yes," Abraham repeated. "Return to me, man of God, and bring the blood…all of it."

The laughter resumed then, but not so loud, or so cold to the heart. Antonio moved quickly to the wine bottles, grabbing the basket quickly, nearly overturning it in his eagerness, and started back down the hall.

Abraham did not speak as he entered the small space, merely watched with a dark, unreadable expression planted on his pale features. The bishop opened the first bottle, stepping closer and tipping it to his captive's lips. The vampire drank like a child from the bottle, gulping the blood greedily. The container was empty in moments, and Antonio was reaching for a second when Abraham spoke again.

"It would be much easier if you untied me and allowed me to open the bottles myself."

Antonio started back with a second bottle, ignoring the words, then stopped as he drew near. He met the vampire's stare, and he found nothing there to fear. The features were fuller, younger, the eyes earnest. He knew he might be making a fatal miscalculation, but if so, at least his end would be swift. If he had to return to the Church with the news that he had lost their most precious treasures, and had no idea what to do about it, that death would be painful and prolonged.

Setting the bottle aside, he moved closer, examining the steel bands that bound Abraham. It was going to be no simple task, even with his freedom, to remove them. He would need time, and tools.

"I will try." Hesitantly, he added, "My friend. I will have to find something that can cut these, and a way to do so without severing any limbs."

"Do not worry too much about wounding me," Abraham replied softly. "I have—amazing recuperative ability."

Antonio met Abraham's gaze full on. He no longer faced a withered, drawn creature fighting for its existence. Staring back at him was a handsome young man, if a bit burned and scarred from the ravages of the sunlight and the flames. Nodding slowly, the bishop moved back into the hall and made his way toward the fire. As he entered the sitting room, his eyes latched onto the wall above the mantle. There, hanging with handles crossed, were a battlestar, and a heavy axe. The blade glistened brightly in the flickering firelight.

Antonio moved to the wall and wrested the weapon free of its mount, nearly losing a foot as the full weight of the heavy blade surprised him. As the blade glanced off the stone floor, he lifted it again, testing the weight. He could lift it, but he knew that to strike the metal bands from Abraham was going to take a steady hand indeed.

He dragged the axe down the hall and through the doorway, leaning on it heavily.

Abraham took in the bishop's pudgy form, the blade, and his eyes flickered darkly.

"Can you even lift that blade, man of God? Have you rescued me only to lop the head from my body with a single mishandled stroke of the axe?"

"I don't know what else to do," Antonio breathed heavily. "I am no blacksmith."

The bishop felt suddenly very weary, although the walk down the hall should not have tired him so, even carrying the unaccustomed weight of the heavy axe. He started to seat himself and relax, just for a moment.

Abraham's gaze was locked onto his, holding him easily now. Antonio thought, just for a moment, that the intensity of the young man's stare was odd. He wanted to turn away, or to rise and make his way to the hall in search of some other tool, some other means of cutting that steel, but he could not bring himself to move.

"I…"

His words trailed off, and darkness swallowed him, the floor wavering, moving closer and at odd angles, the blade slipping from his hand and clattering against stone. He tried with his last coherent thought to drop his hands beneath him and break the fall, but they would not move. Then there was nothing.

Abraham concentrated. He was still weak, and he didn't know how long he could maintain control of the bishop's form, or to what extent that control would allow him to manipulate the other's body. He did know that with the bumbling fool of a clergyman wielding the axe, the chances of surviving his release were minimal.

He closed his eyes against the pain of the bands, which bit into his flesh again as he recovered his strength and his flesh filled out. There was one point where the metal was joined by a single, thick lock. It was there that the blade must strike, and it would have to be a single, hard stroke...backed by stone, or it would be in vain.

He let his mind reach out...tugging at the threads that bound the unconscious bishop's body to his mind, binding them to his own thoughts. He wanted to roll, to position himself more perfectly, but he could not. While he controlled the bishop, his own body lay inert. He could not see it, but he could sense the roughened metal hasp resting against the cool stone.

The bishop's body stirred...then rolled a bit itself. In silence, Antonio Santorini's body rose, eyes dark and vacant. Abraham concentrated hard...and like a huge puppet, Antonio picked up the axe once more. There was a difference. Without the hindrance of his own mind, the axe swung up easily, resting across his shoulders.

One blow, Abraham told himself. *You have one blow, and that's it.*

He kept the images simple and precise, transferring them from his own mind to the bishop's limbs. The axe rose, held steadily over the priest's head. One step closer, then another, focused, the lock, the axe, making that image one…and…now!

The axe sliced through the air, whistling in a steady arc. Abraham closed his eyes…seeing in his mind the lock struck. Time slowed in that instant, his life, and then a second life flashing through his mind like a nightmare jumble of emotion and regret.

Then there was the hard *chink* of metal on metal on stone. He released the bishop and was immediately rolling away, when an excruciating dart of pain ripped through him. The axe clattered to the floor, and Antonio's body slumped beside it, lying in a silent heap.

Abraham opened his eyes, crazed by pain, but free. He brought his arms around before him and stared. There were deep lines where the metal had cut into his skin, and the skin on the back of one hand had been shaved away to the bone by the stroke of the axe. He cursed softly, reaching down and finding the lock on the back of the band that bound his legs. He knew the lock was the weak link, and, taking it firmly in his hand, he twisted hard.

At first nothing happened. Then Montrovant's mocking laughter floated free of Abraham's memory, and he twisted again. The lock snapped, releasing the bands suddenly, and Abraham slumped back against the wall.

As his thoughts cleared, he remembered the bottles of blood, and with a soft groan he began to crawl slowly across the floor, then faster and faster as the hunger gripped him and drew him onward. Knowing his control was weakened, he skirted the bishop's prone form carefully. He had no other ally on earth, and it would not serve his purposes to make that ally a meal.

The first bottle went down in a single long gulp, and the second. No thought accompanied his feeding. His hand began to heal, and the marks from the metal bands slowly disappeared, but he paid them no notice. So long, so long since he'd been full, and even though the animal blood was weak, teasing him with the promise of strength it could not quite deliver, it was like sweet nectar. It had been so long since he'd moved except to scream and to claw with bound, helpless hands at the box that had been his prison, that the freedom was intoxicating.

The ravages of the sun would never completely disappear. There was a scar along one side of his face that he would bear for the rest of his nights. He was unaware of it all until, holding the last bottle high, upturned between his lips, he felt the final drop sink down his throat.

His eyes focused slowly, and he remembered the priest. It would not do to have his new ally awaken to find himself in a heap on the floor. Rising for the first time since the dark one had grabbed him and spirited him away, he stretched his limbs...then leaned down and scooped up Santorini's unconscious form easily, moving into the outer hall and down to where the fire still roared. Abraham didn't care for the fire or its warmth, but he knew it would be comforting to his companion, and after what he'd just done, it might take a considerable effort to achieve that comfort, or any level of trust. The only thing in Abraham's favor was that he had not taken the fool's life.

Laying the bishop out on a small couch, careful not to cause any bruises or lumps, or aggravate those already forming, he seated himself in a chair in the shadows to wait. If he'd learned only one thing from his ordeal it was the ability to be alone with his own thoughts.

❧

Antonio was dragged from the darkness by a throbbing drumbeat that grew clearer and clearer as he approached coherent thought. It was not until his eyes were fluttering open and the dancing light of the fire split the darkness that he knew that beating for his own pulse, and the throbbing from a head that felt as if it had been clubbed into pulp.

He tried to rise, but moved too quickly and fell

back…the motion, and the soft impact on the couch, both served to redouble the pounding, and he closed his eyes a second longer, trying to regroup his thoughts. Then memory flooded in and his eyes flew open once more. In a sudden burst of energy remarkable in one so recently unconscious, Antonio sat upright, his eyes scanning the shadows in sudden terror.

"Calm yourself, my friend," Abraham's voice slipped like silk from the shadows. "If I wanted you dead, trust that you would be."

Antonio spun toward the sound…just able to make out the vampire's shadowed form seated in a chair, off to one side of the fire and set back in an alcove. The urge to rise and to run, not looking back, taking his chances on reaching the courtyard outside and his mount, was strong, but the calming influence of common sense proved the stronger. Antonio leaned back in his seat.

"For one so eager to set me free, you are remarkably unappreciative of your own success," Abraham said, chuckling softly.

Antonio's hand flew to the knot on his head, rubbing it gingerly. He looked dumbly around at the room. "How…"

"You must forgive me, but I did not trust your wielding of the axe. I took…steps…to insure that I would lose as little flesh as possible in my release. Even so, it was not without its danger…or its pain. I find that you have saved me twice now…once by rescuing my body, and the second time by allowing me the use of your own. I thank you, my friend...but I wonder, what is it that you think you can gain by keeping me alive? You have seen how the dark one dealt with me the last time we met...what makes you think another meeting would turn out differently?"

Antonio fought to order his thoughts. He knew he was alive only because this other allowed it, and he wanted very much to ensure that nothing about that situation changed.

"Alone, I have no chance of ever seeing Montrovant again," he said at last. "Not unless he desires it to be so, and when such a meeting comes about at his will, he will triumph. The Church is not without resources that could better handle the dark one than I myself, but I do not wish to call their attention to my own failures or shortcomings.

"I want you to track him for me, and for yourself. I want you to work with me to find a way to either bring him back, along with that which he seeks, returning both to the influence of Mother Church...or I want him dead, and I will present you as the new guardian. It makes little difference to me."

Abraham sat in silence for a while. He sat so long, in fact, that the bishop was about to speak again, fearing he'd failed to make his case.

"You are a fool," the vampire said at last. "You believe Montrovant was working with you, that you had a pact. The dark one is well known to the Order I served, and I have heard a great deal of his history. He has never had a "pact" in his life except with his own desires. If he could make you—or the Church—believe that he was your ally to gain what he wished from you, he would not hesitate. Neither would he hesitate to bring the Vatican to ruin or to hang your plump carcass from a tree and lie beneath it, feasting on the blood as it spilled.

"So," Abraham continued, "what you would have me undertake in your name, or in the name of your Church, who cannot even know I exist if we are to preserve your shaky position, is a fool's errand. You don't know it, but there are those in the Vatican who know of my kind, of Montrovant, even. How will you protect me from them? How do you suggest I go about doing as you ask? You would have the prey chase the hunter across the countryside, supported indirectly by those who will not acknowledge him. You would have me seek a nearly certain second death at the hands of the one I have so narrowly escaped this time. I will ask you then, what is in it for me? An alliance with the Church is a precarious situation at best for one such as I, and hardly worth risking my existence over."

Antonio thought fast. He thought back to Montrovant, sifted through what little he knew. "If Montrovant seeks to be guardian of the Grail," he began, wording his answer carefully, "there must be some personal gain in holding that relic…something he would not share with me. If you return that treasure to the Church, the guardianship could be yours. You could begin your own order, gather your own dark knights. I can offer handsome payment in gold and treasure, but something tells me that if such was your goal you could acquire it easily enough on your own. I could offer you blood—a ready, virgin supply of it, but again, I doubt you need my assistance, for if you did, you would not have lived long enough to be saved by me this time. The sweetest thing I can offer is revenge.

"I won't go so far as to say you owe it to me, even though I dragged you from the wall and the burning of the sun. I will say that you owe it to yourself. You owe yourself a chance for revenge. I have heard the dark one say on many occasions that the one thing that grows more and more scarce in his existence is entertainment. Can you afford to deny yourself this chance?"

Abraham was laughing softly again. Rising slowly, he stepped from the shadows into the flickering light of the fire. His skin was healed in great part, except for the single scar, his hair was clean and luxurious...his eyes bright and reflecting the laughter on his lips as Montrovant's never had.

His hair was blond now, where it had been stringy and graying, and it swept back over his shoulders. He stood half a head taller than the bishop, but more slender, and built with the strength of youth, though there was a hint of experience and age to his eyes that belied that initial impression.

"You speak well, as one would expect from a man of your calling, but your words are unnecessary. Montrovant himself ensured that I would follow him if I survived...he bid me do so, and you yourself have named the reason for his madness. He is bored. He invited me to exact my revenge, though I doubt he expected I would be afforded the opportunity, or that I had the means to carry out that revenge should the opportunity present itself.

"He follows the Order, and I myself must find them again. He has his quest, and I have mine, and now my own is sweetened by the knowledge that I may find what I seek and take my revenge at the same moment. Since I am already planning this adventure," the vampire's eyes began to flicker brightly, as if amused, "I would be a fool to not accept aid from one who could prove a detriment if I refuse."

"I pose no threat to you," Antonio babbled quickly. He would have gone on, but Abraham held up a hand for silence.

"I know that you think this is true, but it is not. If I were to refuse you, and to leave, you would seek another, or another means of carrying this out without my help. That other would be a hindrance—perhaps a serious danger—to my own efforts. It is in my best interest to be your ally, my friend, and I am not ungrateful for the rescue."

Antonio rose then, and Abraham strode closer,

offering his hand, which the bishop took uncertainly.

"It is settled then," the vampire concluded, smiling. "There are things I will need before I can depart, and I must build my strength a bit...but there is little time to lose."

"Whatever you need, if it is within my power, I will provide it," Antonio answered eagerly.

"In that case, I have a request that will test just how far you are willing to go, my friend. It is not a good idea for me to be hunting near here. I might be seen, and, should I return, my mission a success, I would not want the locals to remember me in hatred or fear."

Antonio shivered, knowing what was to come and dreading it.

Abraham watched him closely...a grim smile twisting his lip. "Do not fail me in this, Antonio. I will consider it a gauge of how close our...friendship...is to grow. Make her young...pretty...sweet. Bring me something to make up for those days and hours screaming hopelessly in the darkness of that crate. I am very hungry, Antonio," Abraham's eyes flashed suddenly, yawning before the bishop like an endless cavern and calling out to him to leap into their depths. "I am *starved*."

Antonio turned then and fled. He could sense Abraham's eyes focused on his back, could hear the vampire's mocking laughter floating after him down the hall. In that instant he knew he'd traded one dark master for another, gaining little but his sanity. His heart cried out to him to turn away, but his mind was already working over the details of how he would obtain the girl.

The laughter floated about him like a cloud, seeping up from his mind to haunt him as he rode swiftly back to Rome. His lips began to form the words of a prayer out of habit, but he bit them back suddenly, ashamed, and thrilled at the same time. As he rode the darkness seemed to swallow him whole.

FOUR

Montrovant and his followers were not long on the road before the approaching daylight forced the first halt. His men did not question him, being familiar with his oddities. There were certain places known to them all, safe, hidden places, that allowed for discretion and secrecy. Montrovant wanted to be beyond the annoying, clutching reach of Bishop Santorini and the longer, more insidious grasp of the Church itself. He could easily have spent the night in his own keep, made his farewells the following day, and gone at the sun's next setting, but once the scent was firmly planted, he needed to act. Even the few miles they gained that first night were too much for him to resist.

Rising as he now did to a new night, the day and the pitiful, annoying existence of the weakling Abraham behind him, he felt a freedom he'd not experienced in some time: that of the road. It had been too long since he'd shared time with that finest of companions, and he found himself itching to be gone, far from Rome, far from those who knew him. His old hunger filled his senses.

He had been close enough to grasp the treasure he sought more than once, and the faint scent of it that remained had fermented over the years. Now he felt it growing strong once more. He'd sat too long in that keep, letting the Order's empty words and the "alliance" with the Church numb his senses. He had not followed the Grail so many years to sit and watch others possess it: the time for such foolishness was past.

His followers felt the freedom as well, coveted it. Le Duc in particular glowed with renewed vigor. The dark one's progeny's eyes sparkled and his wit was recovering the sharp, stinging quality Montrovant remembered well from past adventure. The two understood one another in ways that the rest would never comprehend. Dark men, all of them, with secrets and hungers they preferred not to share and pasts that would see each dangling from a dozen scaffolds; none of them had been born to sit and watch the world pass.

The first night they spent in the ruins of an ancient abbey, Montrovant and Le Duc in the cellars below, the others finding what comfort they could among rotted pews and the shattered remnant of stained glass. Many years had passed since any had celebrated the mass between those walls. The only worshipers who remained were buried beneath stone monuments in the cemetery behind the building, overgrown with weeds and vines and crumbling to the dust that had spawned them.

Montrovant led the others out at dusk, keeping off the main roads but paralleling them as he wound their road away from Rome. In the distance the umbrella palms lining the ancient roads were in clear view, marking their way as they set off across country.

With nothing else to guide his choice, Montrovant headed for France. It was there that he'd last encountered the Order, there where he'd faced them down, watched the ancient creature Santos crumble, seen his own sire Eugenio clash with the ages-older Kli Kodesh. There might be no answers waiting in France, but it was home, and there were those there with the wisdom, influence, and contacts to guide him in his quest.

They did not wear the colors of the Templars openly. That order had been banished by King Philip, its leader, Jacques de Molay, put to the stake and torched before Montrovant's own eyes. The Templars had gone underground, their meetings held in secret and their rites closely and jealously guarded from outsiders. Their influence had lessened only slightly, and Montrovant had kept his own ties to the Order as firm as possible without truly involving himself in their affairs.

He was believed to be a direct descendant of another Montrovant, one who'd helped to found the Knights, and who'd saved them more than once from certain destruction at the hands of mythic evils. He was not questioned, and only a very few suspected the truth, that he and that other Montrovant were one and the same, and that the knight who fought most closely at his side, Jean Le Duc, had been one of the first Templars ever to wear the cross.

Their road veered off shortly from the straighter route of the Romans and through a brief range of mountains. It would cut a considerable amount of time off their journey, though the going would be more difficult. Montrovant was indifferent to the difficulty. Either way was the same to him, except that the mountains would bring him more swiftly to his goal.

It was on the second night's travel that they found the passage leading upward and began their ascent, taking the trail more slowly and in single file as it began almost at once to grow more steep.

"This is a lonely way," Le Duc commented, riding up beside him. The moonlight cast long shadows over the way ahead, the sky gray, stark, and the mountains looming overhead were lined with a silvery sheen.

"Our way has always been lonely," Montrovant replied softly. "Whether or not there are others about makes no difference, unless one is hungry."

Le Duc grinned at this, but shook his head. "I know you better than that, dark one. The boredom would drive you underground and you would never surface."

Montrovant grinned. "That much is true, but it has been too long since I got out of that moldy keep and onto the road. It is one thing to crave society and its intrigue, quite another to spend endless dreary nights in the company of the same few."

They rode on in silence for a bit longer, the others filing silently along behind. None could find the energy to break the lethargic silence. The weight of the journey was on their shoulders, as always, at the beginning. Everything lay ahead, nothing behind, and it brought solitary thought and introspection to each.

Finally Le Duc spoke once more.

"Do you know this trail? I have never traveled it myself, and wondered if we would be seeking shelter before sunrise, or if you had a stop in mind?"

"I have not been this way either," Montrovant replied. "I chose this as the shortest route. There are rumors of a monastery up the mountain, odd rumors, to be truthful. We will seek that as our shelter, and if that fails, we will just have to find something else. I want to be over these mountains tomorrow night and on the road to France."

Le Duc nodded. "I will send two of the men ahead to scout," he said softly. He turned to the side then, slowing his mount and dropping back as Montrovant continued on, moving with steady speed, not pushing his mount, but not really caring about it either.

The trappings of mortality sat well on Montrovant's shoulders. He was a large, powerful, striking man...tall, slender and imposing, long dark hair sweeping out behind him like a cloak. He rode with the practiced ease of the warrior, but he did not need the horse to get where he was going...in fact, it slowed him. The others slowed him as well, but in a world growing increasingly dangerous for his kind, it was best to appear as "human" as possible.

Two dark forms trotted by, and took off at a slow gallop up the trail. The scouts. He watched as they passed...felt the steady drumming of their hearts...familiar, comfortable. His men worked as a single unit, a precision that he demanded of them. Among men they were the safest from his hunger. He needed them more for their strength, obedience, and unwavering faith in his own judgment than he did for sustenance. There were meals enough walking the streets of each city, tilling the fields mindlessly.

The trail wound up and between two towering peaks. It was not well-traveled, but there were some indications that others had passed that way recently. Deep ruts from passing tires, the cold ashes of campfires, and occasional animal remains appeared here and there. None of the signs were fresh.

It was nearly an hour before the scouts returned to them, and the moon was beginning to descend from her throne. The two came at a faster gallop, less concerned for safety on a road once traveled. They reined in beside Montrovant.

It was du Puy who spoke.

"We have located the monastery. It is not on the main trail, but up a winding side-road that branches off about two miles ahead. We rode close enough to see the walls, and to note that there appear to be no guards."

Montrovant's eyes gleamed. Two miles. Then there was time to arrive, and make arrangements, before the hour was too late and he was forced to be more…direct.

Nodding to du Puy, he whistled for Le Duc to join him, repeating what the scout had said. "We will ride hard now until we reach the monastery, and we will seek shelter there. Remember that there are rumors of strange things from this place. You and I are no strangers to the odd, or eerie," he grinned at this, "and it will be up to us to look out for the others."

Le Duc nodded. "Perhaps it is just their seclusion that brings the reputation?"

"Perhaps," Montrovant replied, "but we cannot afford to take that kind of a chance."

Le Duc dropped back once more in silence, passing the orders back along the line as Montrovant
spurred his mount and sped up the trail, following
du Puy and the other scout.

It seemed only moments before the branch in the
trail appeared, and du Puy turned down that way
without hesitation. The trail they entered was
wider, more of a road. Montrovant suspected that
the brothers at the monastery would bring carts
down that road to the trail below, meeting merchants and travelers there to do their trading,
rather than trying to negotiate the narrower, more
treacherous passage to the bottom of the pass.

Briefly he wondered at the seclusion of the place.
He hadn't given Le Duc all the facts behind the
rumors. There was talk of travelers not returning,
emissaries of the Church that traveled this way and
either were not seen again, or came back with tales
that caused others to believe them mad. Something
in the tales itched at Montrovant's memory. Something familiar, and at the same time strange.

In any case, there was little that he feared, and
certainly not a group of secluded monks on a
mountain. He would seek their shelter, feed, and
be on his way. There was no time to lose if he
was to find the trail of the Order still warm with
their scent, and this time he intended once and
for all to answer the question of exactly what
treasures they kept and guarded. And he would
taste their blood as well.

DAVID NIALL WILSON

The monastery rose from the base of the highest peak as they rounded a last curve in the road. It was not a tall building, but stretched wider than Montrovant would have expected, spanning an area at the base of the mountain that spoke of depth and size. Hardly what one would expect from a small monastic order.

He rode boldly to the front door of the keep, ignoring the danger of possible ambush, and dismounted, dropping his mount's reins beside the walk. There was no sign that their approach had been noted. The walls were dark and silent, shadowed from even the moon's soft rays by the side of the mountain itself. It was eerie that there were no guards...no sign of a watch. Even such a remote area as the mountain was not without its bandits, and the Church had its share of enemies as well.

There was a huge, ornate iron knocker on the door, and he lifted it with a quick flip of his wrist, smacking it into the solid wood with a resounding thud. He waited impatiently, and moments later struck the door again. He had pulled the knocker back a third time and was about to let it drop when a loud scraping sound echoed from within and he hesitated. Moments later the door swung open wide.

They had been prepared for trouble, but not for the sight that met their eyes. The man was short, perhaps four feet tall, and was cowled so that only his eyes caught the moonlight. One seemed abnormally large, but upon closer examination Montrovant realized the second eye was squinting, nearly closed. Given the uneven curve of his back, they appeared to be facing a gnome, rather than a man.

"Greetings," the short monk said, "I am Maison." His voice was deep, rich, and resonant.

Montrovant stepped forward without hesitation. "We are travelers on the road to France, in the service of the Church. I seek a place for myself, and my men, to rest. We are traveling by night to avoid detection."

Maison looked up at him with the one open eye, tilting his head almost comically to take in Montrovant's tall, lean frame. Then he glanced at the others...head bobbing as he counted, before turning back with a smile.

"We would be pleased to provide shelter, and food. It is not often enough we receive visitors, and even more seldom such distinguished travelers as yourselves...on such dark, mysterious errands..." The man smiled, the open eye twinkling strangely in the moonlight.

"The others are at late devotion," he continued, turning and gesturing for Montrovant to follow him inside.

"In that case," Montrovant replied, "my men will see to the horses before joining me."

Maison nodded. "I will send one of the brothers to fetch them in a bit. The stables are around beside the base of the mountain. They will find everything they need. We keep few animals ourselves, but have facilities available for just such an occasion as this."

Du Puy and another, St. Fond, headed around the side of the building with their mounts, and Montrovant led the others inside slowly. Their host had turned and scuttled off down a long, stonewalled passage that slipped away into shadowed darkness.

Le Duc stayed close to Montrovant's side, and Montrovant knew that his progeny sensed something, as did he. It was nothing he could name, or describe, more a sense of imminent danger. A prickling memory was dancing just beyond his reach. There was more to this place than a monastery, perhaps more to Maison than there appeared, as well, though the man was certainly not Damned.

That had been Montrovant's first thought upon hearing the rumors about the monastery. His own sire, Eugenio, had resided in a monastery for years, under the very noses of the Church. Such a location as this fairly screamed "safe." The only problem would have been the lack of...food.

The passage continued deep into the building, ending in a set of double doors nearly the size of those at the building's front. Here Maison stopped, turning to them with a grin. "You will have to make your own fire in the dining hall. We have long since finished our own meal, and things have been cleaned and prepared for tomorrow."

Montrovant nodded impatiently. The night was still young, but not endless, and he needed to be certain that whatever arrangements they made were secure, and private.

Maison did not seem to present much of a threat, and if the others of the Order resembled him in any way, it would not prove to be a horribly difficult task to hide himself away, rise, feed, and be gone. The others were an unanswered question though. How many? How bright? Most important of all...what was that nagging, bothersome warning bell tolling in his head?

Maison pushed the doors to the dining hall open and they all stepped through at once. It was a large room, the ceiling a bit higher than that in the hall, but not a lot. It was criss-crossed by heavy beams, and these were supported by wide stone columns that lined the center of the room.

Between the columns rested long tables and row upon row of chairs, and beyond these tables, near the door that exited on the far side of the room, was a huge fireplace. A kettle hung over the fire pit, and metal frames held a spit and other utensils, as well as a large flat bit of metal that might once have been a shield, now obviously a surface for heating water, or keeping a meal warm.

The hall was crude, but serviceable, and nothing in the layout or furnishings provided a clue to Montrovant's sense of impending danger. Everything was just as it should be in a house of God…simple and orderly.

Le Duc began to wander about the room immediately, and two of the others made their way to the hearth, grabbing wood from the pile just inside the door and stacking it carefully in the fireplace. Maison watched their activity with mild interest, his one open eye shifting about the room curiously, then he turned at last to Montrovant and spoke:

"All that we have is yours, sir. I must return to my brethren for the moment, but when prayers have been offered for the safety and success of your journey, and your time with us, we will return."

Montrovant nodded. "We can find what we need, and if you will see to guiding my men in from the stables, we will be comfortable enough."

Maison nodded. "Of course. I will have them brought directly here, and once you have made a meal for yourselves, I will personally show you to your quarters. I know if as you say you are traveling by night, you will not want to wait long to rest."

"Thank you," Montrovant answered. His eyes narrowed a bit, and he watched the little man closely. The ready familiarity with moving about by night itched at his mind. Then his gaze focused on the door opposite the one they'd entered through. Most of the squat structure lay beyond that wooden portal. The answers to his questions were there as well.

Maison scooted past him and headed for that

door, and Montrovant watched the short man pull the portal wide, slide through, and close it again behind him. Beyond the doorway, for just a moment, the dark one thought he saw a flicker of candle flame, and for that same instant he thought he heard the sound of voices chanting...but then the door was closed once more and he was alone with his men, and his thoughts.

The fire was going, flames crackling and popping briskly, and the others were moving about the small kitchen, locating a pantry and digging through their own bags to scrape together a meal. What they found were surprisingly meager rations for such a remote site.

Again the nagging warning. Montrovant moved over to where Le Duc was walking along a blank wall, nervously glancing toward the ceiling, then the floor, then pacing the length of the wall and starting again. He reached out to touch Jeanne's shoulder, but before he could make contact the door opened again, and he turned.

They all stood, shocked to silence, as a woman entered. She was young of face and dark of hair, but somehow this seemed wrong. The deep glitter of her eyes and the quick, sure-footed stride spoke of age, power, and wisdom. She was robed, as Maison had been, though hers were more well-tailored, and shimmered with hints of many colored thread, woven deeply into the material. She was taller than Maison, but only a little. Her slender legs and soft breasts pressed curves to the robes that were blasphemously out of place in a monastery.

Montrovant stepped forward—began to speak—and stopped.

Eyes dancing, she broke the silence for him.

"Greetings," she said with a soft, lilting voice. "I am Rachel. I believe you have met my brother?"

Montrovant and Le Duc exchanged a startled glance, then turned back to her as if their heads were joined on a rope as the door opened once again. Figure after cowled figure filed into the room, forming ranks beside and behind the woman's slight form. Maison appeared at her side, grinning widely, but none of the others raised their heads to allow sight of their eyes.

The sensation he'd felt earlier had intensified the second the woman's voice broke the silence, but still it was not exactly clear...not what he remembered.

"Who are you?" he asked softly.

Her eyebrow cocked, and her smile broadened. "I am your hostess, it would seem. Is that so odd? My brother has served in the monastery for years. I am visiting."

Montrovant watched the monks forming tight ranks. His eyes shifted back to hers. "You will forgive me if I do not believe that is the extent of it? It has been a long ride, and perhaps my senses are dulled, but I have weathered many nights in the houses of the brothers of God...and you are the first woman I have encountered in all those years."

"You may find a great number of things about me that will differ from your experience, sir," she replied softly. "I assure you I am as safe here as I would be in the home of my parents."

Le Duc moved as if to step toward the woman...then stopped, shaking his head slowly back and forth.

"Jeanne," Montrovant said softly, "what is it?"

"Santos." Le Duc backed warily toward his sire, eyes locked on the woman, Rachel. "I sense Santos."

Montrovant's mind whirled and in that instant he knew it was both true, and not at all true. Santos, and not—so, what?

Turning to the woman once more, he asked again, "Who are you...or *what?*"

As the monks began to move forward slowly and steadily, eyes still aimed at the ground, Le Duc moved closer to Montrovant, and the other knights slid quickly around from the hearth and the servery, eyes wary.

The woman did not answer, but her laughter rang out loud, long, and devoid of emotion. Then du Puy and the others burst in from behind the monks, and chaos claimed the room.

FIVE

Several things happened at once as du Puy and St. Fond arrived in the dining hall. They burst through the rear ranks of monks, bellowing loudly and cursing. Montrovant did not wait for their would-be captors to react, preferring as always direct action. He leaped into the first rank of monks, scattering them like so many leaves in the wind. Only the woman, Rachel, stood her ground...eyes dancing with angry light, but not with fear. The alarm bells were tolling louder, but there was nothing to be done. He had no intention of just sitting back and allowing anyone to assume control of him or his men.

He did not hesitate to kill. The first two unlucky

assailants who met his assault fell instantly with broken necks, the third was sent flying into a stone wall, his head crushed instantly by the impact. It was not until he was face to face with the fourth, reaching for the man's throat, when he sensed the truth. The front rank was a decoy. The second were Damned, and they were not young. The cloaks were tossed back, and dark, twisted features, long, sharp, talon-like nails, and sharp, glittering fangs were revealed.

With a sharp cry, Montrovant called a warning to the others—"Nosferatu!"

The shock of his discovery was nearly his last emotion as the "monk" directly in front of him lashed out, impossibly long nails raking scant inches from Montrovant's throat. Rolling away, barely avoiding the blow, he spun low and brought his leg around in a long sweep, sending his assailant crashing hard to the ground. Montrovant dropped to the hissing thing's neck, knee making hard contact, crushing through bone…and then he was up again, spinning away, moving unerringly toward where Le Duc was engaged with two others.

Jeanne had managed to get his blade free in time to put it to use, and there was no hint of uncertainty in that strong arm. Montrovant moved to his progeny's side quickly, calling out to the others to do so as well. They were outnumbered, and now that it was less certain just what they faced, or how much danger they were in, he wanted his forces marshaled and focused.

They ended up backed near to the door through which they'd entered, and though one of his knights, a younger man named Louis, fell to the second wave of Cainites, the others held their own well. They had traveled long, dark roads at his side, and the notion they might be killing an enemy for the second time was not new or frightening to them.

They formed a rough semicircle, all with blades drawn now, except Montrovant, whose eyes sparkled with a dark light. He spun to meet the gaze of the woman, asking for a third time.

"Who are you?"

There was no laughter this time. Rachel met his gaze with her own, emotionless glare. Then she spun on Maison and slapped the little man hard, nearly knocking him across the room. The show of strength caught Montrovant off guard. He knew she was not Damned, and yet such a blow was impossible from such a slight woman. Her voice crackled out loudly, and all motion in the room stopped.

"You fool!" she cried, anger rippling across her features, ringing loudly in the tones of her voice, so much softer moments before. "You said they were traveling knights. Nothing more, nothing less. You said 'mortal.'" She was quivering with rage.

Maison rose slowly from where he'd slammed

into the wall, shaking his head groggily. He couldn't answer, but she wasn't really expecting a reply. Turning back to face Montrovant, she calmed suddenly.

"I might ask you the same question, it seems. There appears to have been somewhat of a misunderstanding."

"Misunderstanding?" Jeanne spoke out quickly, the red haze that filmed his eyes and mind in battle releasing him slowly and very reluctantly. *"Misunderstanding?"* His gaze dropped to young Louis, dead and bleeding on the floor, and to the small mound of dead monks beside and around them. He did not drop his blade.

Montrovant was calmer, but the anger shone bright in his eyes. "I think *mistake* is the word. I think you have made a very grave error in judgment. That is what I think."

"I agree," she nodded, turning back to Maison. "I have done exactly that in trusting my 'brother' here to complete a task as simple as greeting you. He is not Damned, nor am I," she shifted her gaze back to meet his coolly, "but he has ways to know that you are. For some reason he didn't think to employ them."

Maison hung his head and shivered, leaving no doubt that his punishment for this transgression was far from over. Rachel continued to meet Montrovant's gaze, taking in his tall, muscled form. Then she smiled slowly.

"If it is possible, I believe we would all be best served by beginning this again."

Montrovant hesitated. They were outnumbered, but he sensed that all of those they faced were not Damned. There were mortals mixed in, making the odds a lot more even. There was also the anger. Only Rachel's eyes, locked to his own gaze, old and young, beautiful and somehow rotten, held him from sneering at her words and leading his own attack.

"I'm not certain it is as simple as that, my lady, now that you have shown your first act of hospitality to be murder."

She smiled again, obviously unconcerned by the situation. "I can understand your feelings, my friend, but you of all people will understand the scarcity of...sustenance...for my followers. If I don't allow them to feed here, then they must hunt in the villages near the base of the mountains, and I don't want to draw more attention to this place than we already have."

"You kill everyone who comes here and think you won't attract attention?" Le Duc could hold in his anger no longer. "You must take us for fools."

"No," she replied calmly, "but I did take you for mortals. And no, I do not let them kill all who come here, but it has been a long time since any other has visited, and Maison led me to believe that you were a solitary group of knights, on Church business, but private Church business.

That meant to me that you would not be expected to appear publicly until you reached whatever you had been sent to do or retrieve. By then the trail would have been cold, and the monastery, while possibly attracting momentary notice from those who lived nearby, would not be suspected as the cause of your disappearance."

Montrovant laughed suddenly. "The Church would not miss us so much at the moment. We have been on better terms with His Eminence in the past."

Then his eyes darkened once more. "You have not told me who you truly are, lady, and if we are to continue this discussion, then I am going to insist. Not a child of Cain, but you know me as I am. You are served by Nosferatu and human alike. You live alone on a mountain, surrounded by stone, like a huge tomb, and yet you live."

Her soft laughter rippled out again. "Let's just say that I am no more truly alive, or mortal, than you yourself, and not as young as I seem. Please," she moved forward toward Montrovant, eyes dancing, "accept my explanation, and my apologies."

Montrovant watched her approach warily, and Le Duc glared at her with barely concealed anger. Neither met her eyes, but as she came closer Jeanne breathed a name the two knew too well, and hated too completely.

"Santos."

She stopped very still for a moment, eyes

darkening, then narrowing in suspicion.

"How do you know Santos?" she asked quickly.

"You are the same as he," Le Duc stated, ignoring her question.

"We do not 'know' Santos," Montrovant rejoined, "though I was present to watch his head severed from his neck, and to see him crumble to the dust that spawned him."

She took half a step back. "Santos is dead?"

"Unless he can reclaim his form from a pile of dust," Montrovant replied, watching her reaction with curiosity and caution, "then he is, yes. He would have done the same for us, I assure you."

She was staring openly now, and the menace they had felt in her approach had shifted to shock, and even a bit of apprehension. She shook her head in silent negation, then focused once more.

"Tell me how it happened? I am sorry for my reaction, but I have known Santos for…a very long time, or known of him. He was chosen as guardian for certain holy objects that have long since been beyond my knowledge. Do you know if these objects have been recovered then, by the mortals, or destroyed?"

"We have a lot more to discuss," Montrovant said softly, "before I share any knowledge or secrets with you. Knowing you are as he was does me little good, since I never fully understood who, or what, Santos was. I find myself in that position again, and I must tell you, he was not a very trustworthy…man."

"Let me have my followers clear these away," she swept her arm back, indicating the dead bodies behind her with an impatient flourish, "and we will sit and talk. I can have them all withdraw if you like, and suitable quarters will be made available."

"You will pardon me," Le Duc cut in, "if I am less than enthusiastic about resting in quarters prepared by one who moments ago wished me dead?"

She shifted her gaze to Jeanne for a long moment, eyes cold, then back to Montrovant, waiting. Her shoulders had squared a little at Le Duc's sarcastic tone. Montrovant watched carefully for a reaction that would give away the woman's intentions. If she wanted them dead still, she had two options, and he was weighing those carefully in his own mind.

He remembered all too well the awesome powers that Santos had wielded, but those powers had seemed to take time and concentration to call upon. There was none of the dark, heavy aura of danger in the air that had accompanied Santos's ritual chanting, and this woman, or whatever she was, had not had the time or opportunity to summon such power. This did little to assure him that she did not have some equally powerful weapons at her disposal, so a frontal assault, attempting to take him by surprise, was still a very real danger.

The second possibility was that she would extend her "hospitality" and then attempt to kill or take them in their rest. Montrovant feared no one, but the hours before daylight grew steadily shorter, as did their options.

"I will speak with you, and we will remain here this night," he said at last. Turning to his men, he nodded at St. Fond and du Puy. The mortals who followed him, while accustomed to odd occurrences and odder meetings, were staring at the woman in open distrust, grouping nearer to Le Duc.

"My men," he continued, "will of course be involved in securing whatever quarters you allot us. Not that I do not trust you, though I do not, but only that I trust my safety to no others."

"Of course," she answered softly. "I am no more fond of the daylight than you, though it does not affect me in the same ways. My more...powerful followers will be disposed as you yourself, and only those fully mortal will be moving about. I will assign you a chamber without light and easily secured against attack. It is the most I can do to assure you of my good intentions."

"We are not in a position to argue with you, my lady," Montrovant replied dryly. "We now have the choice of trusting you, or killing you. The latter choice might lead us too close to the approaching daylight. Besides, I would have you answer a few questions for me while the opportunity presents itself. I have wondered too long about Santos, for instance."

She nodded again, turning to call out to a number of her followers and issue quick instructions. The bodies were already being drained in preparation for hauling them off, and the efficiency of the collection of the blood indicated how often this same scene had unfolded, though with considerably less resistance from those on the receiving end.

"Since one of my men died," Montrovant said softly, "I expect your 'followers' to share that blood."

"Of course," she said, smiling. She snapped her fingers, not looking back, and Maison was at her side. "Bring our guests food and drink, and, for these two," she indicated Montrovant and Le Duc, "something...richer."

The odd little man nodded, rubbing a bruise on the back of his head where he'd struck the wall earlier. He did not speak, either out of respect, or because the red, swelling bruise on his lip made it painful. Among the others he seemed to command the same level of respect as Rachel did with him, and food, wine, and silver chalices filled with rich, still-warm blood were brought forward and served in silence.

St. Fond, du Puy, and the others watched in silence. Things that had been left silent and unspoken for a very long time were being laid bare, and their eyes never shifted from Montrovant as he lifted the chalice, breathing in the heady scent of fresh blood, and tipped it back to empty it in a single gulp. Montrovant felt the weight of their combined gazes, but did not hesitate. The time for such foolishness was over. He intended this journey to be the one that brought him at last to his final goal, to the Grail, and all that might mean to him. They could follow him and join in that moment of triumph and magic, or he would simply kill them, feed again, and move on. He was better served on the road by those who understood his truth.

Not a word was spoken or whispered, and as Montrovant laid his chalice gently on one of the tables, licking his lips clean of the last remnant of blood, the others lifted their own glasses in silent salute. Not one of them dropped his gaze, and Montrovant smiled.

Seating himself on the end of one of the tables, preferring to remain at eye level with his hostess, or higher, he began to speak softly.

"I met Santos while in Jerusalem, pursuing my own quest to possess the Holy Grail. He had set up vaults and labyrinthine tunnels beneath the city, or was taking advantage of those already in place, and somehow he had the sanction of the Church in Rome.

"I knew that he guarded something important. The setup was too obvious to hide that, and my research indicated it was a very likely thing that the Grail was among those objects he kept. Unfortunately, he escaped me that time, and I was forced to track him down, only to watch as he disappeared in one direction, a strange 'head' in his possession, as another, older and more devious still, made off with the treasures and artifacts in question behind my back.

"I met Santos one other time, in the tunnels and vaults beneath the keep of Jacques de Molay, Grand Master of the now very secretive order of the Knights Templar. It was there that his head was removed from his body and silenced, but that act brought me no closer to what I sought."

Rachel had been listening in silence, eyes glittering. She opened her mouth several times as though to interject a question, or make a comment, but in the end held her silence until Montrovant had finished.

"It is possible then," she whispered. "It is possible that you have ended that long, long existence. It is very hard to imagine."

She looked away then, and continued more softly. "You have already surmised that Santos and I have certain things in common." Her gaze shifted quickly to meet Montrovant's head on. "There is a similarity, but it is superficial. It would be like my looking at you and hating another of your...inclination...and passing that hatred on to you. It is unfair.

"Both Santos and I were created, but by very different powers and for very different reasons. He is the guardian. He existed because there are things, artifacts and talismans, that have been created by men, or circumstance, over the centuries of what passes for civilization, that should not be wielded by any mortal. Most believe these objects should be destroyed, wiped from the Earth and the threat ended before it can take root.

"That is not the thought of Santos's makers. They felt that a time would come when they might have use of these items, or when man might be ready to understand and wield them wisely. Thus was Santos conceived.

"What they did not predict was his fanaticism. They could not have known, either, his insatiable thirst for knowledge...for power. He was created with a certain set of abilities, but even in the early years of his charge as guardian, he was learning and growing. Centuries, as you well know, can do that to a man...or woman."

Montrovant nodded, a small smile teasing at the corners of his mouth. His eyes remained dark and unreadable.

"You want to know what the artifacts were. I know this," she continued. "Many have wanted to know...men have died for that knowledge throughout the years. I wish that I could tell you.

"Some of the items come from Santos's homeland, Egypt. There are talismans created by great magi, the bones of pharaohs and kings, scepters and jewels with both the curse of death and the healing touch. These I knew before his creation. The rest, the things that most interest the followers of the Christ? These were added at much later dates, and though the one you know as Santos guarded them as selfishly and jealously as any of the original items placed in his care, they were not announced to the world."

She turned to him a final time. "He was there when those tunnels were dug, my friend; when Jerusalem was young, he was guardian. When the city was taken, mosques rising where temples once had stood, he was there still. The treasures of the God of both Hebrew and Muslim lined his walls.

"I don't have your answer, but I will tell you this. If any on the face of this planet know where your Grail is located, Santos would have been that one. If he did not have it, he coveted it. If it existed, he tracked it from the moment it left the Christ's hand.

"I have my own quests...my own search, and I am frustrated by the news you bring me. I have a companion—you may have heard his name—Owain ap Ieuan? He seeks as you seek, though for different knowledge, different objects and powers. Still, the end is the same...he seeks because the burning desire to know, and to possess, will not let him free, and because he must or die of boredom and disuse."

Montrovant listened to every word, sifting it through his mind and looking for holes, evidence she might be lying, or withholding information that he required. The silence that followed her words was long and filled with the heavy weight of tension, but slipped away slowly.

"Your words make sense," Montrovant said at

last. "I can find no way they differ from what I know, and what I have heard." He turned to Jeanne, but Le Duc was silent as well. It was plain to see that the knight believed what he'd heard.

"Santos was both the beginning of my quest, and its bane. When I detected his activities beneath the mosque of Al Aqsa, I knew he guarded something important. When I realized that the Church allowed him to exist, and to continue his obviously dark practices, my suspicions seemed confirmed.

"But he managed to escape me the first time we met, and another, Kli Kodesh, a very ancient vampire, made off with the treasures Santos and I both sought. He nearly ended my own existence more than once, and I his, but when he existed there was a scent to follow. Since his destruction, the scent has grown colder.

"Kli Kodesh entrusted the treasure to an order he founded. They are led by one once Nosferatu, as your own followers, but since changed in some way, perhaps from a taste of Kodesh's own blood. They have been called by some the Order of the Bitter Ash, and though they seem to have some remarkable traits even for undead, they are not invincible.

"I was the agent of the Church responsible for watching over them. Rome knew they held treasures, they knew when Santos guarded the same, but they were content to know these items were there and kept from the hands of others. Perhaps there are secrets hidden among them that would discredit their faith. This I do not know. I do know that very suddenly, and very completely, they disappeared.

"I waited too long. They held the artifacts, rumored among them the Grail, in a vault beneath a mountain near Rome. By the time I realized it was happening, they were gone. No warning. No trace left behind...just gone. I was able to capture one who followed them, Damned, but not of the Order, but he knew no more than I have already told you. He came to them and they were gone."

"Where is he now?" Rachel asked suddenly...eyes bright.

"Unless his God has a sense of humor," Montrovant answered softly, "he is a small pile of dust, blown from the wall of my keep by the morning breeze, victim to Father Sun."

"A sacrifice to Rah," she breathed.

Montrovant turned to her. "A sacrifice to frustration. He would have joined them, and they are my enemies. I removed an obstacle, that is all."

"I will strive not to become such an obstacle," she replied, eyes dark, but not with fear. "I have no time, nor energy for such a conflict."

Montrovant met her gaze a last time, and laughed suddenly, loudly, the sound filling the room and echoing from the stone walls. "Nor do I, lady. Nor do I."

At that moment Maison reappeared. He shuffled up behind Rachel slowly, holding back beyond her reach. "The quarters are prepared," he said softly. "Very safe...very dark."

Rachel nodded in his direction, not turning from Montrovant to acknowledge her 'brother.' "You will be safe among us," she said. "I know you have no reason to believe this, but it is the truth. I have gained more by not killing you a second time than had you been destroyed, and there is little point to risking my followers in the attempt at a bit of sustenance from yours."

"I understand, and yet, we will keep our watch, lady, and we will be gone when the sun sets again."

Montrovant rose, and Rachel followed suit. "Maison will see you to your rooms," she said, offering a slender, shapely hand.

Montrovant took that hand, holding it for a long moment and studying her eyes, then turned away without another thought, following Maison's shuffling form off down the back passage and into the depths of the monastery in silence.

Rachel watched him go, his men filing in behind and around him, watching carefully over their shoulders. The shadows swallowed them, and still she watched, but she made no move to follow, or to speak to her own followers. Her eyes were vacant and very far away.

❧

Beyond the thick stone walls, a silent, solitary figure made his way up the mountain, walking his mount slowly. He saw the structure looming before him, and his eyes scanned the walls, shifting over each shadowed alcove, and finding nothing. The dawn was not far away, and he passed by the face of the monastery as quickly as he could, making his way to a line of trees at the base of the mountain and moving quickly beyond the cleared courtyard. He continued until a small graveyard appeared, and a smile flickered across his features...then died.

Abraham dismounted and secured his horse, leaving it to graze as he shifted aside the stone entrance to an old tomb and slipped in. He knew that the mount could be discovered, but that the odds it would not be associated with the tomb were in his favor. All that he carried he took with him as he entered to rest through the day. The following night would be soon enough to make his presence known. He had his letters of identification from Bishop Santorini, but they would not aid him against the light of the sun.

He closed the tomb behind himself and lay down on the cool earth beside the bones of those long dead. The wind outside whistled about him like the voice of God...laughing softly.

SIX

Despite the obvious possibility of treachery, Montrovant and Le Duc met and survived the hours of daylight without incident. The others had kept watch, two awake, three asleep, throughout those hours, but it was obvious upon Montrovant's awakening that none of them had gotten much rest. He had been convinced of Rachel's honesty, but it seemed they had been less impressed.

In any case, they rose, and they exited the chamber, making their way to the dining hall in silence. The soft chanting of many voices rose to them from the depths of the monastery, floating out along some hidden passage, or up a shadowed flight of stairs. The cadence was steady and rhythmic, eating at the concentration. Montrovant recognized its essence immediately, but it did not drag at him as when he'd heard it in the past, nor did the energy behind it seem as malevolent.

This did not prevent the sudden shocked glance from Le Duc, or the mumbling, muttered curses of his men. They were not quick to forgive young Louis's death, and more than once he heard words of revenge, or oaths meant as protection. Frowning, he stepped forward more quickly and pushed the doors to the dining hall open wide. There was a soft blaze going in the firepit, and the main table, that nearest the fire, was laid with food and wine. There was no sign of the others, and Montrovant gestured the others forward quickly. He knew they needed the food, and he took that moment to consider what was to come next.

"Eat quickly," he said, turning away and moving to stand near one wall. "We must be up and out of here. The trail grows cooler and more difficult with each passing moment."

Le Duc moved to his side, but kept enough distance to acknowledge his sire's silence. Both knew they would require a very different sort of sustenance soon, another reason for Montrovant's urgency for the road.

They had learned some things from Rachel, but not nearly enough to be of any real help in their quest. Bits and pieces of an ages-old puzzle were falling into place, but the trail, the hunt, was no different than before. The Order had not come this way, had not passed through the monastery. This meant either they had stayed on the main road over the mountain, gone around the mountain, or not headed toward France at all. None of these possibilities made Montrovant's mind easy.

"They would have known," Jeanne said softly from behind him. Montrovant spun, catching Le Duc's gaze.

"The Order were Nosferatu, before they left Kodesh. They are mostly Nosferatu now, though changed. They would have sensed those within the walls...might even have been aware of them all along. They would also know we might stop here. It is not a sign that they did not come this way...if anything it is a sign that they suspected you might follow."

Montrovant considered his progeny's words. It was certainly possible that the Order had had him in mind and led him toward France, but the truth was it was only instinct that had guided him in that direction. Every time he had been near to what he sought, the road had led him home. France.

"You may be right, my friend," he said softly, "but somehow I wonder if I am such an important thing to them? I do not see why they would wish to draw me after them. Kli Kodesh found me entertaining, but he is ancient, and mad. The Order is not so ancient, nor so powerful. I am nothing but a thorn in their side. That being the truth, why would they wish me to follow, unless it was a trap?"

Le Duc grinned. "A trap we will, of course, spring?"

"Of course," Montrovant's grin widened, and a flicker of light danced in his eyes. "How could I resist?"

They turned back to the table to find that the others had made short work of the meat and wine, and were packing away what remained for the road. It seemed that Rachel and her followers had chosen not to be present to wish their guests a friendly good-bye, and that suited Montrovant fine. He sent du Puy and St. Fond for the horses and led the others out the front, letting the heavy wooden doors close behind them with finality. With the walls no longer surrounding him he drank in the freedom of the night, and the road.

They mounted, turning quickly back down the mountain, and were gone, the two scouts moving ahead to their point positions and the others gathering in a tight knot about him. They were one less, and so soon in the journey it was a poor omen, but Montrovant was not moved by omens. Too many bodies were strewn behind him, leaving him strong and free, for one more to make a difference. If he were the only one to reach his goal, the price would be small.

He spurred his horse down the curving road and onto the main trail, moving up the last leg toward the peak of the mountain pass.

❦

As they disappeared from the court, a lone figure appeared from the tree line. Abraham stood for a long moment, watching them ride down the trail. His mind whirled with thoughts of revenge, of anger and pain. His first instinct was to fly down the mountain in their wake.

His horse had been grazing casually where he'd left it. None had come near where he rested, and his passage was unnoted by Montrovant, or those who might or might not still live within the walls of the monastery. Abraham hesitated. He needed to feed, and soon, but if the dark one had already entered, and departed, from the stone structure before him, then the odds were good that there were none left inside to breathe his name in their nightmares. The other possibility was that Montrovant had allies, and that was equally dangerous.

He opened his pack, glancing over the safe passage and the other documents with which Bishop Santorini had presented him, then closed the bag and moved to his mount. There would be others on the mountain, and it would not be the first time he was faced with the possibility of animals as his only sustenance. He would follow, remaining as close as he could without putting himself in danger of discovery.

Glancing over his shoulder as he turned down the mountain toward the trail beyond, he saw shadowed figures slipping over one wall, near the back.

Smooth, sinuous motion and the speed of shadows sliding past on the wind marked the passing of these apparitions, and his eyes remained locked to that panorama as they bled into the deeper shadows of the night and were gone.

"Damned," he breathed.

Turning he moved more quickly down the mountain and away. There was no way now to know what Montrovant had done with or to those within the monastery's walls, but even if there was blood to be had there, it would be jealously guarded. There was nothing to gain and far too much to lose for Abraham to risk a visit within those walls.

His plans, from the beginning, had been nebulous and incomplete. Santorini had ushered him out the door of Montrovant's keep, sent him on this "mission" without thought to how exactly it was to be accomplished. Montrovant was old, powerful, and all that fueled Abraham was the fire of revenge and the hunger to find the Order of the Bitter Ashes once more and to confront them for abandoning him. He had served them long and well on the simple hope of joining. Of knowing for certain truths that he'd long suspected.

His own Embrace had stolen him from a family led by a father with a vision, a vision of religious fervor. Holy relics, and a church gone deaf, dumb, and blind to the heritage that had spawned it were the topics of conversation at their dinners. There were the precious handful of scrolls and books, works by learned men of other nations and times. There were maps, both fraudulent and true, all geared toward the same fixation.

Abraham's father would have understood Montrovant's obsession, but he would have insisted that the focus was off kilter. He had not, of course, felt the draw of the blood, nor had Abraham's father walked the roads or times the dark one had lived and seen. It was within his mind the old man had shone, the conviction of his words, and his thoughts, the things he'd passed on to his adoring son.

"There are powers, Abraham," his father Joseph would say, late at night, a tankard of ale in his hand and an ancient tome of one sort or another open before him, "powers we cannot comprehend. The Church is not the only power in the world, nor the oldest, but it has brought a focus to those powers that others have not. That power is brought together, and hidden away, discovered only to be obscured more thoroughly, shared with a select few...so select, and so few, that even the priests of that faith do not know the complete truth.

"Among the Holy Fathers in Rome, there have been those who knew and those who merely suspected, even those with no notion of what went on between and beneath their own walls. Scrolls, artifacts, bits and pieces of the past, even pieces of the saints themselves, the cross, the Ark of the Covenant.

"These things, Abraham, are the keys to the power. The words in the Bible are cryptograms, hidden now even from those who created their coding. It is an uncertain guide, steeped in twisting roads that lead in endless circles."

It was at this point, usually after more than one of the tankards of ale, that Abraham's life would become clearest to him. The things his father had told him had sent him searching, seeking, seeing things that others did not, or that they ignored, reading the ancient texts with his father and seeing the magic that swirled through their words.

To Joseph, the secrets had been an obsession to be sought in tomes and the quiet sifting of the words and treasures of others. He was content with what he could find, and when the urge to move beyond this called out to him too strongly, he would himself call to the ale. That did not stop the fires from burning free of his eyes and infecting his son, who took that fire and placed it fully in his heart.

Twenty years of age, striking out on his own, Abraham had been filled to bursting with those dreams. The Holy Land, the mosques of the Muslims, the vaults of the Vatican. He'd sought them all, and found none. Not more than a week on the road he'd caught a rumor, a dropped word in a drunken conversation, and his life, and death, had been sealed.

He had been seeking anything that might lead

him toward knowledge of the powers and secrets his father had hinted at, and fate had dumped him near a low valley. It was a place feared by all, a dark, shadowed story used to frighten children at night, and it called to him like a siren to those long lost at sea.

He'd entered that valley that very night, not even waiting for a good night's rest or common sense to point out to him that such stories rarely grew from nothing. They claimed that there was a place within that valley where strange men dwelled, a low-slung fortress cut into a bedrock of deep-set stone. Those who lived within were rarely seen, and never heard from, but had been seen abroad, always by night.

Those who entered the valley in search of them never returned. Very simply. No bodies, no horrible scenes of death or destruction, just nothing. It was as if those foolish enough to seek beyond the rim of that valley vanished from the Earth.

There was a road leading down the sloping trail, but it was overgrown from disuse. There were no ruts from wagon wheels, nor signs of passing riders. Although the valley was a natural bridge to the borders of the next village, the road all used wound around, skirting the valley carefully.

None of this had mattered. His father's dreams carefully tucked away in his heart, Abraham had entered that valley. He'd made his way to the bottom without incident, and through the line of trees toward the center, where he found and followed a clear, bubbling stream that coursed up from beneath the stone and wound into the distance.

Along that stream was another trail, this one more worn, and his heart had quickened. Someone did inhabit that valley, and they did move in and out, just not through the villages. The secrecy of it thrilled him, and he moved down that trail, heedless of the danger, until the structure he'd heard mentioned came into sight.

He'd had a single glimpse of that structure, one moment to impress its image in his mind, before he was grabbed roughly from behind, lifted from the ground like a child and carried screaming into the trees. A powerful hand had slammed into his head then, silencing him, and the pain that followed was both exquisite and intense.

He felt himself dancing weakly in the grip that held him...his throat pierced by twin blades, transfixed, eyes shifting to black and mind fighting for control, for understanding. One thing flashed brightly through his mind. He had sought powers beyond his understanding, and they had found him.

"Please," he'd managed to beg, his breath slipping away, dying from his lips, "Please...show me?"

And for reasons that still itched at his mind, that still tore at his heart and raked through the remnant of his soul, his request had been granted. As he'd fallen, the life seeping from him swiftly, blood no longer his own and eyes going swiftly from bright blue and intense, to gray and dull, a drop of something had fallen, glittering in the bit of moonlight that filtered down through the trees hypnotically, splashing into his lips and slipping within, winding down his parched throat like molten fire...and then another....a small stream.

Before he realized it was blood, he was latched to a slender, torn wrist, and feeding violently, drawing that sustenance into him, that power and sight, that amazing feeling of completion. An eternity passed and he was cuffed again, knocked free as she sprang back, crouching and watching him with dark, feral eyes.

Her hair had swept back over her shoulders wildly, dark and windblown. What remained of her gown was nearly shredded, revealing white, smooth skin. She watched him, not speaking, for a long time.

He could not move, still, though he felt strength returning, surging through his veins...and things shifted, his sight blurred, then clear, thought lucid and incoherent in short bursts.

"Why?" he'd asked her. "Why?"

"You asked me," she replied, a soft lilt to her haunting voice. "None ever asked before."

And so it had begun. Lori, for that was her name, had taken him away, lifting him again as easily as she would a small sack of grain and carrying him over her shoulder to a narrow crevasse in the stone wall of the valley. Beyond that crack was a small cavern, and deeper still another, cool and damp, her steps echoing in his mind like the beating of a huge drum. She'd taken him deep inside, dumped him, and left him, not returning until he'd passed into a deep darkness.

When he saw her again she did not speak immediately. She took him by his hand, led him from the cavern into the valley beyond, and up the side of the valley furthest from the village from which he'd entered. They moved quietly, his own speed and agility nearly a match for hers, though he'd lain ready for death the night before.

That night, he had fed, a young man, out hunting too late and too close to the rim of the valley. She'd been on him in seconds, dragging him down, and the hunger drove Abraham to join her before his mind could attach meaning to his motion. He had pierced the boy's throat and begun to drain that sweet blood, hands clutching hair and clothing, dragging the young, warm body closer, before the reality of his actions slammed home.

Not even looking back, she'd turned and left him there on that trail, the dying body of the boy in his arms, and moved into the shadows toward the village, her own hunger still to be sated. Abraham had watched, wanting to scream, to tear free, to turn and to run and run until his steps had carried him from the valley, through the village, and beyond...back to sanity, to his father, to the world he'd left behind. He did none of that. He held, and he fed, and he reached for tears that were beyond him, failing him as thoroughly as his humanity.

That was the beginning. He'd stayed with Lori for several years, feeding along the rim of the valley, watching those within, but never seeing them move, or leave. The fire within him for knowledge had not died with his heart. He craved even more strongly that which lay just beyond his reach, but those early years were years of learning. Lori was not a patient teacher, but she was fierce, and loyal, and had been too long in those trees and rocks alone.

At times they would talk, in the early morning, just before the sun would rise and press them to the earth with the weight of certain destruction, driving them to the caverns. She told him tales of those within the walls of that small keep, naming them the Order of the Bitter Ash. Great secrets, she said, were what they guarded, jealously and tirelessly, dragged into her valley many years before.

The structure had once lain empty. She could remember a time when the valley had been ruled by her own father, and the keep, not so strong, or secret, had been a place where weary travelers came for rest. It had always been sheltered, and because of that was often overlooked in the violent feudal disputes that rocked France in those times. That seclusion had brought her own sire, seeking a respite from the trials of remaining hidden and active in the world.

He had killed them all, her family, slowly, her father first to go, leaving a wife and daughter to rule in his stead, and that dark presence seeping between the two of them, claiming both and setting them against one another. The tales were dark, and the images they brought softened the lines of Lori's face in Abraham's mind. He knew loneliness, as well, though he'd always had his father. His mother had died at an early age, giving birth to a brother that Abraham was never to know. Mother and child had left as one, and only Abraham and his father had been left to share company, and life, and love.

The keep had been abandoned when her sire left, and he'd not offered to take Lori with him, though he'd Embraced her for the game of seeing her feed on her mother and kill her, whom she'd grown to hate for jealousy of his love. Games, endless, death-filled games that had wiped clean the heritage of her village, her family, and a life she would never see again, and never forget.

The order had come much later. First had been men, small, dark men on whom she'd fed, but who'd remained, despite their fear, and their obvious understanding of who and what she was. They had brought great stones and tools, carting them into the valley by night, never using the main roads from the villages and avoiding outside contact when possible. The keep had been rebuilt, but it was not the structure of her childhood. Squat, powerful, walls thick enough to withstand nearly any assault, and empty.

Those odd, dark little men who'd built it had finished their work, sealed the keep, and departed, leaving few traces of ever having been there at all, and the structure itself, eerie and unopened. Lori had considered many times opening those doors and walking those halls, seeking the ghosts that still haunted her. She had ignored these impulses, at the same time creating the legend that would defend the valley from invasion until the eventual arrival of its owners.

The order had come by day. One moment the keep was empty, solitary and bleak, the next there were watches slinking along the upper walls, and wagon wheel ruts in the road, the sounds of animals and occasional voices filtering down through the ring of trees that she remained hidden behind, watching, listening, and wondering.

Lori had never gone to them. She had existed as always, feeding and remaining alone in the valley, watching. There was no remnant of her previous life to call her to that keep, and something in the aspect of those she caught glimpses of told her that there was no blood to be had by that road, either. She wasn't certain who or what they were, but had sight enough to know they were beyond her power to control.

She also believed that they knew of her, and left her to herself, and she saw no reason to interrupt that silent partnership.

Abraham had seen it differently, and, eventually, had found his way to those gates. Lori had let him go. She'd claimed it was because the hunting had grown so much harder with him along, that the villagers were too restless providing sustenance to them both. The future had been a glimmer in the depths of her eyes.

She'd seen the truth that was Abraham's existence. She'd known that, eventually, he would go to them. She'd seen that blood was not the only hunger that drove him, and that in the end, even the call of her own control would be challenged.

He had gone to the doors, early one evening, and he'd knocked, as if it were the most natural thing in the world that he visit them. The door had swung open reluctantly, at last, and he'd met Gustav for the first time. Very old, that one, very strong. His features bore the deformity and decadence Abraham now knew as Nosferatu, but there was something more. Beyond those twisted features, sparkling from within, softening the effect and the imposition of that taint on once-mortal flesh, a light had shone. There was something magic in the man's motions, in his words.

Abraham knew in an instant that his secret was no secret at all in that one's presence, and so without knowing why, he spilled forth his story. His father, his dreams, his descent to the valley. He considered trying to leave Lori out of the tale, but

Gustav knew. He smiled at the near insult of the attempted lie and assured Abraham that the Order had known of both of them for some time, and that her prowling of their borders provided them with a means of protecting their privacy without involving themselves personally, and that they approved.

Abraham never left those walls to hunt with Lori again. They accepted him as guest, helped to provide his sustenance as he studied, and continually spoke to him of other places and times, things he'd heard or read about, but never hoped to be near or a part of. All that while, he'd begged them to share with him their secret, the power that made them what he was, and more. The power that lessened the weight of the sun's bite on their soul and caused them such scant discomfort from their hunger that they seemed rarely, if ever, to feed.

They had smiled at his questions, feeding him knowledge, telling him legends of power, corruption, and wonder, and slowly indoctrinating him into their own purpose. The vaults remained sealed to him, but they let him know that those vaults contained secrets of the sort of which his father had spoken, and they drove him half mad with the desire to see them, to hold and experience them. He lived and breathed to become as they, and they used this to their advantage.

They sent him out as a spy. They used him to carry messages to other ancients, to other lands. Each time promising a little more, each time seeming sincere, until that one day outside Rome when he'd returned to them, ready to beg, to prostrate himself before Gustav and plead for a single drop of that one's blood, and he'd found them gone. Vanished.

The road ahead wound up the mountain slowly, and on that road was the only man, living, dead, or otherwise, that Abraham hated now more than Gustav. They all seemed drawn by destiny toward some single focal point ahead, and though the hunger was eating at his mind and his thoughts, he kept his mount steady and slow, moving into the mountain's shadow quietly and with patience.

It was his silence that brought the soft footfalls to his ears, his focus that whipped his head about and down the side of the mountain, beyond the trail. He was being followed, clumsily, and the scent of blood was in the air. Turning back to the trail with a soft smile, he slowed his mount further. It was a beautiful night for an ambush.

SEVEN

The footfalls Abraham heard were hurried and uneven, not at all stealthy. He quickly revised his initial image of ambush to one of flight and changed course, plunging his mount off the road on the upward slope of the mountain and moving into the trees...picking his way along parallel to the trail below him, stopping now and again to listen, and to speed or slow in tandem with the one below. There were other sounds now, from further back, more footsteps, and voices. Whoever it was below was being followed, and they were desperate to escape.

Something in that pursuit dropped the temperature in the silent, still organ that was Abraham's heart. It was a relentless pursuit, neither gaining nor losing ground. Whoever was fleeing below was tiring quickly, but the pursuit only slowed. They were not trying to catch up, but to terrify.

The sounds of the pursuit themselves were calculated. Each gave a new direction, a new distance between pursuit and prey. There was no way to pinpoint how closely the others followed. Abraham stopped his mount, concentrating, reaching out with his mind, his senses, seeking those who hunted.

It took him only a moment's concentration to realize that one of those who followed was a vampire. Two heartbeats, one thundering, the other easy and slow, relaxed, but one set of footsteps and two horses. The Cainite traveled with a companion, and that might be information that could be used. Perhaps the human knew the truth about his partner, perhaps he did not. From the terror in the heart and frantic pace of their prey, it seemed likely that, if the pursued did not know *exactly* what he faced, he knew the degree of danger.

Suddenly a figure crashed from the trees beneath the road, staggering onto the surface and whipping his head frantically up and down the trail. His clothing was tattered and torn, his hair matted with dirt and sweat, but it was easy to see that the man was noble. The torn shirt was fine, and the soft leather boots that flapped, ruined under his feet, torn by use they were never meant to see, were finer still. His eyes were wide, mad with fear, and without thought the man plunged off the other side of the trail and up the mountain toward where Abraham sat, obscured from view now by a large outcropping of stone.

Abraham stood his ground. Any sudden motion and he would become prey as well, and though he was not truly fearful of those who followed, neither was he foolish. He'd felt his freedom stolen from him once, and the memory of it was burned deeply into his mind. He did not want to feel that helplessness, that burning hunger eating away at him from the inside out, again.

The man passed well beyond the far side of the stone, heedless of the eyes that marked his passing. Moments stretched to an eternity, and then the sounds of hoofbeats followed.

The two horsemen melted from the shadows, long cloaks stretched back behind them in the night breeze like the wings of giant bats. They rode smoothly and easily, slung low over the necks of their horses. They were dressed in black, head to toe, large black hats with wide brims that stretched to obscure their features further from view. A glint of silver shone on the breast of each, and as they passed, Abraham got a closer look.

They wore crosses. They were ornate, silver crosses, like those worn by the clergy in Rome. Priests. Those who pursued were priests, or agents of Rome. And he who fled? Abraham had meant to let them pass, to wait until they had moved beyond his sight and to return to the road, and his own task, but now his interest was piqued. It was not that uncommon for the Damned to move among the clergy. For agents of the Church to hunt and terrify by night was a centuries-old custom. The two bound together was an altogether different and less likely situation.

Moving very carefully, crossing around the far side of the stone from where the others had passed, Abraham paralleled the pursuers' course. It would not be long, in any case, before their prey fell to exhaustion and the hunt came to an end. There was nothing to be gained by remaining too close behind Montrovant at this point except detection, and that was something Abraham was not yet prepared to face.

The two wound up the mountain a few hundred feet, and very suddenly the easy going fell off and the cliff rose straight up, a sheer face of stone. It was against this backdrop that the chase reached its very sudden finale. Their prey ran to the cliff, looking wildly to the right and left, turning finally back the way he'd come. It was too late.

The two horsemen had ridden into sight, one to the man's left, the other on the right, carefully approaching. The smile of the rider on the right flashed a brilliant white in the moonlight, competing with the silver of his cross for Abraham's attention and nearly distracting him from the sight of the eyes above. Deep eyes…dark, but with glimmers of something, not exactly light, more like flames, dancing deep inside. The light did nothing to ease the darkness of that countenance.

Moving closer to the stone that still obscured him from sight, Abraham watched as the first rider dismounted slowly. The man's gaze locked onto that of the terrified noble cowering against the stone, and once he had the other under the sway of his deep, smoldering eyes, his gaze never wavered. The horse was left behind, and the dark man stalked his prey with eerie precision. His head shifted to one side, nose sniffing the air like an animal seeking a scent, though his eyes were trained steadily.

The distance between hunter and prey lessened steadily, and at last the dark man stopped, no more than a foot away from the other, having said no word, made no gesture other than that of a snake mesmerizing its dinner.

"I smell it," he said at last, gaze whipping around to meet that of his silent companion. "He has the scent on him, the taint of other worlds. The sulfur and the brimstone mix with his blood."

Spinning quickly, face lowered now and back bent, the hunter approached within inches of the other man's face. "You have spoken with them, haven't you?" he hissed sibilantly. "You have followed them into their dens of darkness, watched as they fed on the blood of God's people. You have led their lambs to slaughter, and all under the pretext of being a *godly* man."

The trapped man found his voice finally, head shaking back and forth, eyes both searching and pleading at once. "No, no, I swear to you. I have no idea, no idea what you want, who you are...please?"

"You may save your breath," the second rider said softly. "Noirceuil is not one to make mistakes, or to admit them if his first rule is broken. We know of your affairs, of those who rest beneath the floors of your keep by night and hunt our people by day. We know everything about you, in fact, and we will find them before we are done, with or without your cooperation.

"I would think that after the enormity of your sin, you would be prepared to repent. Your soul is surely damned, but there must be a lesser Hell that awaits those who beg forgiveness."

"But I have done nothing," the man dropped his head into his hands, moaning softly. "I swear to you by all that is holy. For God's sake, my own daughter has been slain, taken to darkness. Surely you must see that I could not be a part of that?"

Noirceuil stood over him for a long moment, watching the man shake and sob, eyes darkening with each heavy, rasping breath his victim took.

"You make a mistake when you take me for a fool, my friend," he hissed. "I can smell them on you, can sense their foul touch on your skin. Do you truly believe that if you keep their secrets they will come for you? I assure you, they will not, and if they do...it will be the last mistake they make in this world."

Reaching down suddenly, Noirceuil grabbed him by his disheveled hair, slamming his head back into the stone and laying bare the man's neck. Even from where Abraham peered from the shadows, the fang marks were obvious.

"They have fed from you, and yet you walk alive on the Earth. Do not do me the disservice of believing I do not know what this means. I assure you, there is little of their foul, damned hearts that I do not know, and well. I make it my business to know, and my business to end their madness wherever it crosses my path, such as it does this night. You will not be returning to their darkness, Dorval. You will not be completing the journey you have begun." At this moment Noirceuil slapped the man's throat hard, hand flat over the twin wounds of sharp truth.

Dorval lurched up and forward then, his courage returning in that last moment, or his sanity departing, and he lunged with his hands curled into claws at the cleric's throat. Noirceuil waited an impossibly long moment, shifting to one side at just the right moment to avoid Dorval's lurching attack. As his attacker stumbled, missing his target by the width of a man's hand, Noirceuil struck, his own hand coming down with massive force on the back of Dorval's skull, driving it harder and faster to the stony ground at their feet.

A sickening thump signaled Dorval's final meeting with the earth. Noirceuil stood over the suddenly inert body, gazing down in silence. As he turned to walk away from Dorval's corpse, his boot shot out suddenly, grinding into the back of the man's skull and driving it more fully into the earth.

"Ashes to ashes," he said, the words breathed softly, "dust to dust."

"You might have left him a breath to tell us which way they went," the second man's voice rang out suddenly. "You might, for once, have controlled that urge of yours to play God. We are here to serve the Lord in all his glory," the voice, now sarcastic, droned on, "not to feed the fires below. It is quite warm enough on this mountain without our help."

Noirceuil's gaze lifted to meet his companion's, and his voice cracked suddenly across the space between them like a whip. "You will be better served by prayer, and by vigilance, than by sarcasm, Lacroix. He was tainted, and he would not have told us anything that we could use, or that I cannot find without his help. I tracked him here to save his soul, and to rid the world of potential evil. We will find those we seek, do not trouble yourself on that account. I am quite unaccustomed to failure."

Lacroix fell silent at Noirceuil's words, but his eyes did not waver. They swam with the fire of the fanatic, and again Abraham pressed more tightly to the stone, stroking his horse's neck gently. He nearly prayed himself that moment, for the animal's silence, and his own safety, but it proved unnecessary.

Noirceuil glanced about the clearing once, shaking his head oddly, and sweeping his gaze over the stone with a curious glint in his eyes, but at last turned he to his mount and slipped easily back into the saddle.

"The trail grows cold," he said softly. "Let us ride, my friend."

The two wheeled, spinning toward the road below and away. Abraham sat as he was. He watched, and he thought about what he'd just witnessed. Noirceuil was Damned. There was no doubt of it, no way it could be denied, and yet, there lay a dead body, filled with fresh, hot blood, and Noirceuil had turned from it, without so much as a backward glance, and ridden away.

One thing was confirmed. Lacroix might know or suspect a great deal of dark things about his partner, but it was becoming glaringly obvious that the one thing that should have set off the alarm bells in that man's brain was the one thing he was ignoring. Noirceuil was hunting the Cainites for the Church. He was putting an end to his own kind without thought, and to those who served them.

After waiting what he felt was a safe amount of time, and then waiting a bit longer, Abraham rode from the shadows and dismounted slowly. He stepped closer, leaning to grab Dorval by his hair, lifting the ruined face from the stone and bringing the inert form limply into his arms.

Without hesitation he latched onto the dead throat, drinking the cooling blood, slaking the hunger that had gripped him the moment he felt the man's heartbeat, fleeing the two priests below the trail. His hunger, unquenched for two solid days, had pounded through him, backdrop to every thought, every image that flitted through his mind tainted by that insidious crimson haze.

That left the question of Noirceuil more prominent in his mind. Who was the man, and what motivated him? How could he walk so calmly from the curse that seared through Abraham's veins? Why did he hunt his own?

The worst of it was the connection to the Church. If there were vampire hunters in the hire of the Church in Rome, and they were on the road at the same time, in the same area, as he, Abraham wondered why it was that Bishop Santorini had failed to mention it. There were two possibilities, neither of which calmed Abraham's nerves.

The Church might not trust Santorini any longer. The bishop had been the liaison between Montrovant and Rome, and Montrovant was gone, as well as the Order he'd been supposed to be "guarding." None of this was likely to have won Santorini points in the Vatican.

The other possibility was that it was Santorini

who lacked trust in his own agent, that he had turned Abraham over to another branch of the Church. The solution of a problem was more certain if it was approached by more than one avenue. What if Santorini was also behind these others, and they were also on Montrovant's trail, or Abraham's own? Too many things left to question, and no answers to be had except through the road ahead.

If he found Montrovant, he knew, things would fall into place, one way or the other. If these others sought the dark one as well, they would find him a bit more of a challenge than Dorval, whose drained, worthless carcass now slipped back to the earth that would eventually claim it. Abraham wiped his sleeve over his lips, cleaning away the last remnant of blood, mind lost in thought.

The night was not so old, despite all that had happened, and Abraham knew he should return to the road soon, but he held back a bit longer, moving back to the stone and seating himself with his back to that solid wall, thinking. Montrovant would waste no time reaching France, but that made the trail easier to follow. A straight line was what the dark one would take, and that is how Abraham would follow.

Abraham wondered at these others. He wondered if this Noirceuil knew as much of those he sought as he claimed, and what could possibly have turned him so against his own that he would hunt them like animals. Most pointedly he wondered why he'd never heard the names Noirceuil or Lacroix before, and what they would mean to his own future.

Mounting at last, he returned slowly to the road and continued on over the mountain, not hurrying his pace, wanting to catch up with neither Noirceuil nor Montrovant until it was at a time and under circumstances of his own choosing.

There would be time to pick up Montrovant's trail once all of them were safely across the border in France. The time in between would allow him to make a few contacts of his own and communicate with Santorini. There were answers he needed now, and he needed them quickly. He was in as much danger from the Church which had sent him on this fool's errand, it seemed, as Montrovant himself. More so, in all likelihood, considering the dark one's age and power. He did not intend to leap in headlong until he at least knew the depth of the hole he was entering.

He moved slowly down the road, lost in thought, as those ahead pulled steadily away, moving to their own designs.

⁂

Noirceuil and Lacroix made good time now that the hunt was over and behind them. Neither spoke, but they moved comfortably together. They had shared long roads, and though neither qualified as *normal* by the standards of the world at large, they were well acquainted with one another's idiosyncrasies.

Lacroix tolerated his partner's odd hours and habits because, whatever dark hunger it was that drove him, the truth was that Noirceuil's methods were the most effective Lacroix had ever seen. To live as they lived, to hunt and sleep by the light of day, to leave behind all that meant the most in life, all for a dream of service to God. All for the good of Rome.

Noirceuil's mind was so attuned to the Damned they hunted that his habits mimicked theirs at times. His violence grew with each hunt, his ability to ferret them intuitively from behind their clever disguises and the many masks they wore was unparalleled. Some of that ability had rubbed off onto Lacroix himself, but most of their success as a team was based on Noirceuil. If not Lacroix himself, there would be others to travel by the hunter's side.

Lacroix's ability was of a more mundane nature. He was well connected in the Church. His own efforts were largely responsible for the recognition of the Damned, and the dangers they presented to Rome. His quiet, whispered praise of Noirceuil, his own name cleverly inserted whenever possible, had led to the founding of their own small branch of the growing power of the Inquisition itself.

The Pope would not be coming to their rescue if they got into trouble. That much he'd not been able to accomplish, but at least they were supported, and cleared for safe passage and assistance wherever possible. It was a start. The more of the evil, blood-sucking monsters they brought down, the further they could push their cause, and their own worth.

Lacroix expected one day to be a bishop. Noirceuil, he knew, would be the hunter still. No amount of success would quell that one's hatred. No amount of revenge would end his pain, whatever it might be.

Lacroix had attempted once to delve into Noirceuil's past. One lonely night, three damned souls rotting back to dust in the wake of their passing, he'd broached the subject of the past. He'd gone so far as to ask the hunter why—why the pain, the fire…the darkness?

It was a mistake he'd never repeated. One glance into those cold, deep, empty eyes, had been enough answer for a lifetime. For several lifetimes. Noirceuil had not said a word. Nothing. He'd turned from the fire, moved into the darkness, and disappeared, not returning until early morning. The fire had burned low, but Lacroix had not slept. Something in his partner's actions had chilled him beyond the ability of simple flame to brush aside.

No words had been spoken. Noirceuil, true to his habit, his ritual, had moved to his horse, grabbed his pack, and secluded himself from the sunlight that morning, leaving Lacroix alone to face the day. The subject had been dropped, and it remained a mystery that Lacroix had decided was better left unsolved.

Now, on the road once more, he was beginning to wonder about the stability of his hunter, and their future together. The hunt for Dorval had been a long one. Months of watching and spying, reports and intrigue, had ferreted this lone human from the ranks of hundreds of others, informant and servant to the one they sought, this Montrovant.

Then they had spent another week in getting the man away from his own people, out alone where he could be separated quietly, and hunted. The hunt had always been a challenge, a glorious moment of hot blood and dark thrill. That had not changed. What had changed was Noirceuil.

The man should not have been killed without questioning. The entire circle of intrigue they'd drawn had become so much wasted effort in that one short moment, and Noirceuil did not even see it. He was blinded now by his rage. The closer they came to this one, this Montrovant, the crazier Noirceuil became.

After this hunt, Lacroix decided, he would be forced to offer his partner a choice. Take a hiatus, regain control of his thoughts and regain the focus that had made him the force for God he'd become...or have his association with Lacroix, Rome, and the protection that came with it all severed. Lacroix did not intend to have his own future plans destroyed in a fit of insane rage.

The only question, he knew, as he watched Noirceuil's mount cut through the night, its grim passenger bent low against the whipping of the wind, was how to break that news and remain alive himself.

EIGHT

The mountain did not hold Montrovant and his followers back for long, though they were getting a bit nervous over the cold and the lack of supplies before they reached the pass on the far side, winding down. Beyond that mountain they could see smoke from scattered settlements and camps, and signs of activity on the road. This side did not seem quite as secluded.

Montrovant took to leaving the others behind as they began moving again each evening, and not returning until late in the night, or early morning, in time for making camp. He took Le Duc with him twice...two other times he went alone. Not a word was spoken to his men of where he'd been, or why.

Since the events in the monastery, and his "feast" with Rachel, they were quiet and subdued in his presence. Their loyalty was not swayed, but the answers to questions they had been content to leave as mysteries had been thrust upon them by fate. Her story was quite a bit to swallow all at once, as well.

The dark one was content to watch them, waiting for them to sort it out. They all knew him, and his ways. They also knew that they would not live long if they chose to cross him. That left the two choices of accepting, or dying. There was little doubt in any mind which they would choose. All that was truly in question was the manner in which they would work it out in their hearts and minds.

Montrovant was lost in his own world. He left like a shadow and returned just as silently. He spoke only when spoken to, and his brief replies left little doubt that his silence was not to be disturbed. So they rode, and they waited. The days slipped slowly away behind them, and they neared the border of France. They were passing small villages now, stopping now and then at an inn, or to awaken the merchants in a small market in order to replace their supplies. Montrovant spent those times in the streets, the alleys, asking questions and slipping gold from his fingers into the hands of those who possessed what he sought—knowledge.

Le Duc watched in silence as well. It was not the first time he'd been left to wait, and to watch, guarding his sire's back. He held the men together, listened to their stories, their jokes, and the mumbled questions, quickly suppressed whenever Montrovant appeared. Although they feared Jeanne as well, each knew that Le Duc himself feared Montrovant. He was their link, their liaison to their leader, and he tried to do what he could to fill that role without betraying the trust of either side.

One of the oldest and truest rules he'd learned since his Embrace was a deep-rooted distrust of mortals. They served their purpose, and they made excellent servants and slaves, but to trust them with your existence was little short of foolish. That was the position Montrovant had put them both in. It was an indication of the dark one's sense that it was all coming to a close. They had sought the Grail for so long that Le Duc could scarcely remember a time when it had not been his focus, or at least a secondary focus.

Through that time Montrovant had run hot and cold. They had been close enough that their goal seemed just beyond their groping reach, and so far away that the entire thing seemed like a foolish dream. None of those times had been like this. Montrovant was drawn inward, concentrated and focused, and they traveled at a pace that indicated Montrovant knew where he was going.

Each time Montrovant left and returned, they shifted their course slightly. He was on the hunt, and he'd caught the scent of his prey; the only thing left was the chase. They slept by day in any shelter they could find that was adequate protection, cemeteries, old abandoned keeps and churches. One night was spent in the root cellar of a farm house. The family, a man, his wife and his daughter, had fallen to Montrovant and Le Duc, and the others had ransacked the place, taking anything of use and disposing of the bodies as Montrovant and Le Duc slipped into the cellar and pulled the strong oak doors closed over their heads. They had left the place with their packs full, leaving no trace whatsoever of a struggle, or their passing. Another mystery for the drunks to debate hotly in the inns by night. Another step closer to their goal.

Eventually their path wound into the city of Grenoble. The lower reaches of the mountain were behind them at last, and the farmland stretched to either side of the road where they passed. The dwellings of the farmers and a few larger homes appeared, near enough to the road to be made out in the hours of darkness, fires lit, smoke rising from chimneys. Montrovant ignored them. He was more careful as they neared the city.

It was necessary to minimize their presence whenever possible. He had little fear from the inhabitants of Grenoble unless he was careless, but there was no reason to spread rumors of strange happenings before he even entered the city's boundary. Grenoble was not a small city, and it was certain to boast Cainites of its own. Le Duc knew nothing of them, but Montrovant was wary. Le Duc had long been aware that anything that made his sire leery was worth looking out for, even if one did not know exactly what it was.

With inns and women and the promise of ale just around the corner, the spirits of the others were picking up as well. Nothing had changed in the way things were between them and their lord. He treated them just as he always had, if a bit more silently than was his norm, and that lack of change was heartening. He had trusted them with his very existence, and he did not seem to be regretting that decision. It made them proud to a man, drawing them slowly closer together than they had been before.

A rumor had even started among them, much to Jeanne's amusement, that Montrovant sought the Grail only so that he might drink blood from it and become human once more, to drink and carouse with them, dying a natural death.

It was a healthy tale, one with no danger that Le Duc could foresee, so he ignored it. When questioned, he merely watched the eyes of whoever asked until they were forced to look away, neither confirming nor denying their theory. He knew that his silence was tantamount to agreement, but was careful to leave it at that. It might come in useful if they needed a rallying point, a standard against which to call loyalty beyond that they already held. Save Montrovant's soul. Find the Grail and make him a man among men once more...bring him back to the sunlight.

Under other circumstances it might have been funny. Montrovant sought a great many things, but a return to mortality was not among them. Jeanne himself had contemplated that subject more than once. He remember riding to battle in daylight, the sun glistening off the armor and weapons of a thousand men. He recalled the subtle pleasures of the flesh, the sweet hot bite of wine and the cool, swiftly heating flesh of a woman. Nothing in all the years since his Embrace had been able to wipe away the memories of those sensations.

It meant nothing. When laid beside the hunt, and the sensation of hot, red blood flowing down the throat, it paled. When the brightness of the day, coupled with its discomfort, sweat, and toil was held to the mirror of cool nights, bright moonlight, and stamina and strength beyond human reckoning, it reflected poorly. Though the images of his life, and the things and people he'd left behind crept into his dreams at times, there were no real regrets. There was nothing to draw them back toward the world of humanity and mortality save the off-kilter promise of salvation and redemption, hard to believe in on the best of nights, and certainly nothing to die for. Not any longer.

No, Montrovant did not seek that. He sought to

rule, to gain more power, to set himself above his own and others and have them acknowledge him as superior. He sought entertainment in all its forms. He had told Eugenio, his own sire, that it was for the "family," the Lasombra. Le Duc knew better. They had left the dark one on his own for so long that he had become quite the renegade, bending his will and energy to abilities not strictly inherent in his blood. Making his own way. Trafficking with Nosferatu and Ventrue alike, sitting late under the moonlight with the gypsy-blooded Gangrel. He knew no boundaries of family, and if it were not for the Blood Oath, he would not bother to acknowledge Eugenio. With the Grail in hand, Le Duc was uncertain that even that bond would hold him.

Now they moved into a city none of them had seen in over a hundred years. Too much could change in such a span of time. Those in power once, even among the Damned, were not so likely to be the same. And there was a banding together among those of like blood; the powers in a city were not as accepting of outsiders. The older one became in the blood—and Montrovant was old—the more valuable they became to those who came after. France was home to both Montrovant and Le Duc, but they had been away too long to expect a cordial welcome.

They entered the narrow streets of the city only about an hour after sunset, walking their horses slowly down the streets, eyes sweeping right and left, taking in businesses and homes, markets and scurrying peasants. None approached them, but all were watching. They moved in silence until at last Montrovant turned down an even narrower side street, almost an alley, and led them to the very end. The road ended at a sheer wall of brick with an alley turning right, and another left. Montrovant swung his mount around to the left and led them into deeper shadows until they reached the rear of the row of dilapidated homes.

Montrovant dismounted, taking the reins of his horse and making it fast to a rail. The others followed more slowly as the dark one mounted the back stairs of the building, produced a key from some dark fold of his cloak, and pressed the door inward, disappearing from view.

They followed him quickly, glancing at one another in consternation. They had been looking forward to a night or two spent in one of the many inns Grenoble boasted. They had dreamed of women, roasted meat and wine. He brought them to cobwebs and dust. The building had obviously housed no one in a number of years.

"We will make this our base," Montrovant said as they joined him inside. "You may move about by day and bring the provisions you will need, but you will at all costs remain absolutely silent about our mission. Leave the questioning to myself, and to Jeanne. I want it to appear in every way as if we are a band of knights, weary of the road, ready to make our home here for an indefinite period of time. When we have all that we need, we will disappear the same way we entered. If I have my way, that will be tomorrow night. Silently and quickly."

There was a moment of silence, but no complaints. The inns would still be there, and he had not forbidden them access. Silence was a small price to pay. Once the initial disappointment wore off, the wisdom of his choice became apparent. They were at the very back end of a street where, if there were any inhabitants at all, they were not showing themselves.

They moved about the large home, poking into closets and shadowed corners, finding some wood still stacked beside the fireplace, which had not been cleaned out in years, and set about making a makeshift camp inside. They knew it was best not to change too much that was visible. The smoke alone would attract some attention, and the idea of slipping into this uninhabited little corner of the city was to attract none. Still, when St. Fond struck a spark and brought a small pile of tinder to a quick blaze, Montrovant said nothing. He turned to the door, Le Duc close behind, and moved into the streets.

※

Jeanne and Montrovant moved very quickly once they left the others behind. Le Duc watched their back, carefully scanning the streets for any

paying too much attention to their passing.
Montrovant moved through streets and back alleys
as if they were his backyard. They were on the far
side of town before he finally slowed and stopped
before the doors of a huge, ancient building. The
edifice had once been a magnificent place, spanning four streets across and two back. Later days
had cost it much of its glory. The lower floors had
become a catacombed conglomeration of taverns,
vendors, and shadowed alcoves.

Montrovant swept his gaze up and down the
building's face, then stepped quickly through a
doorway. Soft light leaked out from the interior,
firelight dancing merrily. Above the door, hanging
crookedly on a bent nail, a sign proclaimed "La
Flambeau." The low hum of voices joined with the
soft throb of heartbeats to draw Jeanne in his sire's
wake.

The scent of roasting meat and that of sweet red
wine drifted to Jeanne, but the blood drowned it,
diluting it to a background haze. He heard the
voices and could make out some of the words, but
that first instant, melting into that moving mass of
life and heat, was always dizzying for him. Jeanne
had spent the earlier years after Montrovant had
Embraced him traveling, secluded. He had never
quite gotten used to the crowds.

Montrovant moved quickly ahead, and Jeanne
concentrated, following as his sire led him toward
the back of the tavern to a table in the shadows.

Here they slid onto benches on opposite sides of a rough-hewn table and leaned against the wall, watching the activity in the room.

Jeanne had no idea what they were looking for, so he let his senses range as widely as possible, feeling he could do the most good by missing nothing. He mentally noted each face, tried to catch the tones of each voice. It distracted him from the growing hunger. Montrovant showed no signs of such an inner struggle. His eyes were clear and deep, sweeping the room with purpose.

The ceiling was high, but hung with nets, the sort you would find on fishing vessels. Lamps were mounted on the walls, soaking the room in mellow, golden light. It was surprisingly busy for such a late hour. It was not a prosperous area of the city, and the surrounding buildings and shops had shown nothing similar in the way of activity.

"Why do they come here?" Jeanne said softly. "What is this place?"

Montrovant turned slowly, eyes still staring across the tavern. "It is an old place, Jeanne. The rest of the city has moved away, but this one tavern remains of the old city. When the Crusaders came through, they drank here. Templars were closeted in the basements and transported safely from these walls when Philip decreed them disbanded. I believe that, should the rest of the city crumble to dust around it, this one place would have light, and music."

Jeanne watched Montrovant carefully as he listened. Such poetic discourse was hardly the dark one's habit.

"You know this place, then," Jeanne prompted.

"I have been here many times. It is a good place to find secrets, my friend. Sometimes one finds secrets that others do not even know are secrets. So many pass through here, it is easy to forget those who stay. Those with eyes and quick wits. These are the ones I seek. If the Order passed through Grenoble, or near the city, information about that passing also passed through here. You may count on that."

Jeanne looked about again, this time watching for those most comfortable…larger groups not attired for travel, or the road. Eventually one of the serving girls made her way to the table and Montrovant ordered mulled wine for them both. The warm, scented drinks filled their senses, the heat enticing, but the aroma fell so far short of blood that it nearly nauseated Jeanne, who was less used to such masquerades.

"There," Montrovant said at last. He nodded toward a man leaning against the far wall, his fist gripping a tall mug of ale tightly. The man's eyes were never still, and each time he shifted his gaze in another direction, his head cocked, as though he listened for sounds on the wind. "He will know, if any do. If not, he will know who does."

The dark one rose, and Jeanne followed. They

136

moved along the wall of the room, carefully avert-
ing their eyes from the one they sought. As they
turned toward the bar, their paths running directly
before the man, Montrovant raised his eyes and
caught the man's attention. At first it seemed the
other would flee, or turn away. His mistake was
meeting the eyes.

They were beside him in seconds, and
Montrovant's arm had snaked around the man's
shoulders in a friendly gesture of camaraderie.

"You will come with us," the dark one whispered.
The man had no chance. He was swept from his
post by the wall, pressed through the crowd and out
the door before he even had a chance to finish his
ale, or set down the mug. None took any notice of
their passing, and they were in an alley moments
later, their new companion pressed tightly to one
stone wall.

"I wish only information," Montrovant said,
voice steady and low. "You will provide it, and then
you will return to your drinking, a much wealthier
man. The other possibility, of course, is that you
will lie to me, or resist, in which case, you will not
return at all."

The man twisted to one side, trying to make a
break, and Montrovant slapped him hard, slamming his head back into the stone. Trembling now,
their prisoner waited, eyes wide.

"I...I have done nothing. I came only for a
drink, please..."

"I am counting, my friend, on the fact that you very often 'come only for a drink,'" Montrovant said, smiling darkly. "Now, no more foolishness. I am seeking a strange group of men. They would have passed through here in the last month, or near here. Probably they traveled in the guise of monks, moving only by night and transporting a cargo in one or two wagons."

The man's eyes shifted. Jeanne saw that the fear, which had ruled the fellow's face seconds before, was swept aside momentarily by greed, then again by a wary, sidelong expression that attempted to avoid Montrovant's eyes.

"I never saw such a group in my life, lord, but might be I've heard tell of such a thing."

The man waited, as if expecting something, and Montrovant lunged forward suddenly, his forearm pressing the man's throat to the wall. "I have no time to play games with you over this. Tell me what you know. If it is what I need, you will be rewarded; if not..."

The man tried to swallow, fought the panic as his air was cut off, then relaxed a bit as Montrovant pulled back. After a harsh coughing wheeze, and a quick rub of his throat, the story poured out quickly.

"I was in the bar, minding my own business as usual, having an ale with Jean Thomas, the bartender's boy, when three men came in looking as if the spirit of Lucifer himself was on their heels.

DAVID NIALL WILSON

These were not timid men now," the man's eyes narrowed, as if testing to be certain Montrovant understood, "they had the look of bandits, and I've seen a few of them in my time."

"Get on with it," Montrovant grated.

"Well," the man cleared his throat, seeing that it was no time for lengthy tales, "they claimed they'd been with a larger group, on the road, when they'd met a small caravan coming the other way, skirting the edge of the city. They said it seemed odd to them, such a group traveling in the dead of night, so they hailed them."

The man stopped here, turning to include Jeanne in his gaze for a moment, then continued. "You ask me, the only greeting offered was a demand for their gold. These were up to no good, that much is certain.

"To make the story short, for they went on a long time, babbling about demons and death, they said it was a group of monks and that their companions had been killed. They only survived because they'd hung back. Me, I think they were cowards. In any case, no one paid much attention to them, except me.

"Not sure exactly why, but I just couldn't imagine them making up such a crazy story. It stuck with me, and now that you mention a group traveling like that, it comes back to me. I hear a lot in that tavern."

"Where might we find these gentlemen?"

Montrovant hissed. "Those who saw?"

The man's eyes widened for just a moment, then he met the dark one's gaze once more and spoke. "I wouldn't know for certain, now," he coughed, still fighting for air, "but there's a forest just outside the city where it is said their like can be found. A place to be avoided."

Montrovant released him suddenly, drawing back with a humorless smile.

"That is exactly what I needed to hear." He reached into his cloak and withdrew his pouch, counting out several gold coins and dropping them into the man's hand. The last of these he held for a moment. "You say you see a lot of things in that tavern," Montrovant's voice had gone very cold...very distant. "You did not see myself, or my companion. Ever. We never asked you questions, and you never answered. Believe me when I tell you that if I find you have forgotten this last bit of information, you will die a very long, slow, painful death...at my own hand. Am I clear?"

The man nodded, gasping as Montrovant's arm pressed again into his throat. The dark one dropped the last gold coin, which bounced off the fellow's hand and into the dirt of the alley with a dull thud.

The informant dived after the coin, scrabbling around in the dark alley for a moment and letting out a soft cry as his hand wrapped around the smooth surface of the coin.

As he turned to rise, his jaw dropped, and his face

140

grew pale. He was alone in the alley. There was no sign of Montrovant, or Jeanne, no sound had marked their passing. He glanced down at the coin once more, shaking. It was real, very real, and the dark one's words slipped back in to haunt his mind as he returned to the bar in search of something stronger than ale.

⁂

The two horsemen approached the rear wall of the cathedral shortly after midnight, drawing up short of the rear wall. Noirceuil remained mounted, staring at the huge edifice fixedly, but Lacroix slid easily from the saddle and approached. He'd been there many times before, and he knew his old friend, Cardinal du Pois, would be expecting them. If they were to make their greetings and be properly welcomed, it was important that they make their way inside at a decent hour.

"We should search the city," Noirceuil said harshly. "If we wait, we will be left behind again."

"We have our orders, my friend," Lacroix reminded his partner with a stern glance. "If we are on the road another few days for the delay, what does it matter? His Eminence, Cardinal du Pois, is expecting us. Who knows, maybe his men have learned something. You know that he is aware of the focus of our mission, if not the...details?"

Noirceuil nodded distractedly, then spoke again. "They are not equipped as we to search. The dark one could slide through their fingers without their

To Dream of Dreamers Lost

even being aware of his passing. You know this, Alexis. I wish only to complete our mission, to rid the Earth of his evil. I burn to do this, and the delays do not sit well with my heart."

"They are necessary delays, Noirceuil," Lacroix answered, tying his horse off near the wall and climbing the stairs to pound on the rear door. "I wonder sometimes what has happened to you, my friend? You act as though hell is going to rise and swallow you in a matter of hours and every blood sucker must be wiped from the Earth before it happens. We have time."

The door opened quickly, and three cowled monks stepped out, exchanging polite greetings with Lacroix. Noirceuil watched them for another long moment, as if he might just turn and ride away, then he reluctantly dismounted, handing the reins over to one of the men who reached for them and following Lacroix into the cathedral.

"If he escapes us," Noirceuil said, as he stepped past Lacroix toward the door, his voice very low, "it will be on your head."

The echo of those words followed them down the vaulted passage beyond the doors, and Lacroix let them die to a silence punctuated only by their footsteps. He could feel the glaring intensity of his partner's eyes seeming to bore into his back, and for the first time since knowing the man, felt a small twinge of fear for himself. Shivering, he continued into the shadows.

DAVID NIALL WILSON

NINE

Abraham approached Grenoble warily. He knew
that it would be difficult for a party the size of
Montrovant's to hide in the city, but the two agents
of the Church were a different story altogether. If
they came from Rome, they might know about
Abraham, and from the looks of the Damned one,
Noirceuil, it would not matter if Abraham were on
a mission from the Church or not. If they met, one
of them would not walk away.

He kept to the shadows, using the roads only
when necessary, and slipped into the city from one
of the side roads. He'd visited Grenoble once before, many years back. He knew which side the
cathedral was located on, and he entered from the

other side. He had his own letters of introduction from Rome, but Noirceuil and Lacroix had changed his perspective on their value. It seemed Abraham was on his own, more so than he'd thought.

It was possible that Santorini was not even alive. The bishop had been in disfavor after Montrovant's departure; if word, somehow, had gotten to the Church that he had hired another of the Damned to join in the hunt, it might have been too much for the venerable cardinals to accept. They weren't above executing their own to preserve their secrets.

There was to have been a communication for Abraham waiting along the road, anything pertinent, but now he decided he would do without it, and Santorini without his answer. He would find Montrovant on his own, and he would do what he could do, but he wouldn't risk being destroyed by those who had sent him.

Up until that night on mountain, the only one who brought fear to Abraham's heart had been Montrovant. Noirceuil had doubled that number.

He slipped out through the entrance of an alley and cantered down the empty street. It was still fairly early in the evening, families were in their homes eating, the day was over and it was still early for those who haunted the streets and taverns by night. He needed to be certain he had a safe haven for the coming day before he could begin his search. It was always the same, and particularly difficult in such a large city. He knew he could just ride out of the city and sink into the earth, but he would almost surely lose his mount doing that, unless he stabled it and walked. The city was no place for a vampire far from anything familiar to wander unannounced, and it was another delay.

Montrovant was no fool. If he'd come to Grenoble he'd done so with a specific plan in mind, and he would not waste a lot of time over it. The dark one had his own agenda, and it did not allow a lot of time for wandering about city streets. Without the refuge of the cathedral to count on, Abraham knew he would be wasting valuable time. He moved through the center of the city quickly, heading for the older part of town. Near the fringes things were falling into disrepair. There were abandoned homes, others gutted by fires, even a church with the wooden doors swinging loosely. The place had been vandalized and looted long before and left to rot.

Beyond that was a small cemetery. Abraham moved closer, considering...but he caught several dark flitting shapes, just out of the line of his vision, and decided against it. There were others there. He could sense them, and knew they had felt his presence as well. They were waiting to see if he would move into their territory, and he had no time for such confrontation. They might offer him sanctuary, or they might drag him off and drain him for their own strength. He moved further to the edge of the town, and he saw what he was looking for.

An old house stood, shutters long rotted away, windows open and gutted, but with a shed still standing out back. There was no sign that any other had set foot on the property for years, but somehow the shed still stood. It would do to hide his horse from the road. As he approached, a second pleasant surprise met his gaze.

There was a rotted wooden door flush with the foundation of the ruined house, angled downward. A wine cellar. It was perfect, if the door did not crumble in his hand. He might not have to take to the earth after all.

He opened the door to the shed, peering inside and inspecting the walls, the floor, looking for any sign of recent inhabitation or use. There were none to be seen. It was empty, musty, and smelled of the musk of cats. Still, for a single day, it would do the animal no harm. He could leave food and water. The beast was well trained…it would not give him away, and if it did, still, there would be no reason for any to search the cellar.

He made a quick circuit of that dank place as well. There was a low table that was still sturdy, and though it was slimed with mold and very old, it would hold his weight nicely. Rats peered out at him from the little cubbyholes that had once held wine, and vermin crawled along the base of the walls. There was not a chink in the wood of the door. No light would enter, and if by some odd fluke the doors were opened, he would be far enough inside that direct sunlight would never reach him.

It would do. He left the majority of his things in the cellar and returned to his mount, heading back into the city. It was later now, and there were lights and sounds rising from the squares and taverns. He smelled the scent of fresh, red blood, and very suddenly realized how long it had actually been since he'd fed. Too long.

Now that he was among mortals again, too close for control, it was driving him mad. He caught a sudden, close scent, and then the sounds reached him. A low, chuckling voice, rang out. The smooth sound of a blade being drawn...a dagger. Muffled cries. Abraham slid from his mount quietly, making it fast to one of the posts that lined the street and slipped along the nearest wall to the mouth of the alley.

Inside Abraham saw two figures, one large, the other slender. He slipped into the mouth of the alley and the scene became clearer. A large bearded man was facing a young woman. She was pressing her back to the wall, and though he stood two heads taller than she, there was a fiery glint in the girl's eyes. She had a very small blade gripped tightly in one hand, and though he was laughing at her, her assailant stood back a bit warily, his own dagger gleaming brilliantly in a small patch of moonlight filtering down between the buildings.

Neither heard Abraham as he approached. He stepped closer, the scent of their blood pounding through him...driving his thoughts deeper as he fought for a few more moments of control.

"Come on," the man grated lazily. "You will like Pierre."

The girl said nothing, but her expression spoke volumes. There was no defeat marring the soft beauty of her features, and her muscles were tensed to spring. She glanced up the alley, watching as the big man foolishly allowed his gaze to track hers along the wall. In that instant she moved. Her blade whipped out in a quick arc, slicing through the back of the man's knee and dropping him instantly, drawing a howl of rage from his throat. He was drunk, and it was possibly numbness brought on by the alcohol that allowed him to react at all.

His massive arm swung, catching her ankle, barely, and sending her tumbling forward. He gripped her by the thigh with his huge paw of a hand and drew her toward him with a roar. She lifted her blade, but he caught her arm easily.

It was then that Abraham moved. He slid from the shadows without thought, his hand gripping the man's before it could snap the girl's arm. Abraham gave a twist and the man released her, yelping in sudden pain, then whipping around to his new opponent in maddened rage.

"You have interfered in the wrong fight, my friend," Pierre grated. "I will kill you now, and then I will kill this little tramp for what she has done to me."

Abraham laughed then, an empty, lost, hungry laughter that echoed up and down the alley and sent the girl cringing against the wall.

"You will kill nothing, ever." Abraham said softly. "You will beg, and you will die, and you will not even die an honorable death, because one who would attack young women deserve no honor."

As he spoke, Abraham twisted the arm he'd grabbed, slowly, feeling it giving way, bones snapping. Pierre was gibbering, then screaming in pain, and Abraham covered the man's mouth with his boot, pressing down to stifle the sound. Then the hunger rose and he could no longer deny it. With a roar more animal than human he fell on the hapless Pierre, latching onto the man's throat, sinking his fangs deep.

He held the bigger man easily...lifting him and arching into the hunger...the pleasure...feeling the warmth and strength flowing through him. He fed quickly, without regard to his surroundings, or the girl. It was not until he staggered back, letting Pierre's near-lifeless form drop to the dirt of the alley floor that he remembered her at all, and then only because she gasped.

He spun. She stood very still, backed against the stone wall as he'd first seen her, but frightened now, trembling like a leaf in the wind and ready to blow off down the alley and run for her life. Only the combined shock of Pierre's attack and the horror she'd just witnessed held her pinned in place.

Something in him brought his mind back to sudden focus, and he managed to speak.

"Wait," he said. "Wait, do not go."

She nearly bolted then, but he'd caught her in his gaze, and she remained, pinned to the wall helplessly.

"Please," she managed to gasp. "Oh please…"

He stepped closer, wiping his lips on his sleeve, trying to steady his nerves. He spoke again, soothingly.

"It is all right, little one. He deserved it. I am sorry you had to see, but surely you do not mourn for Pierre?"

She shook her head slowly back and forth, but Abraham could not tell if it was in negation of mourning or what she'd just witnessed. He moved closer still. He knew he would have to calm her, or kill her. There was no room for such a rumor to spread if he was to reach his goal.

He stopped short of touching her, watching her quietly. "I am sorry to have frightened you, but I assure you, you have nothing to fear from me. What is your name, little one?"

Her eyes went wider for a moment, then some of the steel he'd noted when she faced off against Pierre returned. She cleared her throat, and managed to say, "F-Fleurette, Monsieur."

Abraham grinned at her. "Little flower…a very deadly blossom, it would seem. Another moment and you'd have gotten away from you friend over there," he pointed at what remained of Pierre, "without my help."

She did not answer, only watched him, warily, as if she were ready to turn and run. He decided the direct approach was the only one he could afford time for.

"You did not see what you just saw," he told her matter-of-factly. "You were in a fight, you killed Pierre, if any ask. You never saw me at all."

She shook her head, an almost stubborn light coming to her eyes. "What did you do?" she asked suddenly. "How did you kill him so easily? You broke his arm. I saw you. You broke his arm and you drank his blood. You are vampire…"

He nodded. "Yes…and you never saw me. You don't even believe in me. Pierre was drunk, and slow, and he picked the wrong girl to assault in an alley. I have things I must do this night, others I must find. I cannot let you run off and tell the city to beware of 'the vampire,' so I will tell you a last time. You never saw me."

"I will show you," she said softly. "If there are things to be found in Grenoble, Fleurette can find them faster than you." Her gaze swept up and down him, eyes dancing. She still feared him, but that fear was giving way quickly to something else…recklessness? Curiosity?

"I would be slowed," he started to say.

"You will be slow without me," she retorted before he could finish. "Fleurette knows every tavern, every alley in the city. Tell me what it is you seek." She grew silent for a long moment, then met his gaze once more. "You have saved my life. Let me help you."

He watched her a moment longer, then realized that it was either allow her to guide him, or kill her, and also that she was right. He had not been in Grenoble in years. She would better know where he might find Montrovant, or his men.

"Very well, little flower," he said, letting his hand slip out very, very quickly, so quickly she could neither follow the motion or prevent it. He let his nails slide caressingly over her cheek. "Do not disappoint me. I have a very important task to complete, and I promise you have nothing to fear if you aid me in this."

"I will help you because you saved my life," she said, pulling away from his touch for a moment, then leaning back into it. "I will not betray you. Fleurette is as good as her word."

He nodded again. Then, as quickly as he could, he gave her a description of Montrovant. He had only the vaguest of descriptions of the others, but the dark one's features were imbedded in his memory. He couldn't rid himself of them, even when he tried.

She listened carefully, then nodded. "And he will seek information?" she asked. Her face grew thoughtful for a moment, then she turned to him, very serious. "He is like you, this Montrovant? He is a vampire?"

Abraham nodded. "Montrovant is old...much older than I."

Her smile widened. "Then he would go to the places he remembered...the old places."

She turned and disappeared into the streets, and Abraham followed. In the alley, the final gasp of breath signaled an end to Pierre, but none noted his passing. Not immediately.

⁂

Although he'd acquiesced to Lacroix's insistence that they make their entrance to the cathedral, Noirceuil had no intention of remaining within those walls until the sun rose. He entered, stood patiently by, nodding and affecting the proper deference to the cardinal, and made his exit as swiftly as possible. His needs as far as quarters had been made clear before their arrival. It took only moments to find a servant and order them to show him where he would sleep away the daylight, and less time than that to find another to lead him to a side door and into the streets beyond.

He couldn't brush off a feeling of restlessness. He sensed that their prey was about, the dark one, and possibly others. It was intolerable that Lacroix would have him waste an entire night of the hunt as their prey slunk off behind their backs. The man was weak, and a fool. Both signs of his mortality.

Without a backward glance, Noirceuil pulled his cloak more fully over his dark features and slipped down a side street, moving steadily inward toward the center of the city. He wasn't certain what he sought, but he knew he would not find it in the cathedral. Lacroix could handle the social amenities. Noirceuil had as much respect for the Church as his partner, but a very great deal more respect for the opposition as well.

Evil walked the Earth. He himself had been tainted...soiled. It was his curse, and only the quest, the tireless struggle to rid the Earth of his own kind, gave him even a moment's release from the torture of it. The hunger boiled through his veins, but he channeled that pain, focusing it inward. He would feed. It was as inevitable as the sunrise. No matter his prayers, no matter his strength. He would feed. Noirceuil served many masters, but of them the hunger for blood was master.

That was the basis of his pain. He knew he was Damned. Nothing he could do would erase the suffering he caused others. No single act could redeem the murder and theft of a man's lifeblood. It didn't matter if he chose a beggar, or a king. It was a life, and he was forced to take them, again and again. Each time he did, another bit of what he had been died.

The city was waking to its night face. There were those not comfortable, or safe, moving about by day who would slide from the cracks at each nightfall. These lined the streets, leaned against the stark, shadowed doorframes, gathered in the entrances of taverns and other dark houses.

The shops were closed. The families, children, well-dressed ladies, all in their beds, or the beds of others. Noirceuil prowled these streets unnoticed. He spoke to no one, and most never even noted his passing, or, if they did, they saw him turning in ways he did not, taking paths he ignored. His image was uncertain, there one moment, then seeming to turn away...and yet he moved in a steady line.

He was close enough to the main streets that there was little threat of attack, but far enough in the shadows to avoid the main traffic of the night folk. He avoided the sounds of the bars, turned from the revelry of the whorehouses. They would not hold what he sought. He moved further in, finding the buildings growing steadily older, more corrupt and decayed, the sounds and movements of those awake and alive more scattered.

The scent of blood hit him very suddenly, and he stopped, tottering in his tracks, fighting the sudden wave of hunger, cursing himself for a fool in waiting too long to feed with such an abundance of humanity surrounding him. He calmed himself slowly, fighting the madness...suppressing it. He would not succumb to it.

Slowly his mind calmed. He did not turn toward the scent of blood, not yet. It was old, cooling, and though it would have sufficed, it was not what he needed. It might well be the trail he sought, but he needed to feed before that would be possible. With a sudden leap he was on the first landing of the nearest building, not looking back to see who might have noted his passing, and a second swift movement took him over the ledge of the rooftop. He moved so swiftly that one watching might have believed him an illusion, there one second, gone the next, to reappear atop the next building.

He did not go far. These were old buildings, dilapidated, but still tenanted, and it was not long before he found what he sought, a balcony, just below the level of the rooftop, and an old woman, alone, sitting in her chair and watching the empty streets below. She did not look up as he approached, and he watched her for a long moment, the old war beginning anew in his heart, raging through his veins and melting in the fire of his hunger.

He listened carefully, stilling his senses. There was no movement below, no sign that there was any other in the small room beyond the balcony. She was alone, or if not, the others slept.

He did not hesitate further. It was a life, but if she were a good woman, she would go to eternal glory, a gift forever denied him. If she were not, she had little of her life left to remedy that, and in any case, his work must continue. There was no other the Church could turn to, no other who could survive, who could hunt the blood-sucking demons and bring them to judgment. It was one life; an old life, nearing its end.

Noirceuil dropped to the balcony with the softness of a falling leaf, and though he did not speak, he saw her stiffen. The woman did not turn, but he heard her heart speed, and knew that she sensed his presence, and his approach. Still he did not hesitate; there was nothing she could do.

"So," the woman said, still gazing out over the street below, voice wavering slightly, but strong, "it is true. You come for me in the night, like a shadow, dragging me from this world of pain. I have been waiting for you a long time, monsieur."

He did not immediately understand, but he slowed his steps, listening.

"I will not look upon you yet," she said, rocking gently in her old chair. "I know that is the moment of my end, and though I am prepared for it, I will not leap to your arms, even for the promise of a better world. I will savor my last moments, sir, drink them in like the wine from the market, soft, sweet, warm, and I will await your cold touch on my shoulder."

He knew then. She had recognized him after all, though her mind had painted a more romantic picture than reality would provide. Death. She knew him as the angel of her death, and it was a bittersweet moment. An angel...the only angel he would ever be, the only glory he would ever achieve. Only in bringing death was he proficient and pure.

TO DREAM OF DREAMERS LOST

He moved closer still, but hesitated. "Old mother," he said, guessing of her children, "each lives only a certain allotted time. Yours is done, and yet you will be of service to your Lord, and should be glad."

She nearly turned at the sudden sound of his voice, then settled with a shiver. "I will be glad for the days in the sunlight, and the sound of my daughter's voice. I will remember with pride the things I have done, and those I have helped, and for those who have done me wrong, I will leave forgiveness. I will not be glad for death until I reach the other side and determine the truth of the promise made."

He watched her a moment longer, then the hunger boiled up suddenly, fueled by the reminder of that promise. It was a promise made him as a boy, a boy who had lit candles on the altar of the church each Sunday and sung the hymns with a voice of pure silver. A promise that had been ripped from him cruelly, replaced by a curse.

He fell on her then, clamping onto her wrinkled flesh, fangs biting, driving in deep, hands pressing her forward to hold her still. She cried out softly, once, and then was still, shivering against him, then pressing back, reaching to that damned, dark light that had called to him so long before, and claimed him. He felt it seducing her, felt it drawing her from him even as he drew the life from her veins. He cried out, pulling free, letting her slump against the short wall of the balcony. With a quick flick of his wrists, he flung her over, watching as she tumbled toward the street below, finishing what he'd begun.

He would never Embrace another. He would never pass the curse, but would spend his existence putting it to an end. Turning from the balcony, putting thoughts of the strange old woman and her words from his mind as he climbed swiftly back to the roof and returned the way he'd come, carefully wiping the blood from his lips.

He dropped back to the street, glanced up and down and saw no one. The scent of the blood was still there, but much fainter. It had cooled completely. There was no life in it, no sentience moving it about.

He found the mouth of the alley and slipped inside. The mound of flesh that had been Pierre immediately caught his eye and he moved closer, flipping the body over to its back with one boot. There were no marks, but he had already sensed the truth.

Turning, he let his eyes scan the alley, sweeping the walls, the ground, searching for anything to lead him after the one who had drained the body. There was nothing; nothing, but a faint tingle shivered deep within his mind. He slipped back to the street and away, moving toward the nearest lights. As he neared the first corner he stopped very suddenly.

A single bright red drop glistened on the road at his feet. He leaned, taking that drop on the tip of one fingernail, bringing it to his lips. The same. He moved down the road more quickly, following the scent and trail of death. There were several hours remaining to the night, and the hunt was on.

TEN

The open door of the tavern beckoned and Fleurette dragged Abraham through it without hesitation, spinning to one side and elbowing her way through the crowd like a drunken soldier. Incredibly, a way formed as she bulled and shoved, and Abraham noted both glances of amusement and respect from those she jostled. Apparently his "little flower" had a reputation. More than once he met a glance tinted the green of jealousy, and he grinned despite himself and the circumstances.

They slid up to the bar, and Fleurette ordered wine for them both, handing him his without making any gesture to pay. The bartender stood, watching them, and Abraham reached into his pouch, pulling out a coin and dropping it on the bar. He took the wine as it was offered, holding the cup absently, peering around the interior of the tavern in curiosity.

"Why here?" he asked at last. "There must be a thousand taverns in this city. What makes you think they would come here?"

"If they are after information," she replied, "this is the place. Your Montrovant will know this, if he has ever been to Grenoble."

Then she caught sight of someone and he saw her stiffen slightly. She leaned close, taking his arm and pointing, her hand held in close to her body to keep the gesture hidden. She was pointing to a shifty, dark man leaning against one wall. The man had a flagon of ale in his hand and was watching all that happened in the tavern in silence. He did not speak to those around him, preferring to blend against the wall and observe.

"That one will know if your friend has been here," she said softly, "but it won't be cheap."

Abraham watched the man for a moment longer, then nodded. "I'll wait outside," he said softly. "I wouldn't want to alarm your friend. You bring him along, and we'll talk. I don't want to be seen in here asking questions if I can help it. There are others, besides Montrovant, who are searching. I'd prefer to remain as hidden as possible."

She glanced up at him, placing a small hand against his chest for a moment, then nodded, slipping away. Abraham looked down at the full mug of wine in his hand, then reached out to stop her. He traded her drinks with a smile, seeing that hers was half drained.

"No sense wasting it," he said softly. Her eyes widened for a moment, then she took the mug and turned away. Abraham moved toward the door, leaving her half-full drink on an empty table as he passed and exiting to the street. None took any note at all of his passing.

He moved through the doors and into the street, glancing to the right and left and picking an alley half a block down on the right. There were what appeared to be two abandoned merchant's booths lining the entrance to the place. It would be private and secluded.

He stood at the edge of that alley, waiting and watching the door. It was only moments before Fleurette exited, the man in tow, and she saw him immediately. She had her wine in her hand, not having bothered to leave the cup inside, another sign that she was more well known than he might have suspected. The man stopped at the sight of Abraham, but at a nudge and a few words from Fleurette, moved closer slowly.

Abraham wasted no time.

"I seek a group of men, knights, actually," he said softly. "I believe they may have come through here on a search of their own, and it is important that I find them. Very important."

The man's eyes shifted uneasily, but he did not speak.

"I am willing to pay for the information," Abraham said, slightly annoyed.

Fleurette smacked a hand into the man's chest. "Raul, you are embarrassing me. I told the gentleman speaking to you would be worth his time."

Raul looked down at where she'd struck him with a slightly glazed expression. Abraham smelled the ale then. Moving closer, he took Raul by the shirt, dragging him into the opening of the alley without further discussion and slamming him to the wall just out of sight of the street.

"I have no patience tonight," he said, "for those who love liquor more than life. If you do not wish me to count you among them and rob you of both, you will answer my questions, take my money, and be on your way."

Something in the unnatural strength of Abraham's assault brought a terrified light to the man's eyes. "No," he whispered. "No, they are gone."

Abraham stared at the man, eyes narrowing. "Who has gone? Tell me and be swift, or you will tell no one another thing."

"He was dark…very dark, monsieur," Raul babbled. "His eyes, like pits, and his companion… They told me if I spoke of them, they would return."

Abraham's mind was whirling. Raul could be

speaking of no one but Montrovant, but getting anything useful from this raving drunk might prove more than mere threats of violence could produce.

"If you do not tell me now," Abraham said at last, "it will not matter that they return. They will find a dried, withered husk. Not a man, but a shell, empty…dead…forgotten. Your bones will be all that remain, bones and a thin sack of skin. Is that how you would end your days, Raul, or would you live?"

Slowly the words were sinking in. Perhaps it was the sight of Fleurette, who'd begun to back away at this new approach. Her eyes were glittering, and Abraham saw that her hand was sliding down toward her blade again. In any other circumstance, he would have smiled.

The man's eyes were shifting again, as they had been inside the tavern, looking for avenues of escape. It was a good sign. If his fear could be reached, how far behind could his greed be?

Abraham pulled back a bit, partly to reassure Raul, and partly to let Fleurette know that he wasn't about to kill her friend. He reached slowly for his pouch and lifted it free of his belt. For the first time since leaving Rome he was glad for Santorini's assistance. If nothing else, the bishop had provided a great deal of gold for the undertaking. He opened the pouch and pulled out a pair of gold coins.

"These are for your cooperation," he said softly.

"There are two more if you have the information I require."

Raul's eyes shifted rapidly back and forth from Abraham's eyes to the gold. He wanted to run. The fog of alcohol was fading, and the memory of the threat Montrovant had planted in his mind was fresh. He wanted to run, and to take his chances.

"If you run," Abraham said softly and simply, "I will kill you."

Raul gasped then, slumping against the wall. He laid his head in his hands, and sobbed quietly, then pulled himself together enough to speak. "It does not matter then," he said, voice shaking. "Perhaps they are gone already. Perhaps not. Perhaps they stand on the rooftops above our heads. Either way, I face death."

He raised his gaze to meet Abraham's, eyes haunted and dark. "They have gone to the forest outside of town in search of a group of bandits, men who witnessed the passing of another group."

"The Order…" Abraham breathed.

Raul looked up. "I do not know. I know what they asked, and what I told them, of the passing of a strange caravan, and those who died trying to rob it. That is all I know."

"It is enough," Abraham said, turning and dropping the coins in the dirt where Raul now sat, leaning against the dirty wall. "More than enough." He turned to leave, but Fleurette grabbed his arm suddenly.

"Wait, you will leave?"

He hesitated, then turned to her, ignoring Raul, who was dusting himself off and edging around them toward the entrance to the alley.

"I must. I know where he has gone now, and I must follow while the trail is yet warm."

Her eyes were searching his, and he felt the speeding of her heartbeat. He closed his eyes, firmly restraining the talons of hunger that leaped forth, then opened them once more and met her gaze...held it.

"It is not a road for you, little flower. You would wilt, and wither, and possibly die, all for things that do not matter to you, but only to me. Stay, be strong. You have friends, a life. Perhaps our paths will cross once more?"

She did not speak, but there was a fiery spark in her eye that he could not quite read. She did not answer. No nod, no argument. She watched his eyes, backed away, and as she neared the entrance to the alley spun on her heel and was gone. She was quick for a mortal, and the image of her eyes...the scent of her hot, pounding blood, left Abraham momentarily disoriented.

He frowned, turning and moving to the street with purpose. He did not need distractions, particularly from mortals he had no connection with. There was precious little time to catch Montrovant's trail, and perhaps even less before that of the Order faded away completely. He knew them better than Montrovant. They would have planned this well in advance, and they would have expected pursuit. That in mind, there would be a disappearing act, or a trap, not so far ahead of them. Secrecy was how they maintained their near-mythic "mystery." Whatever their final destination, it had been ready and waiting to receive them for years, perhaps decades, and the cover that went with it would be well established.

The night was dying quickly, the first touches of the dawn threatening the horizon, and Abraham moved swiftly back toward the abandoned home where he'd left his mount. No matter how close he might be to his goal, the hunt would not continue this night. He had barely the time to reach his shelter and secure himself against the sun.

Montrovant would not be traveling either, nor would Noirceuil. Briefly Abraham wondered how a vampire worked in the service of the Church without giving away his damnation. It was an odd marriage, and on the road particularly difficult to disguise.

He left these matters for another time, easing from shadow to shadow until he reached the edges of the city, leaving the remnant of the city's night life behind. There was no sound where he walked, no scent of blood or sound of laughter. He knew this would change when the daylight arrived. The streets would be busy, farmers making their way to market, those up too late and too far from home traveling out of the city. He had to be out of sight and safe before any of that began.

He did not see anyone as he skirted the main road heading out of town, and he made it to the old home without incident, slipping into the shed to check on his horse, gentling the animal and insuring there was a bit of food, and some water available to it. He didn't want it becoming over-heated, or hungry during the day and making noises that might attract someone from the road. Horse thievery was not uncommon, and if any were actively seeking him, which was possible, there now being two mortals running about the city who knew who and what he was, he did not want to make their search any easier.

With the animal tended to, he slipped back into the shadows and opened the doors to the old cellar, a last look around satisfying him that he was alone. He ducked inside and pulled the door closed tightly over him, then dropped down the steps into the dank, dreary interior of the cellar and lay back on the short table to await the coming and passing of the day.

Beyond the confines of the cellar, two sets of eyes watched.

One was young, blazing with energy, and curiosity. The other set was old, old and dark. Neither of these two moved closer to threaten the safety of Abraham's rest. The dawn was slipping sleepy fingers over the horizon, and Noirceuil knew his time was at an end.

He slipped away, vaguely aware of a heartbeat nearby, but certain whoever it was had not seen him. The young "hunter" could wait. Noirceuil needed to know if the boy had information that could be put to use before destroying him, and Lacroix would not remain calm through a second premature slaying. Their orders said nothing of killing this Abraham, though Noirceuil had no intention of letting any of the Damned free once they were in his sight.

He fairly flew down the streets, slipping through shadows, in and out of open areas before any could be certain he had been there at all. The cathedral was not that far away, but the sun was rising with unnatural swiftness, as though scenting him, and he knew he'd waited too long this time.

Cursing himself for a fool, he slid through the outer court and into the side door of the temple, ignoring nods and soft words from those he passed, making his way straight for the stairs leading down to the lower levels. He knew the way to his chambers.

He yanked the huge oak doors open and pulled them closed quickly behind himself. All had been arranged as he'd asked. He moved to the large mahogany armoire, which stood ajar, and slid inside. There were pillows lining the floor of it. He had not ordered them, but decided to leave them.

DAVID NIALL WILSON

To sleep on the rough wood surface would attract attention he could not afford. It was odd enough that he shunned the light. Worse still that none ever saw him eat, or drink. It seemed only a matter of time until his secret was found out.

Lacroix was the key. Lacroix had been with him for a long, long time. He had seen him kill vampires, and men alike. He had never seen the light of hunger in Noirceuil's eyes. He had never seen the trembling horror his partner could become if deprived for too long of the blood of mortals.

Lacroix believed in results, and their partnership had been based on that belief. Noirceuil claimed his methods, his idiosyncrasies, aided him in his hunting. He found the undead, and he destroyed them, with shocking regularity. It lent credibility to his words.

Noirceuil pulled the doors of the armoire closed behind himself, hearing the satisfying click that meant they were closed tightly. He lay back and closed his eyes, mind an immediate blank. In the room beyond, there were no windows. No lights. No candles. The day began, but in that chamber there was no hint of it.

※

Fleurette watched the old shed for a long time, fighting against the urge to go to him. She didn't know what she would say, what she wanted to do, and so she watched. He had saved her life, at the same time frightening her more fully than she had ever been in her nineteen years of life. She had said it so calmly in the alley, *vampire*. The reality of that had not even sunk in as that arrogant pig Pierre's body ceased to breathe, and cooled.

Only when Raul had been slammed to the wall, when the man, monster…Abraham's words rang out so clearly, and softly. *Death*. More than death, drained, a shell, empty. As he'd shaken Raul like a child, her heart had nearly stopped. She had helped him because he helped her, and her mind had been centered on the alley, on Pierre and what he'd nearly done to her.

Abraham was not a man. Not exactly, or not *just* a man, and she'd ignored that until he threatened a repeat performance of Pierre's death with Raul. Now she didn't know how to feel. He had not hurt Raul. He had given the fool money and sent him on his way. That was a good thing. He had killed Pierre, God in heaven, he had drained the man's blood. Did it matter?

She squatted in the shadows at the mouth of an alley, watching the shed as the morning light grew, wondering what she had walked into. She could feel his eyes on her, the skip in her heartbeat as they lingered, wondering what he thought, what he sensed. Did he see her as a woman, a child, or another meal? Again, did it matter?

She turned at last. He had not returned from the ruined home, and it appeared he would be resting during the daylight. She would do the same. He was strong, and fast...and she didn't know if he were dead, or if he could be killed. She knew she should just turn and leave, not looking back and forgetting she'd ever seen him, or heard that low, shivery voice—she knew she could not.

As the morning sun warmed her back, and people began to move back and forth along the street, she rose, crossing the main road and slipping closer to the old, ruined building. She moved to the shed and pulled the door wide softly.

She found a horse, a bit of feed and water. Nothing more. No sign of him, no bags...no weapons. Nothing. He had disappeared. She glanced outside again, sweeping her gaze over the ruined home, but there was nowhere that he could remain hidden. Nowhere that would afford enough shade for sleep.

Did he sleep? So many questions. She closed the door to the makeshift stable softly, and, glancing down, she noted the cellar. She stood there for a long moment, hesitating. She had forgotten again. He would not be sleeping in the sunlight, or even in the shed. He would not truly be sleeping, only hiding from the light of God's day. That is how the priest would tell it, how the stories had passed from father to daughter. Fleurette knew those stories well enough. Now they were not stories, and she wondered how much of what she had heard was truth?

She slipped into the street once more and away toward her own small room. She didn't live far away, and suddenly the thought of her own bed, and a cup of warmed wine seemed very inviting. As she moved, she felt his eyes still locked to hers, watching. She shivered and slipped up the stairs to her loft.

ELEVEN

Montrovant had always been an early riser among his kind. Before Le Duc was even stirring within the shadows of his mind, the dark one was up and moving, readying the others for the road. He had no intention of remaining in the city any longer. He had what he wanted, and he was ready to move. As he waited for Jeanne to rise, he gave instructions to St. Fond and du Puy, sending them on ahead. He knew which direction he needed to take when he departed the city, and why. He and his men had little to fear from bandits, but that in itself was a problem. They would not be attacked, so they needed to find another way to locate those they sought.

The scouts were off and Montrovant was pacing back and forth like a madman by the time Jeanne rose. They were packed, and their mounts had been prepared. Without waiting for a word of explanation, Montrovant headed for the door and mounted. Jeanne and the others, used to such behavior, did not hesitate to follow. If they had, they knew they'd be struggling to catch up. The dark one was not one to wait when he had caught the scent of his prey.

They were moving down to the main street and turning toward the edge of town shortly after Jeanne rose, and they made no attempt to hide their passing. Montrovant was not really worried about being followed, and he knew that furtive movements and an attempt to slip out of town unnoticed would be more likely to attract attention than if they left in a group and said nothing. That is what they did, slipping out the west side of town and heading down the road at a brisk trot toward the forested area beyond.

It was this forest they approached that the little weasel of a man had pointed them toward. Bandits were not uncommon, nor were they difficult to find, but to pinpoint the activities of a particular band was more chancy. The local law would be seeking this particular group as well, along with half the nobility of Grenoble. It was not going to be as simple as riding into the forest and making the group's acquaintance.

Le Duc knew this would actually pose little problem. If du Puy and St. Fond failed to find sign of the raiders, he and Montrovant would be able to trace them by other means. There were advantages, as well as drawbacks, to the hunger. Hot, rich blood would draw them. Such a group as their informant had spoken of would not be easily hidden. It was a large, well-organized band.

They hit the edge of the tree line and disappeared within quickly, the growing shadows sweeping long and eerie across their path. Jeanne let his gaze shift right and left, scanning the trees and shrubbery for a sign of passage. The road itself was well traveled, but the forest was where those they sought would move, parallel to the roads, shifting through the trees and shadows.

By day the road was safe. None would chance a skirmish on a heavily traveled road, unless the booty to be gained was immense. But at night, all was changed. Any who chanced the dark trails of those woods without the benefit of the sun's light, and without heavy guard, invited those who walked among the trees by night. It was an easy life for Jeanne to understand. He had been a man of action, and his very nature, once Embraced, was that of hunter. It was in the blood he stole from those he hunted...the notion that he lived on borrowed life, on borrowed time, and that he would continue to steal and borrow and drain that life and blood until fate managed to wrest it from him.

They moved in deeper, and a few moments later St. Fond melted from the shadows, reining in beside Montrovant and speaking, his voice low. Montrovant lowered his head, listening, then nodded quickly and spurred his mount down the trail. The others followed quickly behind, not questioning the sudden speed, even when St. Fond dropped back into their ranks and du Puy appeared without warning at Le Duc's side.

There was no reason to question. If the information was good enough for Montrovant, then it would be correct, and even if it were not, it was not their place to question. They rushed down the trail in the dark one's wake, and when he veered from the main road, plunging into the shadowed darkness to one side of the trail, they followed without question.

There was a second trail. It was not as clear as the first, nor as wide, but once beyond the dividing line of trail and trees, it was plainly visible. The horses had no trouble moving along it at a reasonable speed. Montrovant pushed that. He had no fear of being unhorsed, and his concern for his men went only far enough that he hoped they served him well. He thundered down the trail and moments later plunged down yet another track, leading straight in toward the center of the trees.

Their approach was not unnoticed. Jeanne felt, even before he heard, the shifting of bodies, the quick tread of horses. They had been spotted, and those who'd seen them would reach their camp before Montrovant could arrive. It was not exactly a trap, but it was certainly not going to be a surprise, either.

Again, there was no fear for Montrovant. No fear, in truth, for Jeanne either, but Jeanne was not so quick to ignore his companions. As he sensed the others moving ahead of them he began to bark orders sharply. There was no need for silence, they were expected. What was important was discipline, and speed. They would not be unannounced, but if they pushed their own speed, there would be little time to mount a defense.

Moments later they burst into a clearing. Arrows were flying the moment they cleared the trees, but most were wild shots, without aim or care. Montrovant took a shot through the shoulder, but it did not even turn him in his saddle. He spurred his mount forward and ran the bowman down without a thought. He was out of the saddle in seconds, leaping to the ground without waiting for his mount to come to a stop, ripping the arrow free, snapping one end and dragging the tip out the other side, tossing both pieces aside with a snarl.

Jeanne followed suit, leaping from his horse to strike another bowman full force, toppling the man to the ground and ripping his throat out with a single swipe of his talons. Le Duc had his blade free of its scabbard as his feet struck the ground, and he had another before him, the steel blade sweeping

in an arc with death at its end, removing a head
and sending it spiraling through the air in slow-
motion.

The battle was short. It appeared that they'd
caught the camp only partially manned, and
though they had not truly had the element of surprise, it had been close. Those they faced were not
prepared for the ferocity of their attack, and they
were not disciplined warriors like Montrovant's
knights. They were bandits, and they had little
loyalty to anything, let alone the risking of their
lives in the defense of an empty camp. They turned
and fled moments after the battle began, and the
chase was on.

"Get one of them," Montrovant bellowed.

The words were unnecessary. Jeanne was already
flying down a side trail in pursuit of a lanky, long-
haired warrior with a bow in one hand and an arrow
in the other. The man had not had the chance to
draw his blade, but had chosen instead to flee and
take his chances on the trail. He'd believed, mis-
takenly, that Montrovant's group sought the
treasure in the camp, and that his own life would
be of little consequence.

Jeanne ran the man down easily, moving more
swiftly without the horse and with the battle rage
seeping into his eyes. He held his arm at the
ready...shivering with the need, the desire to spill
the man's blood. The hunger was eating at his
thoughts, and the battle rage pounded through

him, making the blood he'd already stolen feel weak and thin.

A strong hand fell on Jeanne's shoulder and he spun quickly, his blade ready to slice back and up, but the gaze he met stopped him cold. Montrovant stood there, very still. There was no fear in his sire's eyes. He waited for the blade to slice, and both knew it would never meet its mark. Jeanne's mind cleared in that instant and he released the tension, stepping aside and tossing his captive to the ground with a quick shrug of his shoulder.

"I would not have killed him," he muttered softly.

Montrovant's eyes were dancing now, and Jeanne nearly laughed.

"No, my friend, you would have destroyed him. But it is not to be. Not yet. I need to know where the others have gone, and I need to know if this one was present when they encountered the Order."

Jeanne nodded, walking away slowly. His mind was clear, but the hunger was no less intense. He fought it, listening with only a small part of his mind as Montrovant questioned their prisoner.

"I seek a group that came through your forest recently," he said slowly. "They would have been transporting several wagons, and might have appeared to be monks, or pilgrims."

The prisoner's eyes were wide, frightened. Montrovant regarded him with dark eyes and no visible emotion. When the man did not immediately respond, the dark one slapped him, hard, with the back of one hand. The bandit went sprawling to the ground, a huge red welt rising on his face.

"You will answer me," Montrovant said softly, "and you will do so swiftly and completely, or you will die. It will not be a pretty death. It will not be a quick death either. It will be long, and slow, each moment spent working toward the truth you will reveal eventually. Save yourself the pain. You may die anyway, but it will be swift and final."

The man swallowed once, shook his head, closed his eyes, and then swallowed a second time. "I saw them," he said at last. "Jesus, God, don't kill me, monsieur. I saw them. They wore brown robes, hooded, and I couldn't make out their faces, but it was I and another who spotted them on the road. I brought the word back to Claude, and he led the attack. It is the only time since we came to the forest that we have suffered such a defeat. Nothing was gained that night, and three men were lost. We were lucky that all was not lost."

"You fled, then?" Montrovant made the question an insult, twisting his lips into a sneer as he voiced the question. "You are here to answer my questions because you left your companions to die?"

Anger flared in the man's eyes for just a moment, then faded it the face of Montrovant's gaze. "There was nothing I could do. There was nothing anyone could do. Claude called the retreat, and he called it too late, if you ask me. He tried to get to the oth-

ers, to help them, but we could not. They were
demons. They moved like lightning, and they were
stronger than bears. I saw one of them fling a man
twenty feet through the air. Not human."

Montrovant laughed then. Without warning he
moved after Jeanne, grabbing his progeny under the
arms and flinging him upward without warning.
Jeanne cried out, then realized the game and grew
still in flight, rising higher, focusing and then plum-
meting to the ground. He was so far from the point
where Montrovant had grabbed him that he was
able to grab a low-hanging branch and swing to the
ground, smiling at their prisoner as he landed.

"You will talk to me," Montrovant told the man.
"You will talk to me now, and quickly."

The man swallowed a third time, and then nodded.

"I know very little," he said, shuddering. "They
were too much for us, and after we fled, they
seemed to just disappear. Claude believed they had
taken a different road altogether. I don't know for
sure. None of us do." The man's eyes dropped to the
ground, and he whispered, "We ran like children.
I have no idea what was in those wagons, or where
they took them, but I know they headed in, toward
the mountains."

Montrovant stared off into the darkness in the
direction the man had indicated.

"How long?" he asked. "How long since they
passed this way?"

"Four days," the man said quickly. "It has been four days. Tonight is the first that Claude has ventured out on the roads since then."

"And he is out tonight?" Montrovant asked. "We did not see him on the road."

"He was to go into the city first," the man said softly. "There are supplies we need. He was to pick those up, then to watch the road for a few hours, then come here."

Montrovant smiled. That would take some time, and there was little danger that the bandit chief would come back before they departed.

With a quick toss, he pushed the man toward Jeanne again. "Be quick," he said softly. The others had joined them, two others prisoners in tow. "We will be on the road again in a few moments."

To his men, he gave quick instructions. There was no reason to leave the camp intact. He ordered that any gold, silver, or supplies be quickly removed from the camp. There was no way to know what they would face on the road ahead, and to leave any resource untapped was not Montrovant's style.

As the others trickled away, Jeanne grabbed his prisoner by the throat and dragged him into the trees without a word. It was a matter of seconds before he'd laid the man's throat bare, drinking the rich, hot blood hungrily and tossing the nearly drained corpse aside with a shrug of his shoulders. He knew Montrovant was doing the same in a different set of shadows, and he smiled. It felt like old times. He and Montrovant had shared many roads, but it had been a long time since the two had fed together, and it marked the first time in the close vicinity of the others. A landmark.

They moved back to the clearing at nearly the same moment, filled and sated, ready to continue the chase.

"We must head for the mountains," Montrovant said softly. "We will find them there."

Jeanne nodded, and the two moved back toward the camp quickly. Their men had gathered their mounts, which had not strayed far, and packed everything easily carried into their bags. They would be on the road and gone before the bandits knew they had been robbed.

"There is no reason to wait for the rest of these worthless vermin," Montrovant said as they turned away from the camp, following one of the bandit trails parallel to the road. "We have the information we need. There is little more that could be added by other witnesses, and any time we waste making our way to the mountains is time that Gustav and the others will have ahead of us."

Jeanne nodded. "If they are headed for the mountains from here, they have only one road. We will find word of them along the way. It is difficult to hide such a large group, even traveling by night."

Montrovant nodded. They gathered their men and thundered off through the forest toward the road beyond. Montrovant wanted to be well beyond the borders of the city before daybreak. It would be unfortunate if the bandits were able and of a mind to follow them, less fortunate still if they actually caught up. The forest swallowed them whole, returning to silent shadows.

※

Abraham was out of the cellar and into the shed at the first kiss of shadow. There was no time to lose. If Montrovant had learned of the bandits, and that the trail of the Order led through the woods beyond the town, he would be there, perhaps there and gone. Abraham would have to pick up the trail beyond and hope he could make good enough time to keep the group in tracking distance.

He also wanted to get free of Grenoble before Lacroix and Noirceuil located him. He knew he was not likely to be the pair's prey, but he was certain this fact would not sway Noirceuil one bit from destroying him. Abraham had seen the hunger in the older one's eyes as he worked. There was a hatred there burning, very old and very strong. The last thing Abraham needed was to fall victim before he even had his goal in sight.

He mounted his horse and turned away from the ruins, sweeping his gaze up and down the road to be certain he was not seen. He sensed others moving about, but that was to be expected. The day was ending. Workers returned home, and food would be on tables around the city. A good time to rise and be gone.

DAVID NIALL WILSON

Eyes watched him from the shadows of an alley, but he paid them no mind. His thoughts were focused ahead, on the trees and the dark memory of Montrovant's laughter, and his eyes. Soon, he told himself, there would be a reckoning, for good or ill.

He did not take the road straight to the woods. He swung wide, coming in from the far side, where a line of trees jutted from the side, sliding in among the trees easily, senses alert. Odds were that, traveling alone and by night, the bandits would find him before he traveled too far. He was not worried about an attack, but he did not want to waste too much time, nor did he want to become the next rumor bandied about in the taverns. Lacroix would be on that scent in moments.

He moved quietly, and though he sensed once or twice that there were eyes watching him and heard furtive movements deeper in the trees, sometimes ahead, sometimes behind, he was not molested as he moved in toward the center of the forest and the main road. He slipped from the trees and onto that trail about an hour after sunset, eyes sweeping up and down, watching for signs that others had passed.

At first there was nothing, but as he moved in deeper he saw where a group of horses had sped up, and plunged off the main trail, and he followed those tracks, sliding off the secondary trail and into the trees once more. No sense announcing his arrival. He wanted to get in and out without being seen, if possible.

There were no guards, and that in itself was strange. The trail of the others led boldly up the center of the path, and eventually he came to the edge of the clearing that marked the bandit's camp. He smelled the fresh blood then, and from the shadows of the trees, he could make out the sprawled bodies and disheveled equipment. Montrovant had been here, and gone. He slipped from the trees, walking his horse through the ruins of the place, the beast shying away from the fresh corpses.

There were not many bodies, not as many as he would have expected from Raul's report of the band. Where were the others? Dead? Fled? He dismounted and leaned closer to examine one of the bodies, and it was then that the gates of Hades opened up to flood the clearing.

They burst from the trees all around him, swords drawn, eyes blazing, screaming in a mixture of rage and frustration. Abraham turned in a crouch, saw that he was too late to flee, and leaped straight into the air, clearing the first horse and its rider easily and grabbing a limb of the tree above. He swung out and forward, slamming his boots into the face of the next rider in line. There were too many. He might kill them all, he might not, but it would certainly be a bloodbath. Cursing, he rolled back to his feet, ducking under the blade of his next attacker, yanking the man from his saddle and tossing him to the side.

His own mount was bucking crazily, shying away from the attacking horde, but he managed to slip up beside it and scramble into the saddle, gripping the animal's flanks tightly. He didn't need the ride so much as he did the papers and his few possessions. Slamming his heels into the horse's sides, he launched it forward, leaning low along the neck.

He did not draw a weapon. He slipped past the leader of the bandits, and as he passed his hand shot out, catching the hilt of the man's sword and tearing it from his hand. The bandit snarled, but Abraham backhanded him hard, sending the man sprawling to the ground.

He spun for the edge of the clearing, and was leaping through a break in the trees when another cry drifted to him and he turned. He cursed as he saw her. Fleurette was being dragged, kicking and screaming, from the tree line by a huge warrior. His eyes were filled with death, and the girl's fate was obvious.

Without thinking, Abraham spun again, his mount leaping toward the edge of the clearing. Angry swordsmen converged on him from all sides, but he swept past them, ignoring their charge, eyes fixed on the lone warrior who held Fleurette so tightly by her hair.

The man spotted Abraham, and drew his blade with a cry. Fleurette chose that moment to bring down her boot hard on the man's instep. He ca-

reened to one side, screaming in pain, and she was
on him, her dagger sweeping over his neck, sending a red spurt of blood that made Abraham's senses
swim with its nearness.

He did not hesitate. He stormed up to her, heard
her cry out in fright, leaned and took her by the
same grip the warrior had taken, dragging her up to
the saddle before him as he tore out of the clearing, and away. It was not the direction he'd
intended, and he cursed again, arcing, moving at
an angle to the road, then swinging back.

He'd seen tracks leading out of the clearing just
before the attack, and he knew in which direction
Montrovant had gone. The only questions was,
could he get out of the forest, particularly with his
new, unwanted companion, without being overrun
by the bandits?

He doubled back, and miraculously, the pursuit
seemed to fall into a confusion. He could hear them
bellowing and beating about in the brush, but they
were falling steadily further behind as he moved,
and he pressed his mount to a dizzying speed, ignoring the whipping branches and scratches from the
passing trees. Fleurette clung to him, eyes closed in
terror, and the rapid beating of her heart against his
chest brought him to a further frenzy. He needed
to break free of the trees, and he needed to feed.
These were paramount.

If he did not find another, he would take her. He
didn't know what had possessed him to save the

girl, but whatever it was it was nothing before the hunger. If he hungered, he would feed. If she were the only one there, she would be his meal. He would regret it, but it was a fact of his nature.

They burst from the trees to the south of the road, galloping parallel and skirting behind rocks, trees, whatever cover presented itself, flying off toward the mountains. He watched, letting his senses slip back, feeling for blood, for hearts beating in anger and the thunder of following hooves, but it never came. They were miles down the road when at last he could stand it no more and he reined in.

He'd seen no sign of others along that road, and the hunger was eating at his sanity. He pulled her from his chest, turning her eyes up to meet his gaze.

"Why?" he grated. "Why couldn't you just stay in the city, drink your wine, and be well? Why did you follow me?"

"I...I thought you might need help," she muttered, trying for one long moment to hold his gaze, failing. "The forest is not a good place. I just wanted to see that you made it through. You did save my life."

"And now I may end it," he rasped. "You know what I am. You know I must feed, and yet you came to me."

She gazed at him calmly. "I know your darkness," she said. "I have seen it, felt it when you slammed Raul to the wall." She was shivering uncontrollably.

He growled, dropping suddenly from the saddle and leaving her to scramble for balance and handholds as he staggered away.

"You have no idea," he said, spitting the words back at her. It is not by choice, it is my nature. I will feed. If you are here, and I hunger, your life will become a part of mine, and you will cease to be. I am not strong enough to prevent it."

She watched him warily, but did not back away. She sat in the saddle, gazing down at him with wide, questioning eyes. "If not me, you will take another?"

He returned her gaze, eyes dark, then nodded. "Of course."

She slid from the saddle, moving closer...trembling, but stepping firmly. "Take me then," she said softly. "Take me now, because I intend to follow you, and if not with you, I do not want to go back through that wood to be raped and killed, nor do I have anything, or anyone waiting in Grenoble. I would sit alone and dream of you, and the shadows."

He watched her, shaking his head and backing up a step, but she was quick, and as she approached she tilted her head to one side, tossing her hair back with a quick shrug.

Despite her bravado, she was trembling weakly.

"I will not," he said, though he stood very still. Her heart was hammering wildly, and the scent of her warm blood mixed with the perfume of her hair,

192

the fear and strength in her eyes. He had seen nothing like it since his Embrace. He'd seen fear, and loathing, and hatred, but not this. She was offering him what he needed to sustain his life, offering her own as forfeit, and though it terrified her, she stood fast.

"I..." He lunged. It was too much. He knew then that he should have taken Raul, or another from the tavern, left their husk in the alley beyond and been gone. He had waited too long. Fleurette cried out softly as he fell on her, driving her back, catching her before she could fall away and latching to her soft throat. She struggled, but that struggle twisted until she was pressing into him. He held her, he fed, and as he drained her she weakened...fluttering against him, eyes closing in the sudden ecstasy of the moment. He watched those eyes close, and something inside him snapped. He fought the hunger, drawing back with a snarl at just the last moment, while life yet flickered in her heart. Laying her back quickly, he ran a nail across his wrist sharply, opening his reddening skin, starting a trickle of her blood flowing back out of his veins, and he brought that wrist to her lips with a snarl of frustration at his own weakness.

Her eyes flickered open, and she realized in that second what he intended, but if she'd meant to fight him, she could not. The blood slid over her sweet lips, touched her tongue, and she was lost, and found—born again to him. He held her as she

To Dream of Dreamers Lost

locked to his wrist, sucking the blood back through the rip in his skin, ravaging his flesh hungrily. He gritted his teeth against the pain, closed his eyes, and waited. He wasn't certain how long it would take, how much of his blood he would need to return to her. He'd never Embraced another, had intended never to pass on that curse.

Then he had held this girl in his arms, and watched her eyes close, and in that instant knew that she was the one human who'd looked upon him in anything resembling friendship in longer than he cared to remember. She had been unwilling to leave him to his fate, and in her attempts to aid him, had sealed her own. She might hate him now, most certainly would come to eventually as the truth of her Embrace hit her. These were facts he would have to come to terms with. The simple fact was, he did not wish to be alone, and it was not her choice, but his. He felt a small throb of hunger still, but it had not been so long since he'd fed on Pierre in the alley. He would survive, and so would she.

The extra responsibility of teaching her, and of keeping her alive on the road, were something he could ill afford, but he cast these thoughts from himself angrily. He would catch Montrovant, or he would not, and very likely he would be destroyed if he did. Nothing said he should not enjoy his last few days in the company of another. Poor logic, but he was not of a mind to contest it.

DAVID NIALL WILSON

He withdrew his wrist with a quick snarl, watching the pain in her gaze and pushing her back easily as she scrabbled after him, trying to re-attach herself to his vein, to drain more of his strength. As he denied her, the questions flooded endlessly from the depths of her eyes. He lifted her before him, slipping into the saddle, and turned toward the mountains.

They had to find a place they could rest safely, where he could feed her at least once more and build her strength. The mountains beckoned, but somehow they seemed worlds away, and even Montrovant's mocking laughter was fading to a dull echo.

TWELVE

Lacroix followed Noirceuil's lead as he left the city behind. They did not head into the woods, despite what they'd heard.

"They have been there and gone," Noirceuil explained tersely. "We should have been on the road hours ago. I will catch the trail beyond the wood. They will be heading to the mountains."

"How do you know that?" Lacroix had argued for just a moment. "And don't tell me it is just what your mind tells you, because this is far too important to be trusting little voices in our heads."

Noirceuil had stopped short of his mount, turned to his partner, eyes very cold. "I know because the one I questioned at the tavern told me that they would go to the woods. While you sat and sipped the cardinal's wine, perhaps running over old stories of life in Rome, I left the city and scouted those woods. Beyond the woods they could have gone two ways. One road leads straight inland, cities, people, even an army to contend with. The other road leads to the mountains.

"If you were leading a band of undead demons with the very treasure of God in your wagons, would you head for civilization, or would you hide it away?"

Lacroix did not speak for a long moment. He saw more in the depths of Noirceuil's eyes than he cared to. Things he wondered at not seeing before. For the first time he began to doubt the wisdom of being on the road alone with the man.

He nodded at last, and Noirceuil turned away without a word, mounting his horse and guiding its head away from the cathedral brusquely. Lacroix mounted as well, turning to gaze back at the cardinal for a moment. The priest was standing on a balcony outside his quarters, staring down at them, his hand raised in farewell.

Once beyond the city the two made good time. Noirceuil led them at an angle that cut next to the far side of the trees, but avoided the stand of forest entirely. He was intent on the road beyond, and the mountains that stretched above them, brooding and cold. Lacroix knew Noirceuil was probably right, but the further they turned from the confines of the city, and the church, the less comfortable he became.

It was time, he knew, to trade in his saddle and his sword for a parish of his own, or a chamber in Rome where he could oversee the questing of others. His brand of service had been unique, and there were few as qualified as he in such matters. As long as the Damned walked among them, Lacroix would be needed.

Noirceuil now, that was a different story. It was true to a point that one needed a madman to hunt madmen, but there were limits to everything. If he could arrange it, he knew that Noirceuil should not return from this journey. If not, soon after their return he would have to give the word. It would not be an easy thing. Noirceuil might be mad, but he was not a foolish man. He would feel the growing tension between them, and he would be on his guard.

Lacroix shivered. Perhaps it would not be the dark hunter who did not return. He leaned in close over his mount and gazed into the wind whipping his long hair about his shoulders. Noirceuil rode easily, head up as though the battering of the weather did not affect him. Perhaps it did not. His mind was sealed. Perhaps he saw only his own goal, ignoring the rest of the world. Perhaps he was not what he seemed at all.

They skirted the trees and turned down the road. Noirceuil did not remain long on that main track, but cut off first to one side, then to the other, seeking. He found what he was after far to the right of the road and gave a soft cry for Lacroix to follow, spurring his mount forward. Lacroix saw it then, as he came up behind his partner. Tracks...the tracks of a single horse, heading toward the mountains. They remained to one side of the road, but there was no waver in the direction. Moments later, Noirceuil reined in suddenly, sliding from his saddle so quickly that for a moment Lacroix believed he had fallen.

Slowing his own mount and wheeling back, he gazed down at where Noirceuil was kneeling in the dirt, eyes blazing. Turning his face up to meet Lacroix's gaze, he spoke softly.

"He has bred another," he said softly. "A female, young. He fed here," Noirceuil's boot traced the impression of boots, and a knee, in the soft soil. "He allowed her to feed from himself here." Another quick gesture. Lacroix could see that there had been activity, but he scanned the impressions blankly in search of whatever clues gave Noirceuil his information.

"Montrovant?" Lacroix asked, uncertain.

"No," Noirceuil replied with a smile. "The dark one would have killed her and left her shell here to rot. It is the other, the *hunter* that fool Santorini sent out without consulting us. Sending a vampire alone to hunt a vampire seems a fool's game to me. We must see to his destruction as well, and this new one."

Lacroix watched Noirceuil's eyes. The words jumbled for a moment in his mind. 'Sending a vampire out to hunt a vampire, *alone*.' That last word would not release him as he shivered and fought to keep his breath steady.

"It is not our task," he said at last. "We can't divert ourselves from Montrovant for even a moment, or we may lose him."

Noirceuil laughed then. "You forget, my friend," he said softly, "that this young one hunts Montrovant as well. He is leading us straight to our goal, and I will leave no windows open this time. They will all perish, returning to Satan's shadows."

Lacroix nodded, turning away. Noirceuil knelt in the dirt for another moment, then rose, leaping back to his own saddle. "They have passed here very early. She will slow him down, but we will not catch up with them this night, I think."

He turned back toward the mountain, keeping the road in sight off to their left, riding through the chiaroscuro wash of the midnight moon. Lacroix followed, a dark shadow of a dark shadow, flying over the lower hills. It would be two nights before they reached the mountains, and though they might expect to find Abraham, or even Montrovant, before the mountains were actually reached, it was still a long ride.

Lacroix maintained his silence, watching first the road, then Noirceuil, then the road again, mind whirling. Definitely too old for this.

Abraham knew they would be followed. He also knew that with Fleurette in his care, he could not expect to withstand an attack from Lacroix and Noirceuil. It was uncertain if he could do so even if he had full advantage. He decided to go with his instincts, and just before daylight, he stopped his horse, removed what belongings he had, and sent the animal on its way. He moved off at an angle from the road, carefully erasing his tracks as he went, carrying Fleurette's prone form easily over one shoulder and cursing himself as a fool as he went. Montrovant was right. He was weak. Somehow, though, the limp weight of his companion comforted him.

Things were growing more and more complex. He would need to acquire another horse, and they would both need to feed. He had to do all of this without creating a scene, or costing himself too many days on the road. He frowned, then burst into a quick laugh. It was no more ludicrous than chasing a centuries-old vampire by himself with no aid, followed himself by Christian vampire hunters.

The mountains were not so many nights in the distance. He knew that whatever happened there, Montrovant would not leave until he perished, or found the answers he sought. The Order, if they'd moved there, would be expecting to remain for a good many years. It would be better to have Rome's "hunter" before him than behind him. All of these things he told himself as he rode further and further from the road, catching sight of smoke rising in the distance. He found a cave in one of the larger outcroppings, deep enough to hold them both, and a bit more searching brought him a stone large enough to seal the opening. It would not be perfect, but with the girl helpless his options had thinned.

As dawn approached, he dragged Fleurette into the small alcove, drew the stone seal in behind them, pulling it as snug as possible, and lay on the cool earth, drawing her close against his body. The weight of the sun rose, pressing him downward, pinning him and stealing thought. He drifted to the darkness, and for the first time in many years, he was not alone.

PART TWO

THIRTEEN

It was early evening when Gustav was summoned to the great hall of the keep. He had not been up long, the sun releasing him reluctantly to motion and what passed for life. They had a visitor, but not just any visitor. As he entered the hall, his gaze fixed immediately on the thin, ancient figure standing just inside the great doors. Fine wisps of white hair flowed back over thin shoulders, and the eyes were just as Gustav remembered, wild, with a hint of things so ancient they could scarcely be believed.

"Kli Kodesh," Gustav breathed. His master/mentor smiled at him, moving slowly across the room to meet the aged Nosferatu midway.

"It has been too long, Gustav," Kodesh said quietly. "Far too long."

Gustav only nodded. He had known that things would change once they'd moved to the mountains; that went without saying. They had broken the ancient bond with the Church, and this had set Montrovant in motion once more, generally stirring any force interested in the ancient treasures. He had not expected to see the old one at his doorstep in the midst of it all. It had been a long time.

"You are surprised to see me," Kodesh cackled. "Good. I have entertained you. But wait, I have brought something to add to your responsibilities. The artifacts you hold have been too long without their guardian, and I have decided the time has come to reunite the two."

Gustav's gaze flickered around the room suspiciously, and the ancient burst into cackling laughter.

"Oh, calm yourself my friend. Santos is here, but not as you suspect."

Reaching into his cloak, Kodesh pulled free a small vial. It was corked, and inside, something moved about slowly. Gustav looked more closely. A maggot. The vial contained a single maggot. The old Nosferatu's eyes flickered up to catch Kodesh's grinning visage.

"He did not die in de Molay's keep," Kodesh explained, "though it was very close. He was able to reach out and grasp the true name of the only life form nearby at the time. When I went back in search of the head, I found him." Grinning, Kodesh shook the bottle violently, sending the larval form inside spinning and squirming. "I decided it was best to imprison him before he managed to regain his true form."

Gustav's features were slowly creased by a smile. "The head?" he asked softly. "Have you brought us that to watch as well?"

"No," Kodesh grinned, nearly prancing in circles with delight at his treasure, "I left that in another place. It is of little use to any without knowledge of the spells that bind and animate it, but the attempts to find and recreate those spells have been most amusing."

Gustav shook his head slowly. The things that amused Kli Kodesh would not strike the world at large as amusing, or entertaining. That head had nearly cost each of them their existence at one point or another, by the power of its prophecy and the dark intent of its holder. Gustav glanced once more at the maggot, squirming in the vial.

"We have done as you instructed," Gustav said at last. "Everything has been brought here with as much secrecy as possible. I am certain that Montrovant follows, and at least one other."

Kli Kodesh grinned. "It will be good to see the dark one again," he said softly. "He has never failed to entertain me. No matter how many walls you erect in his path, he is incorrigible in his quest.

Men could learn from his perseverance, if not from his success."

Gustav shook his head again, turning and leading the way deeper into the keep. He moved down a dimly lit hall lined with old paintings, hung with tapestries, carpeted in rich oriental rugs. The keep had been many years in the building, even more in the outfitting and design of the interior. It was a place to spend lifetimes, a refuge from the world. Tucked away as it was in a forbidding range of mountains, joined to the world by only a single, well-guarded road, it was a perfect place to preserve holy relics, or to stand off a siege.

They moved into a smaller, darker space. It was lined with couches and chairs, a large mahogany table running nearly the length of the chamber. Gustav passed by this and moved to the far corner where a large, dark desk sat. There were scrolls and books piled high on the desktop. Gustav sat behind this desk, gesturing to a comfortable chair just opposite him.

Kli Kodesh sat, looking about with an approving smile. "I see that things have gone well with this place. It is so much a thing of chance, putting anything worthwhile together in secrecy, and in such a secluded spot."

"We had plenty of time," Gustav replied. "With money and time we could rebuild Jacob's ladder."

Kodesh grinned, nodding. "That is true, and what an entertaining prospect that would be. A stairway to heaven. So obviously destined to failure, but such a lofty goal. You know what they say, Gustav, old friend. If you set your sights too high, your failures will be more presentable."

Gustav's eyes twinkled. "Someone will always be under that stairway when it falls. Best to leave God to His own devices and build our stairways to guard towers."

Kodesh threw his head back and laughed madly. "Always the practical one, eh Gustav? If God had you on his side, he would have guard towers lining the road to Heaven and a search at the border, just to be certain no demons slipped through."

Gustav nodded. "Are you certain that none of our own demons will slip through this time?" he asked. "Montrovant is no fool, and there are others. I doubt that the Church has entrusted the entire chase to the dark one. There is no telling who will end up in our courtyard."

"That is the beauty of it all, is it not?" Kodesh said brightly. "The not knowing. There are so few things in life that I do not know, so few events I cannot predict. I even have a good idea how all of this will end up, though I have high hopes of being disappointed."

Gustav decided to ignore this. "The vaults are sealed tightly," he went on. "The towers are fortified, and the men armed. This keep is more a fortress than anything else. The framework was built by one of the local lords down below. He

208

wanted to have a commanding view of his holdings. There was not enough labor available, and he was killed before construction could be completed. We improved on his design."

"The entire lower level of the keep is a single huge vault. Within those walls are more walls, and within those still more. Each is protected by traps, and guardians. We have learned a great deal over the years, shunning nothing of value."

Kodesh nodded. "I know how the boredom of the years can make the mundane enticing," he said softly. "I want to see the vaults, and to see the artifacts. We will place our friend here," he patted his pocket, where the vial still rested, "with his treasures, as is fitting."

Gustav rose, clapping his hands twice, and two cowled figures stepped from the shadows. "They will show you the vaults," he said softly. "I do not go near the artifacts if I can help it. The temptation to release their power is too great."

Kodesh laughed. "You are too cautious, old friend," he said with glee. "Power is meant to be unleashed, that is its nature. The longer you bottle it, much like curiosity, the more pressure builds for the eventual release."

"I will let it build a while longer, I believe," Gustav said, chuckling.

Kodesh turned with a shrug, following the hooded figures down the long hall again. Gustav sat in his chair, behind the huge desk, watching the

To Dream of Dreamers Lost

thin, crazed apparition depart. So many years. It seemed an eternity since Kli Kodesh had shared his blood, and his curse, with Gustav and the others. Gustav had been old already, but his followers had been Embraced only that night. The old Nosferatu often wondered what had become of the progeny he'd left behind.

Now his existence was a never-ending string of puzzles and games. There were many besides Montrovant who sought one or another of the treasures he guarded. There were those, as well, who believed that the objects they sought were in Gustav's control. He himself had no true inkling of everything that had been entrusted to him. There was no inventory. There was no way to be in the presence of so many objects of power for any length of time. It corrupted. The strongest of convictions paled when the mere chanting of a few ancient words could bring about ultimate change.

Gustav had lived, and died, and walked the Earth again. Even that had not been the end of his journey. He'd been Embraced by an elder Nosferatu, a vampire killed eventually in a skirmish with Kli Kodesh. From that moment on, Gustav, and his own, had followed Kodesh and his "entertainments." He could not have explained why. There was no bond, not like the blood. Kodesh had not been his sire, nor had he drained that ancient upon killing him, as Gustav would have. It was something else, a hint of mystery, and of power.

DAVID NIALL WILSON

Then the question of loyalty had been erased forever. One dark night, just outside Jerusalem, as Montrovant had fought his own battles with the Egyptian, Santos, Kodesh and the Nosferatu had waylaid a group of knights on their way to the Holy Land. They had fed on each of them, Embracing them, and Kodesh had given each a taste of his own blood. Blood so old, so powerful, that the scent had maddened Gustav, nearly stealing his senses.

Until it was offered to him as well. He was chosen to lead this new band. He was to leave all those he'd known, take this band of new, untested followers on a journey of immense proportion and import. They carried secrets and treasures so old and so powerful that they had fallen into legend, and beyond. Things so old that none remembered the people who had wielded them, let alone the stories behind them. And other things. Many of the treasures Santos had collected and guarded came from the early Christian era. Not so old as others, but carrying immense power drawn from the belief and worship of thousands. There were talismans, bits of the flesh of ancient priests and martyrs, scrolls, objects touched and blessed by men long crumbled to dust.

And there were rumors of other things. Of the Holy Grail, the Ark of the Covenant. Many of the items were boxed and packaged, sealed to prevent their influence over those who guarded them. It was a Pandora's box of magic and corruption.

Gustav kept his distance. It was one thing to know the powers that were under his protection, but quite another to dream of those that might be. He had not seen the light of day in several hundred years. He had not felt breath in his lungs, or blood he could call his own in that same time.

Kli Kodesh's blood had returned a rotted semblance of these to him, but this only served to cause further pain. He could rise earlier than most of his kind, and remain upright and coherent longer as the sun rose. He could go long, almost interminable periods without feeding. That bloodlust, the desire to feed and rend, to hunt, that had been the one thrill left to him. Kodesh had removed it, leaving him nearly immortal on the earth, with a single purpose: to guard the objects entrusted to him, and to do as Kodesh bid. These were small recompense for centuries of boredom, but the Blood Oath was complete. He could not ignore Kodesh's commands.

He watched until his men and the old one were gone from sight, then moved to the hall and turned to the left, making his way to a winding stairway leading up to the walls of the keep. He knew that the dark one would not be far behind. Kodesh would not show himself unless there was something to be done, or seen, a new thing to be experienced. It was the ancient vampire's nature to seek out that which could ease the perpetual boredom of his existence.

DAVID NIALL WILSON

The night had fallen fully, and Gustav moved out onto the wall, gazing down the road into the shadows. So much had changed. The arrangement with Rome had provided a measure of security for a number of years, but at the same time, the constant vigilance of Montrovant and the lack of activity had been stifling. Nothing had changed during that time. There were those who approached the Order, young Cainites with their own stories, a bit of something to add, but nothing of substance. Gustav had been ready to slip out one day, slide into the earth, and rest for eternity. Nothing was worth that kind of stagnancy.

The order to move, at last, had seemed a godsend. Gustav had been traveling back and forth from their old mountain hideaway to this keep for decades. He had planned each step of the reconstruction, been there when the stone walls were laid between the layers of the vault. He had picked and purchased the decorations, what furnishings were provided.

The library was one of the most fully stocked in the world. He had scrolls and tomes from every society that had walked the Earth, and a few in question. He had secrets that should have died with those who discovered them. He had read words in tongues long withered from the memory of men, and still there was nothing to hold his interest.

Only action served Gustav, and at long last there was action brewing on his horizon. Montrovant was no match for Kli Kodesh, but Gustav knew his master would exclude himself from what was to come if it was possible. It would be a matter left to Gustav and his followers. The old one would sit back and watch, waiting to see how much entertainment could be gleaned from the conflict.

That was fine with Gustav. He was ready for something different. If it was the last such thing ever to happen in his long years of existence, that was fine as well. The alternative was that he would remain in this keep, alone with his followers, until the world rotted around him, or another came along to attempt to claim the duties and make off with that which he guarded.

So many things he would have traded for a return to times past. He moved along the wall slowly, nodding to the guards as he passed them, slipping around the corner of the wall and away in silence.

❧

Kli Kodesh moved through the stone doors quickly. They had slid open at the soft touch of his guide's hand in a certain sequence against the stones of the wall. The old one memorized that sequence quickly. He needed to know that he could access that which he controlled. They moved inward, and a few feet beyond the stone doors, the guide's hand returned to the wall, opposite side, and another sequence of stones was pressed. The door slid open silently, huge stone slabs slipping to the sides with no more evidence of their passing than if a fly had landed on his cloak. Again he watched carefully.

There were four levels of security in all. Each time they moved inward he matched the pattern of the other's steps. There were traps planted, this he knew. Concentrating, he let his mind grow blank, redirected his thoughts to his physical senses. He could sense the potential danger of the trip mechanisms, and though he did not know their exact nature, he knew enough to be certain they were designed to guard against both mortal and undead intrusion.

The final portal slid wide, and he entered the inner vault. The same wagons that had transported the goods to the keep had been rolled inside. The wide passageways of the keep itself and the huge stone doors had facilitated this passage. The treasures themselves, many packed away from air and the sight of man for so many years their packing had rotted away around them, were still tucked safely in the wooden crates that had transported them since their exodus from Jerusalem so many years before.

Santos had been an excellent guardian. Gustav did him one better. While Santos had been created to guard the treasures, he had had no desire to use them himself. He had his own powers and his own artifacts, some he'd designed, others he'd taken from those who'd tested him through the years. The secrets he'd guarded were sacred to him.

Gustav was different. The old Nosferatu was so careful not to be tempted, so worried that he would slip and break his trust, that the treasures were not even unpacked. Kli Kodesh had seen most of them at one time or another. He had a good idea what the cache held, what sort of chaos that horde of secrets and power could unleash upon the earth if it was released. The tension this created made it so much more delicious to Kodesh.

He had hoped, actually, that his protégé might slip. He had wondered for years how much more fun the world might be if some of the old powers were unleashed. Gustav had proven stronger than he'd believed. The treasures were intact, and now he moved forward, wrapping the vial carefully in a bit of silk from the packing material, and laying it on its side among the rest.

"Farewell, old friend," he said softly, moving back and smiling at the guards. He made a quick circuit of the stone chamber, checking each wall, seeing how strong and complete the they were, then moving back toward the entrance.

He turned without a word, backtracking through the maze of trips and traps without a hitch. The two who'd led him to the vault followed as quickly as they could, watching his retreating form with concern. They were to guide him, but he seemed oblivious to their existence. It was obvious that his one trip through their security had been enough to etch it in his memory.

Kodesh made his way to the main passageway, and, sensing Gustav's presence above him, made his own way up toward the walls. The dawn was not far away, but there was enough time remaining to him for a few moments' meditation. He was not so much in fear of the sun as the others. The blood hunger did not sing in his veins…he could take or leave the feeding. He had walked the Earth for so long that very little could be offered to catch his interest, and the curse he bore had robbed him even of the pleasure of the blood. The curse, and the years.

He did not follow Gustav, but instead stepped up onto the wall and turned, leaping to the walls of the keep and climbing, hand over hand, until he'd reached the highest point of stone. Here he sat, staring out at the shadows, thinking. His eyes closed slowly, and his mind grew blank, seeking, stretching out his senses. He knew they would come, knew them as well as he knew his own mind.

Montrovant. The dark one would come as surely as the sun would rise, his progeny in tow. The Church had its own emissaries on the roads, both Damned and living, and as Kli Kodesh stretched his awareness, he became aware of that other.

His eyes popped open for a moment, and a slow smile crept over his face. "Noirceuil," he muttered with glee. Such a long time, and he'd not been aware that particular Cainite still walked the road of the Earth. It seemed so unlikely, given his particular habits.

Then his eyes closed again, and he did not move until the first fingers of dawn's light slid over his legs, itching at his skin and drawing him from his reverie.

As he climbed down, seeking the shadows and protection of the keep, he smiled again. "Noirceuil. Oh, this is so sweet."

Then he disappeared into the depths of the keep, and silence reigned.

FOURTEEN

Montrovant and his men came to a fork in the road two nights away from the forest. The left fork wound down into a small valley, and the right snaked up the mountain into mist and shadows. He stopped at that crossroad, staring upward, letting his mind go blank. He knew it was the way. There was no other place nearby, no way he could be tricked into the wrong turn. Yet he hesitated.

Kli Kodesh was behind it all. He had been behind it all from the beginning. Sometimes Montrovant wondered if the old one had even been behind his own determination to follow what had turned into a fool's quest for so many years. He watched the weatherbeaten trail, his horse shifting slightly beneath his weight, then turned to Jeanne.

"The Order will be there, but they are not going anywhere," he said. "I think we would be best served by a short visit to the village below. We have not fed in two nights, and the others are growing weary. Tired men are careless men, and we cannot afford to be careless. Not now."

Jeanne grinned back at him. "I was thinking much the same thing, but did not know how you would take such a suggestion. You are right, though. If there is one ally that serves us now as it has always served us, it is time. Neither Gustav, nor Kli Kodesh is in danger of succumbing to old age. The artifacts, and the Grail itself, are timeless."

Montrovant turned to the others. "We will spend this night, tomorrow, and possibly another night beyond that in the village. St. Fond, ride ahead and have quarters prepared, see to the service of our mounts. Have the innkeeper prepare food and wine. Our time on the road may be near an end, and we need our strength, and our wits, for what is to come."

There were murmurs of assent, and a general appreciative rumble at his words. The road was a place they all felt comfortable, but part of the appeal of the road was the wine, women, and food awaiting them at its end. If Montrovant was going to allow them that space, it would be savored and appreciated, binding each to him a bit more fully than he had been before.

Montrovant took the left fork and pressed his horse to a slow canter, heading down to where white spirals of smoke showed the boundaries of the village. St. Fond took off at a faster pace, widening the gap between himself and the main party rapidly and soon disappearing from sight altogether. Jeanne watched him go, considering for a long moment taking off after the knight and joining him.

He could sense that they were near mortals, could almost taste the hot blood on his lips. Two nights was not a horribly long time for him to have gone without feeding. He'd been longer, but for some reason the knowledge of what was to come was spurring him onward, increasing the appeal. Jeanne loved battle. He lived for the red haze that robbed him of everything but the moment. He had the berserker's blood in his soul; his Embrace had not cost him that, but had heightened it. He was not himself once the battle was joined. It was a hunger skewed slightly from the ache that had shivered through his veins since his death. He felt the imminence of fate. He felt powers larger than those he commanded at work, pieces fitting together, and it was all building to a focus of energy that permeated the air. That aura of coming change built within his mind and his thoughts, and it charged his senses, feeding the hunger.

He followed closely behind Montrovant, who

was leading the small group slowly down the mountain, and he noted with a quick smile how the dark one shifted in his own saddle. They held their pace for a while, as though to give in to the urge for speed would be a sign of weakness, but in the end it was too much, even, for Montrovant. They sped their slow progress to a canter, and then a slow gallop, rushing down the softly rolling hills in a tight pack.

As they neared the break in the trees and brush that signaled the border of the small village, Montrovant reined in a bit, slowing to a trot. There was no sense bursting into the village like an angry mob. It was enough that they approached openly. If any came searching, or if they ran into any of Gustav's spies, then their cover was blown.

Montrovant did not seem to be concerned any longer with secrecy. From the moment he'd glanced up that trail to the mountains he'd acted differently, his eyes shining, his step more lively. The dark one was not afraid of Gustav, or his Nosferatu. He was not concerned with the *how* of getting into whatever safe house Kli Kodesh had dreamed up. He was already holding the Grail in his hand as far as he was concerned, his arrogance peaking. This was the moment he'd been born for, and he was loving it, reveling in the excitement.

Jeanne knew that, as usual, he would have to be the practical one. When the trouble started, and their enemies surrounded them, it was Jeanne who would watch the rear, who would seek the safe route through whatever maze presented itself. Montrovant would be the one to charge through that opening, and the trick was to point the dark one in the right direction before he led them into a trap.

Jeanne had no illusions of their destined success. Kli Kodesh was the most ancient vampire he had encountered, so old that the things Jeanne knew as true for himself and Montrovant did not apply in the same way when you thought of him. Gustav himself was not young to the Blood, and they had come across both characters enough times in the past to know that whatever was to take place on that mountain, it would not be simple, if it was possible at all, to break through to where whatever was being kept by the Order was stashed.

Odd as it seemed, Kli Kodesh was their one hope for success. The ancient had created the Order of the Bitter Ash with his own blood, but he could not be trusted to back them completely. He had lived too long, seen too many born and ground to dust. Very little in the world could hold his interest for any length of time, and Montrovant, for all his faults, had proven to be one of those things that could.

Kodesh might not ever allow the dark one close enough to truly get his hands on the Grail, but he would certainly make it possible for him to try. It was more entertaining that way, and Kodesh lived for entertainment. Without his little intrigues and games, Jeanne was certain that the ancient would have sunk to the earth and never risen long before.

The one constant in all their dealings with Kli Kodesh was that none involved could trust him. He would send one group one way, another the opposite, stand in the middle and laugh as a third group neither of the others suspected marched up the center and tilted the odds. The thing to do, then, was not to look for a way through to the treasures. Not to try to beat the puzzle the old one would pose, or to fall into the game he would begin. The secret was to try to anticipate which were the pieces of this game, and to avoid them altogether, while appearing to fall into the trap.

They had never succeeded in getting within hand's reach of the treasures the Order guarded, but they had come much closer than Kodesh and Santos, now apparently destroyed, would have cared to see them. This time had to be different. This time they would need intrigue of their own, and a good measure of luck, because Jeanne knew that, for good or ill, Montrovant had set his mind on this. He had decided it was to end, and here. That meant the stakes, and the risks, would be going up.

As they walked their horses into town, they noted that St. Fond had worked quickly. He stood beside his mount in front of the one inn in the town, two local boys beside him, staring up at the approaching knights as if God Himself had come to call.

Montrovant smiled, slipping from the saddle and handing over his reins to the first of them. "Food, and water," he told the boy, "plenty of it. I expect each horse to be brushed and cared for properly, and the bridles and saddles oiled."

The boy nodded dumbly.

His partner, a bit bolder, chimed in, "Yes sir. We'll take good care of them for you, sir. You'll have no complaints with us."

"That I am sure of," Montrovant replied, almost smiling. "I am not a man you want to displease."

Both boys gulped at this, taking in the tall, imposing figure that towered over them, then nodded. "Yes sir."

Montrovant did laugh then, and turned toward the inn. The others dismounted behind him, dropping the reins of their mounts and following their leader. The horses, trained for battle and camp alike, did not move once their reins touched the ground, but the animals watched, eyes rolling in hunger, as their companions were led off to the stables.

The two stable hands scurried back and forth as if possessed, struggling to get the animals sheltered quickly so they could be about their work. To tend five such magnificent animals in one night was surely the highlight of their past year, but with the threat of Montrovant's anger hovering over them, and the thought of the recompense such a man might offer if he were pleased growing in their minds, they hurried quickly about their tasks.

Montrovant entered the inn with the others close behind. The interior was cheery, a large warm fire centered on the far wall of one large room, several rough wooden tables with matching chairs, and a series of sleeping furs near the fire.

St. Fond had arranged for the only two rooms, both large and spacious, to be readied for them, and Jeanne moved off with the innkeeper's son, who was seeing to the preparations, to modify the one he and Montrovant would share. Du Puy would join them, as guardian, but it was important to know how they would spend the coming day before taking any time to decide what to do with the night.

The room was low-ceilinged, and there was only a single window, heavily shuttered. Thick curtains lined the portal's sides, and Jeanne moved to it, sliding them closed in the center with a quick shrug of his shoulders. He turned, catching the innkeeper's son's eye over his shoulder, and grinned.

"You can go, boy, we will handle it from here. If we need anything, be certain you will be the first to know."

The boy hesitated. It was obvious he'd expected to leave with more information on their magnificent guests. Jeanne watched him for a moment, then turned, taking a step toward the door, and the boy fled. Laughing, Le Duc turned next to the closet. As he'd hoped, it was large. The room was designed to house a group of travelers, as the inn was too small to offer individual quarters, and the closet was large enough for the belongings of several. It was sealed from the room by a very solid oak door, and Jeanne stepped inside, closing this, testing the cracks above and below. There was so little space that as he closed it he could feel the pressure in the small space resisting.

He stepped out, nodding to himself. It would do nicely. This taken care of, he closed the door behind himself and headed back to the main room of the inn. He knew that, with du Puy stationed outside the closet, and the room's door and window closed tightly, they were as safe as they were likely to be in a public, mortal dwelling. Unless the innkeeper was abnormally curious, or some other mishap befell, it would be a smooth visit.

He wanted to get outside. He wanted to get beyond the confines of the city, to the outlying homes, the hunters and farmers. He needed to feel the scent of the hunt, the fear of a victim, needed the hot coppery taste of life sliding over his lips and down his throat; the warmth of another's life.

Montrovant was seated at a table positioned by a shuttered window, as far from the blazing fire as possible. St. Fond and the others were gathered about that fire, with a small group of locals, work-

7

ing on what must have been, from the empty mugs arrayed before them, their third ale apiece.

Jeanne shook his head in silent laughter and joined his sire at the table.

"I need to go out," he said at last.

Montrovant nodded. "I will wait until you have been gone for a while, then follow. We will need our wits, and our full strength. I can't shake the feeling that he has done it again, that Kli Kodesh has manipulated us across the country to this spot like unsuspecting children."

"Not unsuspecting, then," Jeanne grinned. "If he did, what is the difference? We are here, they are here, and the old game has begun again. It is good to be back in the fire," he added. "I have missed the excitement."

Montrovant laughed softly. "Go. You begin now to sound like Kli Kodesh himself. Next you will tell me how it is so much more entertaining."

Jeanne laughed too, then rose and turned toward the door. The night was still young, but he knew he'd need to get far away from that inn not to bring suspicion upon himself, or the others. That meant a quick start, and swift travel. He was aching to begin.

As Jeanne slipped silently away from the inn, and Montrovant turned back to watch the group at the fire, lost in thought, two other travelers reached the crossroads beneath the mountain. They shared a single mount, and Abraham stared longingly up

---

the mountain as his companion, leaning up behind him, clung to his back, dark eyes scanning the road in both directions.

Fleurette had not said a word since awakening. He had fed and shared the blood with her the night after her Embrace, and she'd not questioned it, or struggled. Now she was silent, watching everything with her new sight, taking in every nuance of the landscape, and clinging to him for support, though at the same time Abraham could feel her pushing him away.

He knew they weren't too far behind Montrovant, despite the delay, but what worried him the most was the others. He'd seen no evidence of Lacroix or Noirceuil, and that meant one of two things. Either the two had lost the scent, or they knew exactly where he was, and his time before that confrontation was limited. If the latter were true, then there were choices to be made.

He stared down at the curling smoke from the village, then up the mountain. He could feel them. The Order was up there, waiting, watching. Below, who knew? He could question the locals on Montrovant's passing, but there was little point. The dark one would be going up the mountain. If he was not already there, he would go soon. Abraham only needed to go, and to watch. If he arrived first, then perhaps he could renew his old acquaintances. At the very least he might find some answers about why he'd been left behind.

To Dream of Dreamers Lost

He turned his mount upward, mounting the trail at a slow walk. The way was shadowed and curved around to the left quickly. He rounded that curve and disappeared from the crossroad. The moon was only just rising, and there was plenty of time to scout the hillside above, then make his plans. He wanted to make Fleurette understand as well. He had drawn her into his dark world; that was enough to make her hate him eternally, once the significance of it hit her. Now he was riding into the face of almost certain destruction, either from Lacroix and Noirceuil, Montrovant, or the Order itself...a second death, much more painful and final than the first, and without the promise of salvation.

He planned to offer her freedom, such as it was. He could force her to do as he wished. She was so young to the Blood, and his childe. He had never created another of his kind, and the responsibility was an unfamiliar, uncomfortable weight on his shoulders. She was not going to be much use against Noirceuil except possibly as a momentary distraction. She did not know how to hunt, or what to expect when they reached whatever stronghold the Order had created. She was a burden, and an enigma, with her dark eyes and her silence. Not for the first time, Abraham cursed himself as a fool for not killing her and being done with it when he had the chance. He still didn't know exactly why he had not, except that something deep inside had not allowed him to betray her. It was one thing to feed from those who didn't matter, or who hated you; quite another to end the existence of the only one to care about your own.

He continued up the sloping trail for a few hundred yards, then glanced back down and made a decision. The road was open as far as he could see upward, and below it stretched around that one bend, but was otherwise bare. If any were following, they would spot him and his companion in seconds after rounding that bend.

He turned off the trail to the left, where it was only about twenty yards to where the tree line rose beside them, cutting off their view of the road ahead, but shielding them from prying eyes. The way became steeper and more rocky soon after he veered to the side, but a bit more effort in climbing was a small price to pay for possibly protecting of their lives.

He climbed steadily, shifting from side to side, slipping around rocky outcrops and avoiding stands of trees and overgrown brush. It slowed them to a walk, eventually bringing them to a nearly sheer cliff face. He noted that there was a very dark patch to his right, at the base of that cliff, and he turned his mount toward it curiously.

It was a shallow cave. The hole sank deep into the earth, but was no taller than a small child. He stared at it for a long moment, glanced to the sky, and sighed. It would do. There was still over an hour until the sun would rise, but he needed time to go back over their tracks and be certain they'd not left a trail, and he needed time to talk with his silent progeny.

He turned, pressing her to one side gently and indicating that she should dismount, then joined her, tying the horse loosely to a nearby tree. No way to hide it, or their location. The only hope lay in keeping any from following them to that dark hole. He thought of Noirceuil for a moment, and he shivered. Laying his hands on Fleurette's shoulders, he led her to a small cleared space before the cavern, pressing her down so that she sat opposite him.

"You have to listen to me," he said softly. "Things will never be the same for you. There is no way back from what has been done. You are like I am now, your hunger will follow you and haunt you, the sun is denied you, and you are bound to do as I ask."

Fleurette did not answer, but, meeting his gaze, she nodded. Her gaze was wary. Her wits did not appear to have been dimmed, but she was guarded, turned deeply inward.

"That is the good news," he said softly. "I have to tell you why I am here, and who else will follow."

As he spoke, leaning in closer so that he could keep his voice very low, she watched him intently, listening. He did not stop talking for a very long time, and the night slipped away, stealing the time he had planned to spend on other things. The wind picked up some, and in the distance, a storm was brewing.

⁂

Below, at the crossroads, that same wind was kicking leaves and sand up in small spiraling gusts, dancing it around and over Noirceuil's boots as he dismounted and led his horse to where the roads up and down the mountain met.

Lacroix sat on his horse, watching, and waiting. Noirceuil had calmed somewhat once they were back on the road, and things were nearly back to their usual level of comfort, such as it was. Noirceuil was controlled and silent as he hunted, it was his way, and now he had two trails to follow.

The hunter spun slowly, and spoke in a low voice. "The new one has gone up the mountain," he said softly. "I sense others there, a great number. I believe we are very near our goal, my friend."

"Montrovant?" Lacroix asked.

Noirceuil watched his partner for a long moment, then shifted his gaze up the trail again. "I do not sense the dark one. There is a light trace, but the young one, Abraham, has gone up this mountain, and there is something waiting there. I don't know what has distracted Montrovant, but the Order, and whatever they guard so jealously, is up the mountain."

Lacroix looked troubled for a moment. He knew that Montrovant would not easily turn from this quest. Something did not seem right, and he'd learned over the years to trust his instincts.

"The other way," Lacroix said at last. "There is a village below…"

"The village is a diversion," Noirceuil replied, eyes glittering. "We were to find the Order, my friend, and if possible, to put Montrovant out of the way at the same time. I agreed to this mission because it allows me the opportunity to do as I do best, and that is to hunt the Cainites, to send them to their final damnation. That mountain is crawling with them, and it is there that I will go. You are free to check the village below first, if you like."

Lacroix started to reply. He was nominally in charge of the mission, and while Noirceuil was, in a sense, correct that the Order and their secrets were the primary goal, to ignore Montrovant as if the dark one had faded from the world was just not wise. "I do not want the dark one behind us, is all," he said at last.

"He will not catch us if we continue up now," Noirceuil said softly. "I can sense them not so far distant. Not tonight, but early tomorrow evening we can reach them. If Montrovant is in that village, he can't get there before we do, and we will be able to watch the road below for his approach.

"As far as we know, the dark one does not even know we follow him. There is no reason to fear that he will track us up the mountain, and if we can arrive ahead of him, we can scout the ground above and pick our battlefield. Make no mistake, my friend. This will be no slaying, but a battle. We may well never walk away from this mountain."

Lacroix shivered, then nodded. "I know that, Noirceuil. I have known that each and every time we have begun a hunt, and yet we walk, still. So many have gone the way of dust at our hands I can scarcely recall them all. It changes nothing when this moment arrives. I feel that chill breath on the back of my throat…have felt it since we left that city a while back."

Noirceuil nodded, whether merely in acknowledgment of Lacroix's words or in agreement, it was impossible to tell. Turning away, the hunter leaped back into his saddle with incredible agility, and turned his mount up the trail, moving into the shadows.

There was a quick bend, and Lacroix found himself dreading what might lay around it. He was so shaken he held his breath until they'd passed beyond the turn, but there was nothing to see. The trail stretched up and away into the darkness so far that his sight failed long before it reached either a turn or a goal. Noirceuil started up that trail slowly, and he followed, wondering if it would be the last time he followed that dark form into the unknown, or merely another chapter in an ongoing saga.

He was just starting to relax when Noirceuil stopped again, his nose to the air, as if on a scent. The hunter closed his eyes, spun for just a moment to pass a white flash of smile to Lacroix, and turned his mount from the road. He started off through the trees to the left of the trail at a pace a bit faster than Lacroix would have set. Lacroix spurred his own mount so that he could come nearly abreast of his partner.

"What is it?"

Noirceuil turned to him again, eyes blazing. "They are near. Abraham, Santorini's fool, and the young one. They are very close. I believe we can catch them tonight."

Lacroix's eyes grew dark for a moment. "They are not our mission."

Noirceuil turned to him again, and those eye blazed now, afire with a burning, possessive drive that Lacroix would never understand. "They are my mission. All of them."

He turned away again, and headed off through the trees a bit more quickly.

⁂

Abraham heard the hoofbeats pounding through the trees just in time. There was no time to prepare a defense, or to flee, so he did the one thing that occurred to him that might not spell immediate death. He grabbed Fleurette, drove her ahead of him, and dove for the small cave in the cliff. Scrambling under the rim, he pushed her ahead of him, whispering tersely.

"Go. Don't stop until you feel my touch on your ankle, or you are as far in as you can be." She did not hesitate, sensing his agitation, and he slid in behind her, leaving his bags, his horse, everything he'd brought with him, to whoever was approaching.

He thought of Montrovant, but somehow knew it was not the dark one. It had to be Noirceuil, and if it was, crawling into the cavern was no true escape. They moved steadily inward, and eventually he felt Fleurette hesitate, then slide to one side. He slipped ahead, and found that he'd come up nearly beside her...the tunnel was widening.

Silently, she nodded at the wall to his right. There was a stone slab there, pushed aside, large enough to slide back over the tunnel. It was not a natural cavern then, but a tunnel, and that tunnel could lead but one place. Pressing her ahead a bit further, he grabbed the stone slab and slid it slowly across the opening. It moved smoothly and easily, but when it hit the far side, there was a sudden CLICK! It would not budge either way after that. The tunnel, effectively, no longer existed. He stared into the pitch-black void where the stone blocked their way for a long moment, then turned to crawl ahead again, tapping Fleurette on the thigh so she would know to follow.

It was only a little before dawn, he could sense the weight of the sun's rising, and when they reached a hollowed-out area about twice the width of the original tunnel, he chose to stop, dragging his progeny to him and holding her there in darkness and silence. If none used the tunnel on a regular basis, they could rest through the daylight. He only hoped that whoever was following would not figure out the mechanism to move the stone door.

⁂

Noirceuil came up to the cliff, seeing the horse and its baggage, and noting the cavern moments later. His eyes narrowed. It would be a moment of reckoning if he followed as he desired. Lacroix would not fail to see him as he was if he crawled into the belly of a mountain and dragged the Cainites out without dying himself in the process. It was not yet time for such a revelation as that would be.

He placed his hand to the stone over the opening. He called into it loudly…listening carefully to the echo. His eyes flashed as the echo returned quickly. Not hollow. It had an end, and that meant they would have to come out. Eventually. He would wait.

Turning to Lacroix, he smiled for the first time in days.

"Let's make camp here," he said. "They are holed up for the night, and we will be safe enough until tomorrow evening."

Lacroix nodded. He dismounted quickly, eyeing the hole in the mountain warily, then moving to place a silver crucifix across that opening. He reached to his pack and brought forth a vial of water, blessed by the cardinal in Grenoble, and dripped it in a tight semicircle around the cross. Noirceuil watched in amusement for a moment, then turned once more.

"I will keep watch on the perimeter until it is too light for Montrovant to surprise us," he said.

Lacroix found that he was more weary than he'd realized. Nodding, he sought the shelter of a nearby outcrop of stone with a small bent tree dangling over it for shade. He brought down his pack, placing it beneath his head and drawing his long cloak about himself tightly, lying back to watch the way they'd come.

Noirceuil slipped off into the trees, moving swiftly and leaving his mount behind. When he was certain he'd put enough distance between himself and Lacroix, he stopped. Closing his eyes, he allowed his mind to slow, and his feet slipped softly through the earth, to the heels...ankles... thighs...disappearing slowly into the embrace of the soil of the mountain. He would rise before Lacroix grew suspicious, and then he would find a way to flush his rabbits from their hole. The hunt was on.

FIFTEEN

Jeanne returned to their room in the inn to find that Montrovant was already there. The dark one sat by a window, staring out into the darkness in meditative silence. Jeanne slid into the chair opposite his sire, leaning back and waiting. He was full, sated and feeling the first vitality-sapping effects of the coming dawn steal through his limbs.

"It is coming full circle," Montrovant said softly, turning from the window to meet Jeanne's gaze. "I can feel it. I've hunted this thing for so long, followed this fool's errand until I have begun to see myself as the fool. I cannot continue as we have."

"They have not all been bad times, my friend," Jeanne said softly.

"No," Montrovant said, laughing suddenly, "no, they have not. But there has always been this at the root of it all. The Grail has been fixed in my mind for so long that I feel it with me, even though I've never set eyes on it. I can sense it, calling to me, mocking me, and that eats at me constantly. I was a rational man in life, a bit impulsive, but a good leader. I was destined for great things, I believe. That ended, and even after death, I was cautious, learning, seeking knowledge if I did not possess it."

"Then Eugenio told me the story of Kli Kodesh, and of the Grail. I still dreamed of the sunlight then...did you know that? I still thought of the times I walked carefree with women, stealing away with them, not to drain their life and continue my own, but to share hot, sweaty moments and secrets by moonlight. When he told me the legends about the Grail, it was the beginning of a dream.

"I believed it might bring some of that back to me. I believed that, with the Grail, I might be able to free myself from the shadows, return to that light. Certainly all those I knew would be dead and buried, but what did that matter to one who was eternally young, and handsome? I saw myself as a king in the world of the living, and that intoxicated me.

"Over the years," his voice lowered, and his gaze shifted back to the window, "I have come to a different perspective, though the fire to possess the Grail is no less intense. I know now that there is no going back to what has been. I would no more fit into the world of the living than I would wish to join it. My Embrace did not lessen me, Jeanne, it fulfilled me. This is who I am, what I am.

"That is why I will go to that mountain. I know, as well you do, that in a true test, we have no chance to wrest the Grail from Kli Kodesh. There is no power on Earth I would wager on pitted against him. But he is a mad old fool, and he will give us a chance. I will take that chance. I have taken it before, and it has done nothing but extend the chase, but somehow I feel this is different. He grows weary of the game as I do. He will not play it any longer, but will work the pattern to a close."

"Do not be comfortable with that," Jeanne said, leaning forward suddenly. "He has always woven the patterns, and we have always done just as he knew we would, have always woven ourselves into the tapestry of his little games without considering options that might have changed the outcome.

"You are not a chess piece. You do not have a set move that you cannot deviate from. You need to anticipate the pattern. Probably more than once. He will expect us to try something new, and we must do that, but perhaps there are several things we can do to change the pattern. Maybe there are ways to alter it altogether.

"The goal will remain, and that part of the puzzle is his to command, but the pathway to that goal, that depends entirely on you."

DAVID NIALL WILSON

Montrovant continued to stare out the window, but Jeanne could tell that his words were getting through.

"The trick," Jeanne added softly, "is to know just what would amuse the old one the most. That will be the pattern, and once we know it, we can work to upset it."

Montrovant spoke then, voice low and thoughtful. "If we can find a way to disrupt his pleasure, a way to make things swerve toward an end that will not satisfy him, we might tip his hand. He might move too swiftly, trying to rectify that which we shift, trying to fill what would be a horrible void in his existence, a dull ending to a long, drawn-out game. It is possible that if he believes he is winning too easily that he will tip the scales on our side to balance things, and we might take advantage of that moment.

"One thing I do believe. If we win, he will let us go. He will see the Grail in my hand, and he will smile, and he will begin to scheme with that new knowledge and image in his mind. The changes that could be possible if even half of what I've learned of the Grail are true would be enormous. The entertainment value of it all cannot have been lost on him.

"If not me, he must plan to unleash those artifacts one day. I have to believe that his design for the game includes both possible endings. He certainly did not seem concerned whether I killed

Santos, or Santos ended my existence, so long as we met and clashed. Neither does he care so much about his own followers, since he has pitted them against powers they cannot possibly face more times than I can count, only to pull them out at the last moment."

"Well, whatever we do must wait for nightfall," Jeanne said, rising slowly, "and the dawn is growing too close for my comfort."

He moved slowly to the closet, pulling the door wide and making his way inside. Montrovant watched, then turned to the window again before he rose as well.

"There is something else," he said softly. "I sensed it as I hunted this evening, a presence, a power. Not Kodesh, I would recognize that. Something different, dangerous. I wonder if it is a part of the old one's puzzle that we haven't seen, or a new piece yet to be fitted, one that we can work to our advantage."

Jeanne smiled. "If there is a way, we will find it. I have grown quite fond of the notion of holding the Grail myself. I would hate to be disappointed so near the end."

Montrovant laughed softly. "We will drink from that cup together then, my friend. You have been with me longer than any, been more supportive even than my own sire, and his 'family.' When the time comes, we will end our existence, or begin anew, together."

Then they closed the door quietly behind them. Du Puy was already asleep, half drunk and snoring, along the wall beside the closet door. As it was closed, the knight stirred, scanning the room in silence without rising, then resumed his slumber. His rest was deceptive. Even a few flagons of wine would not be enough to prevent instinct from taking over if any opened the outer door to their room. It was locked, and there were strict orders to prevent any entering, even the others who traveled with them. If that door stirred (and it would not give easily, since one of the stout wooden chairs had been propped at an angle beneath the handle) du Puy would be on his feet and ready before any could gain access.

It was probably an unnecessary precaution. There was no reason for the villagers to suspect anything, and the innkeeper was certainly going to be loath to do anything to end the steady flow of gold that had been flowing into his purse since they entered his establishment.

Montrovant was not one to take chances, and du Puy needed a place to sleep it off in any case. The room fell to soft shadows and the only sound was the tall knight's heavy breathing. From the closet, nothing.

On the mountain, deep within the earth, Noirceuil's body rested, but his mind roamed. He could not find the rest the light should have brought, though he was beyond its reach. He could not find peace in any form, but only endure until the night fell once more and the hunt could begin anew. It was the only time the ache would stop, the only way he could reconcile his existence in any way that did not lead to madness.

He tried to pray. Where he'd once felt his God very close to his heart, holding him up and supporting his mind and heart, he felt a void. Where his voice had seemed to take wings each morning and night, his thoughts and dreams making their way to realms beyond his understanding, where answers had always been waiting to fill his mind with peace, there were no answers now. The words, prayers, and dreams shot off into a deep, dark pit from which there was no return.

He remembered the church so vividly. He could still remember the feel of the sun, warm in the morning, shining in through stained-glass windows to fall over the altar as he prayed. It had been a small church, a parish of so few that there were Sundays he shared the Mass with no more than one other, but it had been so precious, so complete. Now nothing was complete.

Every thought brought the anger. Every memory brought the rage. He knew what he was, and he knew he was Damned. He knew the void would never be warm, or filled, or complete, but he did not lose sight of his God, for all that. If he could not serve and be redeemed, he could serve and save the souls of others. With his own soul forfeit, the means justified the ends. He would put them all to rest, one by one. He would kill them finally and completely, preventing them from stealing the lives and souls and afterlives of others. He would not rest until they all crumbled in the sunlight, or until he himself ceased, at last, to exist. His prayers were no longer for a place in Heaven, but for the nonexistence of Hell.

Lacroix did not understand. He saw the raw edge of Noirceuil's anger, his rage, but he did not see the pain at its base. He saw the dark hunter, but he did not see the angry young priest, robbed of salvation. He saw the obsession, and the growing lack of concern for the Church, and these things angered and frightened him. Lacroix was a man with his mind and heart set on a very worldly future. A nice, soft job in Rome, and a long, opulent retirement.

He had been so vibrant when Noirceuil first met him, so full of fire and the love of the hunt. Lacroix would have been a knight instead of a priest, if it had not been for the hunt. The notion that darkness existed, and was powerful and loose in the world fascinated and intrigued him. When Noirceuil had shown him how it could be hunted, ferreted out, and exterminated, the seeds were sown. Rome had known for years, possibly centuries, of the Damned.

There were legends and stories to frighten children, had been since the beginnings of time. There were no stories without some sort of basis in reality. Noirceuil had heard those words; now he lived them.

Lacroix had never questioned his partner's idiosyncrasies, though others in the Church had certainly cast some odd glances in his direction. It was the results that had kept things moving and relatively safe. Some suspected Noirceuil's secret— how could they not? Rumors were rampant. Though he had what seemed a logical explanation for his odd actions, the lack of deviance in his routine had been noted more than once. It was unnatural, to say the least, to never see the light of day, even if one were obsessed with the night.

To exist as the Damned existed. To walk only when they walked, see only what they saw, and to end their foul existence at every opportunity, all in the name of God. That was his story, his tainted *afterlife*, all that remained of his dreams, and the glory of the love he'd felt for a God who had long abandoned him.

If there was hope for him, he would seek it in revenge. If there were truly "many rooms in his father's house," he would seek his through the hearts of as many of the filthy, bloodsucking demons as he could bring along for the journey. They were Damned, as he, and they should not be walking the earth. They should not be borrowing the lives and souls of others to continue their own unclean existence. They should, in fact, not be at all. That was his goal, to make that a reality.

The sun rose, and kissed the earth, the trees, the wind stirring the grass and animals slipping from their holes and dens to scamper about the clearings in search of food. Noirceuil waited. No rest, no peace, only the agony of knowing that the time would be wasted until again the sun dropped.

⁂

For once, Noirceuil's little jaunt into the forest, from which he never returned before morning, did not upset Lacroix. He still watched the opening in the cliff warily, but he did not believe that, if Abraham and his young one had entered there, that they would be exiting into the bright sun, so he was safe from them.

Sadly, it was the partner with whom he'd spent long years on the road who brought his fear. He was losing trust in Noirceuil fast; and in their work, that could prove fatal very quickly. They had to be able to depend on one another, and without Noirceuil's uncanny ability to spot, flush, and destroy the Damned, Lacroix would have been dead, or risen to a darker unlife, a hundred times over. He focused on that as he rolled into his blanket beneath the stone ledge. They had come so far, and this was to be their most important mission. He could not afford to become the weak link over some childish fears.

Surprisingly he felt his eyelids growing heavy, and it was not long before he drifted off, ignoring the dangers that surrounded them. One thing that had characterized his time with Noirceuil was their enemy. During the daylight, there was no enemy. They hunted by night, a practice he now thought, at last, to question, but by day it was as if the entire madness of it all slipped away and disappeared.

The sun missed him as the shadow of the stone wrapped around him, and he slept, though dark shadows chased him through his dreams.

SIXTEEN

Abraham felt the weight of the sun release him with a slow reluctance. He shook Fleurette gently, knowing she would be slower to rise, but needing her to move as quickly as possible. If this was a way into the new stronghold of the Order, two things were fairly certain. Those inside would know it was there, and they would use it as a way of exiting. Neither fact was cheering to him as they lay side by side covered by a mountain of earth. It was not a good place from which to negotiate.

As soon as Fleurette stirred against him he urged her forward. There was no going back, and he had no way to be certain that Noirceuil would not find a way to open the portal from the far side. Even less than the Order did he want to meet that one in such a dark, confined space.

So they moved on and in. It was no more than fifty feet before the passage turned, and around that turn they came to another portal. This one was already closed, but Abraham did not panic. He slid forward, gesturing for his companion to stay as she was for a moment. The passage had widened considerably, and there was a bit more room over his head as well, so maneuvering was less of a problem. Abraham examined the stone door carefully, fingers pressing into it here and there, sliding around the edges, then walking across the center, looking for a latch. He found nothing, and as he continued to search, growing a bit more frantic, he felt Fleurette moving up beside him.

She remained quiet for a long moment, then her hands shot out, sliding past his outstretched arms and pressing against the stone. With a quick shrug of her shoulders, she pressed the stone slab to the side hard. It slid easily, sinking into a slot in the tunnel wall. She looked at him again, and he thought for just a second that the smallest flicker of a smile had danced across her eyes, but then it was gone, and she was still as silent and unreadable as she'd been since the morning she awoke to death.

Without a word Abraham slid through the small entrance and she followed. Once they were inside, he carefully pulled the stone slab back across to hide the fact of their entrance as long as possible. There were those among the Order who would re-member Abraham, even those he'd thought he could call friend. Now he was less certain, and it made sense not to rock the boat until one knew how deep the water was.

He slipped along the nearest wall, Fleurette moving easily behind him, and found that they were at the end of a long, narrow passage. It curved around to the left, then evened out and opened into a larger passage. Along this larger way he could feel air moving. He turned into that slight breeze, still staying as close to one wall as possible, and moved carefully inward. It was only moments later that he caught sight of the stairway ahead. There were torches flickering along the walls, illuminating the passageway dimly. Abraham knew they would be on the lowest level of their stronghold that was feasible.

The core of the Order had been Embraced by Gustav's original band of Nosferatu. Abraham had heard the story over and over again, though it was endlessly fascinating. Upon their being Embraced, the old one, Kli Kodesh, who seemed little more than a legend to Abraham, had shared with them of his own blood, and it had altered them somehow, binding them to him, and changing their makeup. Gustav had been Nosferatu, and old, at the time of his transformation, and his features still bore the scars of that odd, decayed group.

The others were more fortunate. Their skin fairly glowed. While other Damned were pale, even white at times, these were opaque and milky. Even Gustav had lost much of the harshness of his features, his deformities somehow becoming less obvious. There were other changes.

During his stay with the Order, Abraham had not once seen one of them feed. It was possible that their rituals forbade public blood-taking, but Abraham was certain it was more than that. They did not feed because they needed much less blood than other Damned. They felt the hunger, but it was more of a nagging itch than a consuming fire.

There was also an uncanny ability to be remain awake in the morning, before dawn, and to rise before it seemed possible. Never had Abraham seen one of them retire for the evening, and every time he'd risen, they had been there, alert and busy, moving about their business as though they'd been there all along.

They spent their nights, when not moving about on business that had never included Abraham, in study. In the mountain where they'd abandoned him the libraries and laboratories had been extensive, even astonishing. The wisdom of many ages had been contained within those walls, and Abraham was willing to wager it had come along with them as well, or been moved slowly, a bit at a time, the entire time they'd been under that mountain.

Now he was pitting himself against this group of powerful Cainites, with a newly Embraced companion at his side, and to remain behind with a monster like Noirceuil about was an even more certain destruction than that which they faced. Not for the first time Abraham wondered why, when Santorini had given him the letters and the gold and sent him on his way, he had not turned toward some faraway land and never looked back.

Abraham cared nothing for the Church. He'd given up on that form of salvation when his life was taken, then handed back to him warped and darkened. When he'd walked about as a man it had seemed well and good to offer his life to God and his trust to salvation. Damned as he now knew himself, it mattered little and seemed nothing short of frivolous to worry over it at all.

But the Order promised something more. Their existence, their odd powers, their secrets and knowledge, these were goals worth latching onto and following. These were things worth believing in.

Moving more slowly, he came to the bottom of the stone stairs that led up into the shadows above. There was still no sound, no sign that any save himself and Fleurette inhabited the huge building. For the first time since coming up the trail he wondered if he'd been wrong. Was this where they'd come, or was it an elaborate hoax? It was not beyond the Order to raise this huge stronghold, fill it with nothing for years, then slip in and back out of it, escaping down the far side of the mountain and into oblivion.

These thoughts brought a hint of desperation to his movements, and he began to climb the stairs, moving more rapidly. Fleurette reached out, placing a hand on his shoulder, slowing him. He turned to bat her arm away, but her eyes stayed his hand. She was right. He could not go barreling up those stairs without regard to what might be waiting. Not that he had a plan in any case. So close to his goal, and yet still so far from any resolution.

They made the top of the stairs, and here the passageway branched in both directions, with another stair leading further up directly opposite where they stood. Abraham glanced down the passage in either direction. There were doors lining this passage, and by the spacing he determined that they were probably the private chambers. It was a lower level still, completely cut off from the sun during the day.

"We have to go higher," he said softly. "They won't be here by night."

Fleurette nodded, and as he moved across the passage, taking the second set of stairs upward, she followed closely. He had not bothered to explain to her exactly what they were doing, or what sort of danger they now faced. It would have taken far too long to make her understand, and her silence had begun to wear on his nerves. He was half convinced she'd lost her faculties during her Embrace.

He moved even more slowly than before. There was no way to know how far down into the mountain the structure reached, or how far they would have to climb to be near the top. He climbed steadily, pressing to the shadows along the wall, watching and listening for even the tiniest breath of motion, the softest passage of air.

Ahead, he saw that the stairs ended in another wide passage, and he stepped up to the frame of the doorway, glancing to the right, then turning left, and stopping. Gustav stood not ten feet from him, watching him intently. The old Nosferatu did not move to attack him, nor did he seem particularly disturbed or surprised to see his young would-be follower.

"Hello, Abraham," Gustav said softly. "It has been a long time."

Abraham froze in place, and Fleurette, who had moved up beside him at the sound of a voice, watched Gustav in silence.

"Not so long," Abraham said at last. "Not long enough to forget my name at least. Why did you leave me, Gustav? Why abandon me after so many months of my company? Am I that contemptible?"

"You are not of the Order," Gustav replied simply. "I did not form the Order, and it is not my place, though I oversee the actions of those here, to add to that number. I did as I had to do, as do you. It is good to see you again."

"Who are you?" Fleurette spoke, and Abraham turned as if he'd been bitten.

Gustav watched the childe in amusement. "If you have a few hundred years, girl, I would be happy to sit back and tell you. Unfortunately, however, none of us can afford too much time for idle banter at this juncture."

"What do you mean?" Abraham asked.

"Montrovant, of course," Gustav replied, turning away and heading down the passage slowly, leaving them to stand or to follow, as they chose. "He is right on your heels, you know. He and another. It would not do for us to underestimate the dark one when he takes the time to make his way to our very doorstep."

"It is all a trap then," Abraham called after him, following the old vampire down the hall, his fear of moments before replaced by curiosity, tinged with anger. "It is all to draw the dark one here, and myself in the bargain, if I survived, that is. Tell me, Gustav, why you couldn't have just stayed in the mountain, guarded the treasures, and waited? Why go? Why now? Surely you know the church is aware of your leaving? Rome is filled with those who want to hunt you down, not all of whom are powerless to do so."

Gustav did not look back, but he replied softly.

"It was not my choice, Abraham. It is seldom my choice. Come, in moments you will understand more fully."

It was then that they rounded a corner and came to a massive open doorway, leading into a large chamber. In the center of the room sat a long, oblong table of dark, solid wood. Around that table many chairs were ranged. In each of these chairs one of the Order sat, watching the doorway as though they'd been waiting for Abraham to arrive all evening. At the head of the table, a figure Abraham had never seen lounged indolently.

The vampire was old and brittle, thin to the point of emaciation, his long, wispy white hair sweeping back from his drawn face like a dandelion blossom past its prime, looking as though it might be blown away by a strong gust of wind.

Even from that distance, the vampire's eyes stood out. In a room where every feature appeared a bit off kilter, warped, or rotted, where nothing should have amazed, where the norm was far more bizarre than any other gathering Abraham could imagine, those eyes stood out. They smiled without humor, latching onto Abraham's gaze and drawing him to a silent halt. If Fleurette had not noticed the sudden lack of motion and kicked his leg softly, Abraham might have stood in that one spot and stared for hours.

"Kli Kodesh," he breathed. It was not a question. There was no other it could be, and with all that was happening in and around the keep, there was no other place one might expect the ancient one to be found.

"And you are Abraham," Kodesh replied, grinning back. "I hear you have led my friend Montrovant right to my doorstep."

Abraham watched the old one for a long moment of silence before replying, trying to reconcile the sight of him with the words and stories he'd used to build his own image. It was difficult.

"I did not lead him anywhere," Abraham said at last. "I followed him here."

"I see that," Kodesh replied, eyes dancing, "and yet you have arrived first. An interesting method of tracking, one we shall have to discuss at a later date. It is enough that he has come, as I knew he would."

Abraham found the old one's humor at the situation less than amusing, and would have said more if given the chance, but Kodesh went on.

"It seems, according to our scouts, that Montrovant and his men have departed the village below and are making their way up the mountain. It is nearly time to make ready for their arrival, not to mention a fitting welcome for Noirceuil, whom I haven't seen in years. It should be an interesting diversion if I can arrange for a meeting between those two on the mountain."

"Noirceuil is a hunter," Abraham cut in. "He kills his own kind."

"I believe that he would argue that one with you, my young, impetuous friend," Kodesh replied quickly. "Noirceuil is fighting in God's army, and to hear him tell the tale he is the only qualified warrior in that group. He will do his best to send our dark one to his final rest, you can be assured of that. It is in the interest of the salvation of souls that Noirceuil kills, and while a bit overzealous in his methods, he has proven very effective over the years. I would hate to have to sit down and count the number of Damned he has put to rest since his Embrace. What a delicious irony his existence has been!"

"Why bring him here?" Abraham insisted. "If your goal was to lure Montrovant here, a final confrontation, why invite more trouble? The hunter is not here on his own, he was sent by the Church, the Inquisition. If he does not return, he or his partner, Lacroix, this area will soon be swarming with agents of Rome, poking under every rock and tree, searching for what they only vaguely comprehend. Why ask for that so blatantly?"

Kodesh threw his head back and began to cackle madly, leaning over the arm of his chair and nearly falling to the floor in the sudden, out-of-control burst of amusement.

"If you have heard anything at all of me, boy," Kodesh turned to grin at Gustav, who sat to his right, "and in this company I am assured that you have, then you know that I do things for one reason, and one reason alone. They relieve my endless, tedious boredom. They give me a reason to continue on, though everything has been done that there is to do, and everything seen that can be seen. The only thing left is the mind, the subtle nuance of one will, one heart placed against the resistance of another. It keeps me moving, makes me whole...and it amuses me to no end."

Then the laughter returned once more and the old one lay back in his chair, surrendering himself to it.

"Let me help then," Abraham called out boldly. "I have as much reason to hate Montrovant as any who walk the earth by day or by night. I have seen the hunger take the existence of another just because it suited him. I want to be a part of their end, if such is your plan. I want to be a part of the Order."

Kodesh leaped suddenly from his chair, landing on his feet on the table in an incredible display of speed and agility, made all the more ludicrous by his fragile, aged aspect. His eyes were burning, and his lips were curled back in a sneer.

"You would be one of them?" Kodesh's eyes swept first over Abraham's features, then over the gathered throng of his own followers. "You would walk with Gustav, study and control the secrets of the ages? You would stand against Montrovant, and those who think to take these treasures and make them their own?"

Abraham tried to speak, but Kodesh caught him easily in that magnetic gaze, advancing on him with the grace of a large, predatory cat. Abraham wanted to flee, but at the same time would not have moved granted the strength. It was the moment he'd waited for since he'd come from Lori's caverns to the doorstep of the Order so many years before. He would die now a second time, or he would rise to be something more.

"It will work," Kodesh grinned, nodding. "I will give you what I have given them, on the condition that you will then become the bait. You will go to them both, Montrovant, Noirceuil, and you will let them see what you have become, what has been offered you and denied them. Then you will lead them to their destruction, or be destroyed yourself in the attempt. At least, for that moment, you will have what you have sought for so long, what you have dreamed of late into the night and during your rest by the light of day. You will be one of the Order of the Bitter Ashes, guardian of secrets."

Fleurette had drawn close behind Abraham, and she clutched him suddenly. "Do not do it," she said fiercely. "He is making it sound like a good thing, a special thing. He will send you to your death."

"And what if he does?" Abraham replied, tearing his gaze from Kodesh's dark, deep-set eyes to meet hers. "If I die, I will die accomplishing what I set out to do."

"Not if you die at Montrovant's hand, you won't," she said, shaking him by his arm. "You will do as that one," she turned to Gustav, pointing a slender finger at the ancient, eyes blazing, words snapping free of her lips as if spat. "You will turn your back on what you have created, on the one you now lead. You will do as they all did to you, abandoning me as soon as you took my life and hope of salvation. You will take this new Damnation, and you will leave me here...to do what? To serve? To make my own way in the world, feeding off those I once called friend? Alone?"

She screeched then, diving at Abraham with such sudden fury that he was driven back several steps and took a deep gash below his eye before he managed to grab her wrists and hold her. Still she struggled to get at him, eyes awash in cold fury. His mind whirled. What she said was true.

"Stop," he commanded, and though the fire barely dimmed in her eyes, she did as he commanded. She had no choice, bonded by the blood, or she would have continued to fight until he was forced to do something more permanent to stop her.

"She is full of fire," Kodesh cackled. "You will be better off without her."

"No," Abraham turned back. "I will do as you ask, and I will lead them here, but you must make your offer to us both. I swore long ago that I'd not bring another to this hellish existence, but now I have done so. I will not become what I have loathed. I will not leave her to suffer as I have."

Kodesh hesitated. It was not his plan, but it was clear that Fleurette's actions had caught his eye.

Diversion. Entertainment.

He nodded. "So be it. I will double the stakes. If you lose her on the mountain, that will be on your own conscience. Come to me now, both of you."

Leaping from the table, Kodesh stood before them, holding out one withered hand, and they both started forward instantly, compelled. Fleurette tried to fight at first, but it was futile. Abraham moved in a trance, mesmerized by the moment, the odd twists of events that had led him to where he stood.

They moved steadily and as they came near, Kodesh wrapped each in one ancient arm, his face alight with—madness. It was the only way to describe it. As his arms wrapped them, he brought a wrist to each of their lips, not waiting for them to bite, but impaling himself on their fangs, lifting them from the floor with the violence and suddenness of his action. They both struggled then, for just an instant, then their expressions shifted subtly…completely.

Their eyes stared, glazed, and their jaws clamped hard, as if in unison. Kodesh stiffened for a long moment, feeling the blood flow, the twin bites piercing his wrists in an odd mockery of the nails biting in the crucifixion, symbol of the very Church that now hunted them. Then he shook himself, and they fell away as if thrown, tumbling to the floor. Neither moved at first, and Kodesh drew his arms in toward his body, closed his eyes and lowered his head for a moment, then raised it again, the dark grin having spread to a maniacal expression of something much wilder.

"It has begun," he said softly, as first Abraham, then Fleurette rose to their knees, and then to their feet.

Abraham stared at his hands, then turned, his gaze rising to meet Kodesh's. He tried to speak, but words failed him. "I…"

"Go," Kodesh said gently. "Go back the way you entered, through the tunnel, and find them. If you come first to Noirceuil, as he is hunting you, use that to draw Montrovant's attention."

"And if we draw too much attention?" Fleurette's voice was smoother now, cooler. Her eyes did not drop when Kodesh turned to catch her once more in his gaze.

"Then you had better be prepared to fight, young one," he replied with a smile. "Noirceuil will not be impressed with your fancy new blood. He will want to prevent you from damning any more souls."

Fleurette nodded, and as Abraham watched in consternation, she turned from the ancient without a backward glance and headed toward the passageway through which they'd entered. He watched her for a moment, then turned back to the table as Kodesh started laughing again.

"You'd better catch her, friend Abraham," Kodesh cackled, "she doesn't appear to be waiting for you."

Abraham turned and quickly followed Fleurette into the passage and down the stairs, quickening his steps as the mad laughter rang out behind him. Everything about the way he thought and felt had changed in a single instant. He had yearned and waited, dreamed and now...now it was his. The gift. He was one of them, and there was no chance to savor it. He could sense things around him acutely. He could feel how the hunger, so maddening before, had peeled back. It was there, but so faint, so tiny that it was difficult at first to recognize it as the hunger at all.

Fleurette had no experience to gauge it against, but still her actions were aggravating. As she reached the bottom of the second stair and headed around the curve in the passage back toward the tunnel, he took her by the shoulder suddenly, spinning her to face him. He did not speak at first, only met her steady gaze.

"What are you doing?" he asked her after a moment of silence. "Why do you just walk away?"

"If I could truly walk away, I would do so now," she spat at him. "You have twice, in less than the span of a single week, altered my fate without a choice on my behalf. I came here because your will compelled me, and with my new hunger, I needed your teaching, your support. You would have abandoned me here as surely as we speak. Then, in a fit of guilt at my accusations, all true, you drag me into this as well. Did you ask if I wished to be granted this *gift*? You did not."

"I..." He stared at her, and for the second time that night, realized she was right. "I am sorry," he said, too late, and too pointlessly.

Turning from him, she made her way to the tunnel entrance and pulled the stone slab aside, peering into the darkness beyond. "We will discuss it when this is done," she said in a toneless voice. "I feel that the hold you had on me has been broken. We may need to test that."

Then she was gone, crawling swiftly into the tunnel, and Abraham was left to follow as he could, hoping her anger did not rush them both into something they were not prepared to face. The worst of it was the knowledge that she did not appear to care if she did so or not. For her, Noirceuil might be the best answer of all. At least his mind was clear and focused.

The shadows swallowed them quickly.

SEVENTEEN

Noirceuil returned to the small cave's entrance immediately after the sun had set, as Lacroix had known he would. There were no words spoken, but the hunter crouched immediately at the entrance. Lacroix himself had been awake for only moments, the rigors of their journey having caught up with him finally and bringing a long, sound sleep. Possibly the last for some time to come.

Noirceuil sniffed at the opening, started slightly, shifting back on his heels, his head swaying from side to side. He had the aspect of an animal that had lost the scent, and that bothered Lacroix more than anything since the two had become partners. Something was wrong, or at the very least not as

Noirceuil had expected. Theirs was a precise art. If their enemy got even a moment's advantage, it could easily be the last moment of their existence.

Without hesitation Lacroix pulled back against the stone where he'd been sleeping, drawing his weapon and scanning the shadows surrounding the small clearing with narrowed eyes.

"What is it?" he called out softly.

Noirceuil did not answer immediately. When at last he nodded, moving back from the entrance, his voice was low. "They are not there. They may have come back this way, or gone in deeper. I can't be certain. I think I detect them here…in the past hour or so, but it is too weak a trail to be certain."

Noirceuil turned to Lacroix, eyes blazing, "Why did you not watch the entrance?"

Lacroix's eyes narrowed as he watched his partner back away from the cave entrance. "You were not back yet, and I have never seen one of them before I saw you. I did not think it was late enough to worry yet."

Noirceuil looked about ready to say something more, then stopped, cocking his head to one side.

"Well, they are gone. We can't rule out the idea that they rise earlier than most, and that they may be out here with us."

The hunter cursed quietly, scanning the shadows. Lacroix's heart was calming somewhat. With Noirceuil back at his side, he at least felt on even ground with their prey, if they had not metamor-

270

phosed into the prey themselves. He'd seen too many fall to believe the odds were now stacked too heavily against them, but he hated being caught off guard. He also hated appearing as a fool, and Noirceuil's expression moments before had called him that quite eloquently.

There was no movement anywhere near them, but something prickled along the hairs at the back of Lacroix's neck, and he knew they were not alone. "They are here," he breathed.

Noirceuil only nodded. He had shifted back against the stone, and his stance was that of an upright, coiled snake about to strike. There was no fear in him, no thought of defeat. He wanted only a target. Lacroix wasn't as eager to meet vampires who could rise so early as his partner seemed to be, but he knew he'd be happier once he had them in sight. If he were to die, he preferred to see the instrument of that death.

Then there was a rustle to their left, and the wait was over. The girl stepped into full view, hands on her hips, staring at them as if they were vermin cowering in a corner of her kitchen.

Another sound to the right, and Abraham stood at the edge of the clearing as well, his eyes dark and unreadable. Noirceuil shifted back and forth, watching first one, then the other, poised.

Then Noirceuil stiffened.

"What is it?" Lacroix asked quickly. His first thought was that the two were not alone, and he shifted his gaze about the clearing wildly, but there were no others to see.

"Something is wrong," Noirceuil said quietly. "They are not as they should be. They are stronger. Look at their skin…"

Lacroix did, forcing his gaze to cut the dim light. He chose the girl, the more pleasant to look at. At first she looked no different than any girl, if a bit more pale, but he looked more closely. Noirceuil was not one to cry wolf if they did not face a wolf.

Then he noticed two things. First, the girl showed not the slightest trace of fear. By this time it was certain she knew who Noirceuil was, and why he had come after them, new as she was to her damnation. The other was that her skin was even more pale than he'd first believed, translucent and pale, her eyes glowing with a deep, inner light. Lacroix had seen plenty of vampires, but there was something different, wholly unnerving, in her aspect. He shifted his gaze to where Abraham had appeared, but there was no one there.

In that same instant, Noirceuil leapt from the stone, moving with uncanny speed toward where the girl still stood, staring at them. She did not move, and somehow that tipped Lacroix at the last second, and he lunged, trying to snatch his partner's cape and knowing he was far too slow, and too late.

Abraham slid from the shadows like a dark knife, slicing into Noirceuil from the side and driving the hunter swiftly to the ground. The girl simply melted from sight, and as Lacroix heard a deep snarl of rage from his partner and an answering cry from the vampire, he shifted to his own right, diving and rolling along the wall of the cliff, eyes scanning the gathering darkness wildly.

Rising as quickly as he could into a crouch, he glanced back to where Noirceuil had met the shadows. Nothing. The two had rolled out of sight, and now Lacroix was alone. He drew the wooden blade he carried from its scabbard, worn close to his heart, and without thought his hand slipped up to grip the silver crucifix about his neck. He knew both were likely futile gestures if he could not at least catch sight of his prey, and the longer he went with no sound from his partner, the more certain he became that Noirceuil had finally met his match.

Then there was a sharp cry, and Lacroix knew the voice as Abraham's from the first outcry earlier. It was a yelp of pain, and Lacroix moved. He didn't know what was happening, but he did know that if he could keep Noirceuil alive, and by his side, he had a better chance of facing his judgment at St. Peter's gate and less of meeting it in that dark clearing.

He moved close to the ground, watching warily for signs of the girl, and as he reached the line of trees, he plunged through with a soft curse, following the line the two antagonists had fallen along moments before. There was a sound ahead, scuffling feet, and another cry, this time Noirceuil. Lacroix moved quickly, breaking free of the trees once more to see Noirceuil and Abraham locked, hands on one another's throats, eyes inches apart, rolling in the dirt.

Their exertion was plain to see, but what stopped Lacroix in his tracks was Noirceuil's face. The eyes were deeper, wider, and glowed with a deep red hatred. The man's hands, more like claws, latched on with equal ferocity to those of his foe. Lacroix stopped in his tracks, then took a step back.

"No," Lacroix breathed.

Noirceuil heard him, turning those feral eyes toward his partner. "Get over here and help me, you fool," he gasped.

Lacroix shook his head, not advancing. His lips were moving, but no sound was coming forth. Facts and events were clicking, placing themselves in his mind and memory, stealing his concentration.

"No," he repeated. He backed another step, and it was then that he felt the soft brush of a hand on his shoulder.

Spinning, he saw the girl, hunger washing through her eyes, stepping closer, and he swung with his blade, meaning to drive it straight into her heart and to turn, running to his horse and then away down the mountain, to Rome, to wherever, anywhere but there.

She caught his wrist easily, twisting it and sending the sharp wooden knife flying off into the shadows with a contemptuous flick of her wrist. She seemed in no hurry to go to the aid of her partner, but was instead fixated on Lacroix, on his throat, the soft pulse of his blood growing stronger and wilder with each passing second.

She grabbed his wrist, dragging him to her breast with a sudden yank, and he nearly lost his footing.

"Dive, you fool," Noirceuil hissed at his back.

He didn't know what else to do, so he obeyed. As she dragged on his arm, he dove forward, passing her and leaving her grip as she spun after him, startled. He ignored his lost blade, spinning to the side and plunging into the shadows.

Behind him he heard her hiss once, heard several soft steps follow, then she stopped. The battle behind her must have been sliding in Noirceuil's favor. She did not follow, and Lacroix was back to the clearing and moving toward his mount in a matter of seconds, Noirceuil, their mission, everything forgotten but flight.

He leaped to his saddle and spun the horse, dragging the reins free of where he'd secured them the night before. The animal, frightened, whinnied loudly and bucked, but Lacroix held on tightly, and moments later was flying through the trees, branches whipping and slapping at his arms and face. He prayed not to lose a knee against one of the trees as the horse plummeted through the darkness.

He hadn't gone far when his mind registered another sound. He tried to focus, but the terror was gripping his thoughts, and he didn't hear the pounding hooves until he burst onto the trail and nearly ran over St. Fond and du Puy, who shouted at him hoarsely. He noted them in passing, realizing who it must be, and spurred his mount to breakneck speed as he turned down the mountain. St. Fond turned as if to give chase, but du Puy shook his head, and the two turned instead to the side of the trail, retracing the path that Lacroix had taken out of the trees.

Down the trail, Montrovant and the others saw the man burst into sight, pounding down the trail straight at them, now screaming at the top of his lungs, and without a sound they moved aside.

Le Duc watched the mad horseman flash past them, and he glanced at Montrovant, a question in his eyes. The dark one shook his head.

"Let him go. It is whatever chases him we are concerned with."

Turning upward once more, Montrovant drove his heels into his horse's flanks and launched up the trail, shifting off to the side where his men had left the trail and plunged into the darkness. With a shrug, Jeanne and the others followed.

They burst into the clearing moments later to find a wild scene. Fleurette had dragged Noirceuil from Abraham roughly, but Abraham was slow in rising, and the hunter had turned on her, readying himself to strike.

In that moment, St. Fond and du Puy had burst from the trees, charging straight at the two antagonists. Abraham, though injured, had managed to roll to the side and slip into the shadows once more, and the two knights, filled with the energy and adrenaline of the charge, drew their blades and wheeled, ready to face down whoever got in their way.

Noirceuil cried out in frustration, turning to face this new danger with a snarl. He hesitated, wanting to leap on Fleurette and ignoring the knights, but at the same time wanting to charge them head on. The decision was made moot seconds later when Montrovant appeared behind the two, Le Duc at his side.

It took only seconds for the dark one to assess the situation, and he drove his mount forward quickly, letting the animal's shoulder strike Noirceuil a solid blow and send him stumbling into the shadows. The hunter did not go down, and he managed a quick, deadly swipe of sharp claws over Fleurette's face as he passed, but the blow was glancing, and she stepped away easily, turning toward the trees. Le Duc intercepted her, pulling her up short, and though she tried to leap back the other way, St. Fond appeared behind her, blade drawn.

Noirceuil slipped into the darkness surrounding them with a cry of rage.

"He isn't gone," Montrovant called out. The dark

one shifted about the clearing, taking in the signs of struggle, then glanced for a moment at the girl.

"There is another. Stay close. Whatever you do, don't get out of sight of one another, and don't get too close to the shadows."

He moved then, very quickly, dismounting and making his way to Fleurette's side. He swept his gaze up and down her quickly, taking in her young form, the depth of her eyes, and the cool, unwavering strength of her gaze.

"How long?" he asked her softly.

She did not answer, only returned his gaze. He moved closer, reaching as if to touch her shoulder, then pulling up short.

"How long since your Embrace?"

She still didn't answer, and a cry from the surrounding trees brought a soft curse to Montrovant's lips. He leaped to the side, plunging into the darkness, and Le Duc took several steps to follow. In that instant, when their attention was diverted, she was gone. St. Fond and du Puy stared at one another in consternation, but they did not give chase. Montrovant's word was law, and they were in no hurry to find out what it was that the dark one feared in the shadows. Better to have at least a bit of open ground on which to fight.

Montrovant and Le Duc moved from opposite sides and found Noirceuil locked with Abraham, one of whose arms hung limp at his side. The hunter had him pinned against a tree, but could not seem to gather the strength for a killing blow. Montrovant reined in, watching for a moment, then spun quickly.

"Now," the dark one said softly. "Now is the time."

Without another word he plunged toward the cliff. Le Duc, used to such shifts, followed the dark one's lead, leaving the two vampires to end their struggle as they might. The cliff rose above them moments later, stark and impassable, but before Jeanne could comment on this, Montrovant was on his feet, then on his knees, moving toward the low opening in the stone wall.

It was a cave. There was an opening in the wall, and Jeanne smiled, dropping quickly from the saddle to follow. Montrovant was already disappearing into that black hole when Le Duc dropped to the ground and slid from the clearing, leaving his horse, his belongings, and probably his existence behind.

"Where does it lead?" he asked hoarsely.

"In and up," Montrovant replied tersely. "Did you see them, Jeanne? That was Abraham, the one I left to die at the keep, and the girl was no more than a week to the blood, and yet they were strong. Their blood was powerful, different."

"The Order," Jeanne breathed.

"Yes," Montrovant replied, "and this is the only way they could have come so quickly back from that Order. I sensed the horses of those other two, the hunters, here by the wall and guessed what I would find. If they had come down the trail, it is we they would have met, not that strange one."

"Why did you come here and not remain to help the others?" Jeanne asked, a twinge of guilt tugging at his heart.

"Your words," Montrovant grunted, sliding quickly deeper into the mountain. "Kodesh would expect me to fight. That one was a hunter, and from the glance I had at the equipment on his mount, sent by Rome. He hunts his own, Jeanne. Kli Kodesh knows this will anger me, and I'm hoping that he is counting on it keeping me busy for a while. I turned away from the battle because it is the last thing I wanted to do. We will soon see if I am right, or if, once again, he has played me for a fool."

Jeanne grinned into the shadows, and followed. They soon came to the first, open portal and slid through it. Jeanne hesitated, thinking of closing it behind himself, then shrugged. Once they were inside, it did not matter who followed. If others came behind and caused more of a stir, they might make for a good distraction when one was needed.

They made their way to the inner portal, which was closed, and Montrovant fussed with it until, with a soft cry, he rolled it aside. They slid through and into the lower levels of the keep in silence, rolling the stone back into place. Then they slid out into the hall and to the stairs beyond.

Fleurette watched the two knights from the shadows beneath a huge old oak tree, eyes dark. The hunger was only a distant pulse, and she did not feel the urge to feed, but neither did it seem right to just stay there. Melting into the shadows, she circled the clearing, and finally made out the sounds of struggle once more.

Hurrying her steps, she burst into the clearing and saw Noirceuil, seated on Abraham's inert form, raising his arm high above him, a blade glittering brightly in his grip. There was no fight left in Abraham, but Fleurette knew he had not been destroyed. She wasn't certain how, exactly, but she knew that the moment he ceased to exist on the Earth, she would know, and it would hurt, very deeply.

With a soft snarl she leaped from the shadows and drew her small blade. It rode right where it had in life, strapped to her upper thigh, and the curved bone of the hilt felt good in her hand as she drew it for the first time since Abraham had come to her aid in that alley so far back in time, so many miles in the past.

Noirceuil started, half turning, but it was too late to avoid her charge. The blade caught him flush in the throat and drove him over to the ground. She followed, rolling with the momentum of the plunge and dragged the dagger free as she returned to her feet. Her movements were quicker than she could have believed in life, her agility that of a large cat, but Noirceuil was older, faster, and he'd been fighting to the death for much longer.

He snarled in rage, shifting his own blade to the other hand and rolling away and up. His hand slid to his throat, pressing to the wound, which oozed for a moment, the blood glistening in the soft moonlight filtering through the cover of the trees. Then he moved. He came at her directly, no sidestepping or feints. He was stronger, and he intended to make full use of that, to drive her back and down and finish her quickly.

It angered her. She had faced down older brothers, warriors, drunks in the taverns. She did not back down as Noirceuil charged, but waited, letting herself go limp and feigning fright. His eyes glittered, and as he leaped, she shifted subtly, her boot kicking out quickly and her body shifting just enough to the side that he missed.

His blade sliced through the air, but that was all it sliced, and he tumbled past her, her backhand stab plunging her blade deep into his shoulder and dragging it in a jagged line toward her. She cried out as it was ripped from her hand, and she danced back to the clearing. Noirceuil bellowed in frustration and pain.

Spinning, he was back at her quickly, moving straight for her again, but watching more carefully. She knew the trick would not work a second time, and she had no more weapons. Her eyes shifted around, looking for something, anything she might use to defend herself, but the only thing she saw was Abraham's limp form, sprawled in the grass.

She stood her ground, and Noirceuil smiled then, moving in.

"You are an evil, agile little thing," he said sibilantly, "but it will do you no good with me, girl. I will send you to your dark master, you and your Damned maker. No more innocent blood will flow at your hand. No more of God's chosen will fall to your hunger."

"You are a fool," she said softly. "You are no different, no better. You will feed on those I leave behind, using their blood to fuel your own warped existence as you play God and judge to the Damned."

"Damned I may be," Noirceuil replied, "But I do God's work. Make no mistake of that. You are an abomination in His eyes, and I will wipe you from His Earth."

Fleurette noticed a slight shift in Abraham's form, and she stood her ground. "You do no work but your own, or Satan's, if there is such a creature," she spat. "You know no more of God than I do, and I know no God who would allow his children to become such as we. Who are you to decide what is evil, and what is not?"

Noirceuil hesitated. It was not often he could tell one he intended to kill why. Pride was his fondest sin.

"I know God better than you would believe, girl.

I knew his love, and his salvation. It has been torn from me, but I remember that pain. I will not allow you to continue, and thus rip it from the hearts of others. You must be laid to rest."

Abraham's cry was loud, and chilling. He rose only to a crouch, and his one good arm shot back, grabbing the sword he'd dropped moments before and gripping the blade, ignoring the cuts in his hand as he raised it, whipping his arm forward with a massive, all-encompassing burst of anger, frustration, and rage.

The blade whirled through the air like an oversized dagger. Fleurette watched it, hypnotized by the glittering steel. Noirceuil was too slow. The blade spun, shifted, striking him sideways with impossible accuracy, and the steel slid easily into his neck, severing it and sending his head spinning off into the darkness with the snarl still in place and a dumfounded expression of outrage etched into his dark features.

His body moved a step forward, arms outstretched, still reaching for Fleurette, who stood and watched its approach. Then it fell away, and she turned, moving to Abraham's side quickly and wrapping him in her arms.

"Quickly," he gasped, trying to rise. She helped him to his feet, and they stumbled from the clearing together. "Where is Montrovant?"

"I don't know," she said quietly. "He and the other left the clearing as soon as Noirceuil slipped out after you."

Cursing, Abraham turned toward the mountain's face. "It may be too late to stop him, then," he gasped. His arm was healing slowly, but he still couldn't get any use of it, and the imbalance of it dragging at his side slowed his progress, but he forged ahead.

"What is it?" Fleurette asked softly.

"He didn't fight," Abraham cursed. "He went for the Grail. We have to be there to stop him."

Although she silently believed that Kli Kodesh was well aware of the possibilities, she supported him on her shoulder and the two of them hurried back to the cliff face and the tunnel. He had, for good or ill, saved her yet again. The least she could do was escort him to whatever the fates had in store. They slid into the tunnel and disappeared from sight.

EIGHTEEN

Gustav and Kli Kodesh stood on the wall of the keep, staring down the mountain. Neither had spoken since they exited to that walkway, but the tension in the air was thick.

Finally Gustav could stand no more.

"You led them here, all of them. You spent years building this place, hiding it, fortifying it through me. We have labored long and put more into this than I care to think of."

"Yes," Kodesh nodded, not really paying attention, "you have done well."

Gustav stopped, spinning the ancient one against the stone wall, his eyes blazing. "*Why* have we done it? Why do you move us around this ridiculous chessboard as if you knew your opponent, then laugh and toss us away, sacrificed before the game truly begins?"

Kodesh was taken aback for a moment. Blinking slowly, he glanced at Gustav, a slow smile sliding across his face. "You are not sacrificed, old friend. You are not even set up to lose. If you think about it, there are very few who might have found you out, who might have presented a danger, eventually, to what you have accomplished. I have brought them here all at once to be rid of them. That is all."

Gustav stared at the old one darkly. "That is insane," he said softly. "I could have done away with any of them at any point in Rome, and you know it. I had more than enough knowledge and power to lure Montrovant in and trap him, and he would have come. The others would not have come at all with Montrovant out of the way."

Kodesh watched him for a moment before answering.

"You have indeed learned a lot, Gustav, secrets guarded by Santos for so long that they might have crumbled to dust had we not wrested them from his grip. The books, the learning, the years, they have served you well. I am very happy to have chosen you when I did, and you have done a remarkable job as guardian thus far.

"Know this though, those secrets are guarded for good reasons. I have caused them to be locked away here, beyond even your reach, because I am not ready to be responsible for them being unleashed on the world."

"I was not planning on releasing anything to the world," Gustav said, his anger boiling over again. "I would have used them to rid us of Montrovant, and that is all."

"You don't understand the nature of such objects Gustav," Kodesh replied, his eyes far away. "I truly believe you think that is what you would have done, and I truly believe you would have accomplished your goal. There are some very powerful objects in your control.

"The power would have corrupted you. Not soon, perhaps, but what is time to us, Gustav? The sheer boredom of existence would have done you in. Then there would have been none left to stand before you. It is a losing battle, Gustav, with the years. Each passing decade, or century, a bit more of what you were slips away, and you grow a bit more frantic to replace it with something, anything. The problem is that nothing will do it. Nothing can fill the gaps left as you disintegrate into a monster."

The anger had not burned out of Gustav's gaze at this outburst, but he had calmed. Shaking his head and turning away, he spat his answer.

"You have made me nothing, then, but a feeble, failed attempt to fill gaps in your own decay. You have brought them here and given them half a chance at success, leaving it to me to entertain you by repelling their advance. Your words about power might be true, my friend, but if they are, you are the prime example of all history. My only sorrow is that once I was proud to be part of this."

Striding away quickly, Gustav slipped through one of the stone arches and down the stairs into the huge keep. He did not look back, and Kodesh made no move to follow, or to speak further. His eyes darkened for just a moment, then the glitter returned, and an odd half-smile, half-sneer rippled across his lips. Moving slowly he made his way along the wall, reached the corner, and slipped up onto the stone edge, peering down into the shadows below.

Without a sound he slid over that edge and was gone, crawling down the sheer wall as if it there were steps carved in the stone. Below the only sounds were those of the two knights, beating through the brush, looking for evidence of where their companions had gone, or if they lived.

A hoarse shout indicated that St. Fond had come across the withered corpse that had been Noirceuil. Kodesh slid through the trees quickly, making his way to the edge of the clearing where the battle had taken place. It was a surprise. He'd thought the hunter would finish Abraham. In fact, he'd been right. It was the girl he'd underestimated, and he chuckled.

He'd hoped he might get a good skirmish between Noirceuil and Montrovant, but that would not have been so interesting, in the end. The dark one was much older, and he was very focused just now. Noirceuil would have fallen quickly and easily. This way he got to go with a fight.

The two knights who'd followed Montrovant were sitting quietly side by side on their horses, looking about the clearing in confusion. There was no sign of any of the others, no good indication of where they'd gone.

Du Puy rode slowly around the clearing, passing near where Kodesh watched from the shadows. His horse shied, then calmed and he called out softly.

"Here. Someone has gone this way, toward the mountain." The knight spurred his mount forward, and St. Fond was quick to follow. Kodesh watched them go, and once they were out of sight, he moved into the clearing to stand over Noirceuil's remains, staring down. He leaned in close, gripping a gold chain that hung about the hunter's neck and yanking it free with a jerk. The cross dangled before his eyes, and he smiled. It was made of bone, very old, and the old one knew its story.

It was carved from the finger bone of the last victim of the first vampire Noirceuil had killed, a very long while back, and while the hunter had not understood its significance, Kodesh did. That vampire should have been much harder to kill; had been, in fact, ancient.

Kodesh pocketed the amulet, knowing it would

eventually need to end up with the rest. He then took up Noirceuil's blade. It should be returned to the Church, he thought, grinning at the notion of the faces of those who'd sent the hunter in the first place.

Turning, he moved to the base of the cliff. The two knights had dismounted. They stood by the entrance, staring at it dubiously. They would not enter. It was too much to expect of them.

Slipping from the shadows, Kodesh spoke softly, standing just beyond the line of trees lining the wooded slope.

"They will be back, or they will not, but there is nothing you can do," he said. His voice was quiet, but the words passed his lips with such force, such presence, that neither St. Fond nor du Puy could react immediately. Kodesh took a few steps forward, presenting Noirceuil's blade.

"I believe you might want to keep this," he said. "Rome will be interested to know the fate of their hunter, no matter how this turns out."

"Who are you?" du Puy grated, reaching for his blade with a sudden lurch. "Who are you and how do you know so much about this? If you are Montrovant's friend, why do you not help him...and if you are his enemy, why have you not tried to kill us instead of talking?"

Kodesh laughed. "Both good questions," he said, chuckling harder. "I am not Montrovant's friend, nor am I his enemy. I am one who watches, and waits, and I have known him a long time. He will fail, or succeed without me, and I'm afraid, without you this once. If I were you I'd settle in, watch that exit very carefully, and wait. It is really your only option."

Then he was gone. He moved so swiftly that, blinking, du Puy saw the old one standing against a backdrop of trees one moment, and the next only a sword, blade tip imbedded in the rocky soil, shivering from the impact of being thrust there. No sign remained that they had been anything but alone.

St. Fond cursed softly, letting his sword arm drop to his side. He turned and started to speak, then fell silent. Turning to his mount, he grabbed his bags and lifted them free, moving to the side and finding the same stone outcropping that had shielded Lacroix the night before.

Du Puy stared off among the trees without moving for a long time. There was nothing to see, and as the night continued to slip slowly past them, he settled back beside the cavern's opening with a heavy sigh of frustration, his sword across his knees. Noirceuil's blade stood where it had been left, like a gravestone, or a thin cross, its moon-shadow lengthening as the hours slipped by with interminable slowness.

Montrovant reached the first landing of the stairs and glanced up and down the corridor, eyes narrowed. What he sought was not those who inhabited this place, but the treasures they protected. Logic led him down and in, and since they were already at the lowest levels, he needed to move toward the mountain's heart. He glanced for a long moment at the stairs leading up, then shook his head, turning to the right.

Jeanne was at his heels, moving quickly, but pressed tightly to the wall. Each knew that stealth was likely pointless. If they were correct, and they were not expected this way, this soon, they had a chance. If they were discovered, the only way in would be through Gustav and his brood...possibly Kli Kodesh in the bargain. The outcome of such a battle was not in doubt.

They rounded the first corner and found that the passage ahead widened. "It is headed inward," Montrovant said softly. "The vaults will be at the deepest, most secure point."

Jeanne nodded. They moved down the hall, letting their eyes wander over the walls and down each side passage. There was little sign of the keep's inhabitants at this level, though there were dusty footprints leading inward. Montrovant followed these, not knowing exactly why. The footprints led them in a winding path toward the mountain's center, and suddenly, Montrovant stopped, pressing Jeanne to the wall quickly.

Ahead the hall shifted again, continuing straight and turning again to the right. Around that corner, where the footprints led, Montrovant sensed others.

"Guards," he hissed softly.

Jeanne nodded, eyes bright. If there were guards, then this was the place they sought. But how to get past the guards? They would be members of the Order, strong, not too old; in fact, not much older than Jeanne himself, but they would not be easy targets. The sounds of the scuffle might alert the rest of the keep.

"Wait," Montrovant said. The dark one's eyes were glittering, but he was smiling, and Jeanne watched in wonder as his sire stepped quickly around the corner, walking straight for the doors as though he had every right in the world to be there.

There was a startled gasp, but no cry. The two guards stood, watching Montrovant approach, for a long moment.

"So," Montrovant said jovially, "this is it. This is what Gustav has been ranting about all these years."

The guards were confused for only a moment, but it was enough. As they moved to the sides, crouching at his approach, Montrovant sprang.

He was a dark blur, and the guard to the left of the door was in his grasp before Jeanne registered the motion. Leaping around the corner, Le Duc distracted the second, and that was all it took. A head rolled past Jeanne's feet as he moved, and he dodged it, springing at the second guard. He was too late. Montrovant was there already, the vampire hoisted high over his head, and then drawn down.

With a single rippling jerk of strong shoulders, the dark one lashed out with his hand, nails curled to claws, and ripped the throat from the second guard, flinging the remains against the wall with a sickening crunch and following through, boot placed on the guard's ruined throat, hands gripping long hair, He yanked hard, wrenching the head from the body with a single motion and flinging it back toward the passage beyond.

The entire battle had taken only seconds, and Jeanne stood, the rage seeping back out of his mind before it had fully bloomed. He stared at Montrovant in wonder. He'd never seen his sire move with such single-minded purpose, nor had he seen him display that sort of viciousness toward another of the Damned.

"It ends this night," Montrovant said softly. He turned to the huge stone doors and moved closer, gaze sliding quickly over the surface of the door. Jeanne watched carefully. There was no evidence of a latch, or a lock, but it was obvious that this huge stone slab was the door. The question was how to get past it.

"It is a puzzle," Montrovant said at last. He pointed quickly at several spots on the stone surface, and as Jeanne looked more closely, he could see small smudges where the dust had been disturbed.

"It is a code. There are so many combinations it

would take years to try them one by one...and they know this. We have to figure out what sequence would be chosen."

Jeanne's eyes widened. "And how do we do that?"

Montrovant thought hard. His fingers shot out and pressed in a certain sequence. Nothing. Frowning, he tried again. Jeanne watched, wondering how many attempts it would take before the futility of it struck home.

Then, with a soft cry, the dark one pressed a third sequence, and without a sound, the huge stone began to slide to the side. Jeanne stepped back, crying out. "What," he started, "what in hell's name did you press?"

Grinning, Montrovant moved through the open portal into the shadows beyond. "There were more than five depressions," he said softly. "There were twenty-two, as in the Hebrew alphabet. It was just a matter of figuring which name would be the code...Kli Kodesh is too fond of games to make it more difficult than that."

Jeanne still stared.

"I tried Gustav first," he explained. "Nothing. Then I tried Gustav backward to be certain. Next it hit me. Who guards the treasures here, or who is the guardian?"

"Santos?" Jeanne breathed the name with sudden distaste, but then started to laugh softly. "He still guarded it all then, even beyond his destruction."

Montrovant nodded, turning toward the interior

and scanning the room beyond carefully. It was empty, a stone floor leading to another door, this one of wood, and not so large. There was a large, open expanse of stone floor between where they stood and that door, and the very barren nature of the room stopped Montrovant in his tracks.

He glanced down and cursed softly. He could just make out the footprints they'd been following down the passage beyond the door. They minced back and forth, first here, then three feet to the right, then back the left, an odd, dancing pattern.

"Don't move," he said softly. He placed his feet directly on the first of the prints, then dodged left, meeting the floor where the next smudge showed itself and leaping to the right suddenly. Jeanne watched carefully, and when Montrovant was safely ahead, followed the same motions.

It was slow going, but there was no way to hurry it. Any wrong step would set off whatever security was in place, and both knew that it would be designed for both human and vampiric intruders. The short span seemed to stretch on forever, but it was actually only a few moments before they stood, side by side, in front of the second door. This one had a large, ornate brass handle, and Jeanne reached for it, ready to press the portal inward and move on. Montrovant grabbed his wrist suddenly and very hard.

"No," the dark one hissed. He pointed to the handle. It was glistening, shining and smooth, and seconds later, Jeanne understood. There were no smudges. The handle had never been touched, or not recently, and yet someone had entered the vault ahead of them.

Scanning the door, Jeanne saw a small square indentation. Leaning in closer he noted the small smudge in the center of it, and he pressed it softly. The door swung open easily. They both stood very still, waiting to see what would lie beyond before moving inward.

The second chamber was smaller and narrower. There was a single short passage leading to the door beyond. No wide floor for dancing cryptic steps, and yet, something about it sent a tingle down Jeanne's spine.

Montrovant looked carefully at the floor. He examined each stone, but found nothing. There was no dust this far in; the sealed doors had kept the floors and walls smooth and clean. He glanced at each wall. There were shadowy alcoves all along the short passage, but it was impossible to make out what lay inside each from where he stood. The stone corners blocked his view effectively.

Reaching into his pocket, he pulled free a pouch full of gold coins. Glancing back at Jeanne for a second, Montrovant shrugged and turned to the passage, tossing the pouch ahead of him and ducking back against the frame of the door. The pouch landed on the stone floor directly between two of the alcoves. Nothing. They waited only seconds, then Montrovant took a step into the hall and another.

Jeanne somehow heard the sound first and, taking Montrovant roughly by the hair, dragged him back. The dark one cried out, spinning and slashing at Jeanne as if he were being attacked, but in that instant a long, razor-thin blade sliced the air where his neck had been moments before, disappearing into the stone alcove on the far side, directly over the pouch. A delay.

Rising quickly, Montrovant grinned at Jeanne, who returned it. They stepped into the hall, moving toward the pouch, and the first set of alcoves…and Montrovant glanced up. Handles had been imbedded in the stone and cleverly disguised as cracks and niches. He smiled and leaped, moving across the ceiling like a huge bat. Jeanne, feeling a bit more cautious, waited until his sire had crossed the passage and dropped before the next door before he leaped, following after. No traps were set off, and they reached the door unhindered.

This one had a plain brass push-plate, and a hand print was clearly visible. With a shrug, Montrovant pushed it inward and stepped through.

They both stopped still, gazing into the room, silent, and overwhelmed. Chests lined the walls. There were tarpaulins thrown over each, and none were open, but both knew they had reached their goal. This was it, the vault. One of those chests, if they had not been chasing fool's gold all these years, contained what they sought.

There was a sound behind them, and Montrovant moved quickly...without thought. He closed the door tightly, and leaped to the first of the chests, that nearest to the door. It was heavy, very heavy, and he pressed it against the door at an angle, tilting it up on end.

"Move," he cried. "Quickly, search them all."

Jeanne leaped to obey, knowing they had little time now, and suddenly catching the fire that had held his sire in its sway for so long, the Grail. It was here, he sensed it, so close they could touch it if they could only find the correct crate.

He dove for the first, tearing up the lid and digging into the contents quickly, knocking a small vial to the side carelessly. The glass cracked, but did not break, and the maggot inside began to squirm about in silent rage as the vial rolled against the stone wall, forgotten.

NINETEEN

Gustav had wasted no time in gathering his men and making his way to the lower levels. Montrovant would be finding his way into the keep soon enough, if he hadn't already, and though the vaults were very secure, this didn't still the sudden fear in Gustav's heart that they had not done enough. That vault would have held off an army of men, and most vampires would be shuddering in their final death from the myriad of traps that lined the floor and walls leading to and inside the vault.

Montrovant was not a man, had not been for centuries, and he was certainly not most vampires either. Had that been the case, Kli Kodesh would have tired of the dark one long before this. There were five of them that descended the stairs, the others clustered and spreading out in different directions, searching each level and the walls above. Gustav and his five made straight for the vault.

The tunnel that Abraham and the girl would have taken could still be open. There was really no way to know without crawling in to check, and there was no time for that. If the dark one was in already, he would have gone straight for the thing he sought. If not, that was still where Gustav wanted to be if Montrovant *did* appear.

They rounded the corner and Gustav growled low in his throat, leaping forward. He saw what remained of the two guards and their severed heads, crumpled on the floor and rotting, turning to dust. Too late. The door was open, which meant the first code had been broken. Sliding around the corner, he eyed the first room carefully. There was nothing. Somehow, despite the intricate pattern needed to pass through, Montrovant was not there, and not destroyed...and the door beyond was open as well.

Gustav stepped carefully through the doorway, placing his feet and concentrating. This was no time to give in to the temptation to leap and charge. He would die the death he'd intended for Montrovant, and spring the traps in the bargain, making escape that much easier. He took the first steps, leaped to the side, then back, counting slowly to himself and moving like a darker bit of shadow across the floor.

DAVID NIALL WILSON

His followers kept back until he'd started, then followed, mimicking his steps carefully. They made little sound, but even so, there was a sudden scuffling sound ahead, and Gustav knew that the dark one had heard them. Cursing, he doubled his speed, taking chances. He'd done this a thousand times, perhaps more...he would make it through, and when he did, he would bring this to an end.

The first time he'd faced the dark one, there had been no chance to test him. The second time they'd met under the gaze of Montrovant's sire, and Kli Kodesh, and no conflict had been allowed. This time it would be decided once and for all. He was nearing the door when one of his followers missed a step. It wasn't a large mistake, a single stone on the floor, less than a foot from where he should have stepped.

Gustav cursed and leaped, leaving the ground and stretching toward the doors ahead, leaping too late. The floor gave way, and from where the stone had lain seconds before, sharp wooden stakes shot up viciously. There were not a few scattered spikes to be avoided, but a forest of them. There was one every foot, their wicked points gleaming, polished and hardened by fire.

There were screeches all around him as he pivoted in the air, trying to reach the door frame with his fingers, to drag himself free of that forest of pikes. He was soaring, just beyond the sharp points, the wails of those behind him drowning his thoughts. Then he had it. He touched the frame, extended his hands fully, and drove claws into the door frame. He lifted himself up and over the spikes, twisting and coming to his feet just inside the frame, spinning quickly to scan the room behind.

All were five gone. The one who had misstepped stood still, a spike driven up straight through his body, another through is leg, a third splitting his arm. The first spike protruded from his head, holding him fast, and though he struggled feebly, there was no way to save him...nothing to be done. The mechanism to lower the pikes was on the far side of the room now. There was nowhere to go but forward.

Turning, a low growl starting deep in his chest, Gustav leaped, gripping the handholds in the ceiling easily, swinging across as quickly as his arms could move him. The door at the far end was closed, but that would not stop him for long. If he had to break it from the hinges, he would get through it and he would get to Montrovant. The dark one would not win after so many years, so much effort and pain. Not unless Gustav died in the process.

Gustav dropped and slammed into the door, only to bounce back, nearly falling to the floor behind from the momentum, into the very traps he'd just avoided. Frustrated, he dove forward again, pressing harder into the door. He felt it rattle, felt it bow, but it did not give. It was blocked somehow on the far side, and it was stout. It had been made to withstand a violent assault from an enormously strong being.

Beyond the door he could hear movements, and he knew the dark one was ransacking the room. He also knew the things that would be found, and the impact that could have, not only on himself, but on the world. In at least one thing Kli Kodesh had been correct. There were some secrets it was better that the world forget, and many of those secrets lay just beyond this wooden door.

It would be worse if the dark one were not searching so hard for one item. In that room there were many crates and chests, many treasures and wonders. None would be easy to find without knowledge of where to look, and the fourth protection had still to be broken. Gustav wondered if, after all, his precautions might not prove enough.

Abraham limped through the door with Fleurette's help, and they turned right down the passageway. There were enough recent scuff marks on the floor to indicate which direction the others had all gone, and they wasted no time. There was probably little the two of them could do if Montrovant had won through to his objective, but Abraham intended to be there at the end. His arm was still healing slowly. There had been no good opportunity to feed before they entered the tunnel, not without wasting valuable time, but he found that the blood he'd taken from Kli Kodesh had other properties.

He didn't have full use of the arm, but it was close, and he found he didn't need to lean so hard on Fleurette for balance. The crawl through the tunnel had been taxing, but not in a way that he couldn't handle. Abraham didn't need his arm so much to slither through the darkness, and Fleurette had come behind, pressing him when he lagged. It had taken a remarkably short amount of time to return to the lower levels of the keep.

Still, it was obvious as they moved down the passage that things had begun to happen without them. They could see that several sets of footsteps led inward along a way that had shown no sign of any moving along it when they'd passed the first time.

"The vault," Abraham said simply.

Fleurette nodded. They moved quickly, keeping to the wall, not wanting to present any more of a target than they had to, and having no idea what they would be breaking in on when they reached their goal.

They rounded the first corner and stopped. Inhuman cries met their ears, sounds of utter torment, and the bodies of the guards caught their eyes first, then the open door. Moving slowly, they slipped around the corner of the passage, along the wall, and peered carefully around the doorframe.

Abraham staggered back, and Fleurette could only stare, transfixed by the sight that met her eyes. The closest of those impaled was only a few yards from the door, and his head was turned back toward them, his face contorted, a wooden pike protruding from his temple at a lewd, disturbing angle, and his eyes, still moving, watching them, beseeching them.

Finally Fleurette wrenched away from the scene, and for the first time since she'd carried him on her shoulder through the forest, Abraham felt her collapsing into his arms. He held her for a long moment, then lifted her to her feet.

"We have to get past it," he said softly. "There has to be a way to lower those pikes, and we have to find it. Montrovant is in there, possibly the Grail as well. It can't end this way."

Fleurette's eyes had a glazed expression, and he shook her roughly. She moved then, drawing back a bit and staring at him.

"Now!" he cried.

Moving to the doorway, he began to work his hands over the frame, seeking, searching. Fleurette just watched him for a long time, her expression deep and unreadable. Then she moved to the far side of the door from where he stood, and began a search of her own.

They moved methodically and quickly, but the door frame yielded nothing. Frowning, Abraham moved to the wall beside the door frame. Here he found, after only moments, a series of indentations. Two of them were smudged, and without thought, he pressed them both at once.

The stone door began to slide slowly and inexorably closed, and he saw that as it moved, the pikes retreated slowly into the floor as well. Whoever died that way was meant to be trapped within as well.

Fleurette saw the door closing, and she moved quickly, before Abraham knew what she was doing. She grabbed a sword that had been dropped by one of the dead guards, moving to the door as swiftly as she could. Turning the blade sideways, she slid it between the closing halves of stone.

There was a horrible grinding, and Abraham dragged her back. The blade held, then bowed in the center, impossibly, and it looked as though it would snap. The pikes had not disappeared, but they were nearly at floor level now, and the bodies of those impaled had dropped to lie flat over the hideous spikes, none of them moving and the horrid cries thankfully silent as the throats that had emitted them turned slowly to dust.

They stood and watched. The stone had grown silent, and the pressure seemed, if not to dissipate, to grow no more powerful. The doors were stopped.

"We can't walk on that," Fleurette said softly. "The floor did not close."

He nodded, thinking. Then his eyes fell on the bodies of the guards, dried and withered, and swallowing hard, he knew he had the answer.

He didn't speak, and he didn't ask what she thought. If she'd fought him, he didn't know if he could do what had to be done. He hefted the crumbling remains of the first body, moved to the door, and carefully heaved it, tossing it just far enough into the room beyond that he could leap the distance with no trouble. The bones and skin-sack impaled themselves quickly and came to rest.

Fleurette's eyes had gone wide as he lifted the corpse, but he saw that they had gone cold again as he turned to her. She moved to the second guard, dragged the body closer, and between the two of them they lifted it and tossed it toward the first. Gritting his teeth and trying not to think about it, Abraham leaped into the room, coming to rest on the first body as lightly as he could, and reached for the second before he could truly think about it. It was far enough to the second door that they would need to use each twice.

As he tossed the second body again, Fleurette alighted behind him, grabbing his shoulders for support. He moved as soon as she was stable, allowing her to slide around him.

One of those that had been impaled lay near him, and he reached out, taking the corpse by the hand, and dragging hard toward himself.

The body split with a wet sound, like a ripe melon being pulped, and he shuddered but held fast, tossing the torso toward Fleurette, who watched it smack onto the stakes, then reached for it and tossed it ahead of herself.

They continued across the room, using the grisly stepping stones and eventually both were near enough to the second doorway to leap to the threshold. Here they stopped. They could see the length of the short passage, and at the other end stood Gustav. The old vampire was tearing at the wooden door in front of him like a mad beast.

"Gustav!" Abraham cried. "Gustav, wait! How do we pass?"

The old Nosferatu turned, eyes glazed with anger and madness, barely seeing the two who stood across from him. He watched them for a moment, stopping his scrabbling against the stone door, then turned away with a grunt.

"You do not," he called back. "You stay there. I will stop him. It is my destiny to stop him. The treasures have been in my custody. When it is over, if I do not survive, that job will be yours."

He returned to the door and with a sudden massive *crash* he slammed his fists into the door and staggered into the room. The chest that had been angled against the door spun crazily into the room, and the two inside turned, twin snarls and glittering eyes as Gustav fell headlong, staggering and forcing himself by the power of his will alone to rise and to face those within.

Montrovant spun as the door gave way at last, watching as Gustav fell forward into the room, then diverted his eyes for just an instant. One chest remained. They had ransacked the room, digging through each chest, tossing the contents about the room, but no sign of anything that resembled a cup. No Grail. One chest between Montrovant and his fate, his destiny. One chest and Gustav, who was rolling back to his feet.

Jeanne moved. Le Duc was not as old as Gustav, who was nearly as old to the Blood as the dark one himself, but he had other advantages. The moment the door had begun to buckle, he'd moved for his weapon. Montrovant had moved toward the chests, but Jeanne was ready for something more, something certain.

As Gustav came back to his feet, Le Duc was on him, pouncing with amazing agility. A low, guttural growl roared up from deep in Jeanne's throat as he moved, and as he swung his blade in a glittering arc at the older vampire's neck, he cried out loudly, his sight clouded by the red haze of battle, and the room slowing, nearly stopping, around him.

Gustav heard him at just the last second, rolling down and away again with a grunt, Le Duc's blade tearing away a hunk of his cloak as it passed. There was no hesitation after the miss—the blade did a quick figure eight in the air and drove down to where Gustav rolled, following, slicing sideways and this time finding the old Nosferatu's thigh.

Screeching, Gustav changed tactics, sliding into the stroke, taking the damage to his leg and swiping his arm at Jeanne's leg. Jeanne saw the motion, moved with it, leaping into the air and whirling. He came to rest, feet spread wide, balanced, and raised the sword again. Though Gustav moved with incredible speed, the battle haze had settled firmly, and to Jeanne, the entire scene seemed one of slow motion, blurred images. He saw his opponent lunge toward him, saw a long, wicked dagger slip from the folds of his cloak, all as if it were happening one image at a time, and he avoided the thrust easily, sliding to one side, feeling Gustav glance past, and driving his fist, which still gripped the pommel tightly, into the side of Gustav's head, sending him reeling toward Montrovant.

The dark one looked up with a growl. He had his hands on the lock of the final chest, preparing to rip the lid away, but there was no time. Gustav, seeing that the momentum of his stumble would take him to his goal, moved with it, dagger and hand extended, eyes deep with hate.

Montrovant dove to meet Gustav's charge, glaring in fury. He was there, and Gustav stabbed, but the blade cut only air and what had seemed to be the dark one proved only a wisp of shadow, as its owner stood high behind Gustav, arms raised and crashing down hard over the Nosferatu's back, driving him to the floor. Montrovant moved forward as if to finish what he'd started, but Gustav rolled away, and then there was another distraction, voices, from the door, and Abraham, followed closely by a girl who stank of Kli Kodesh's blood, swung through the portal from the hand holds on the ceiling beyond.

Crying out in frustrated rage, Montrovant slammed his boot down where Gustav's skull had been seconds before. Gustav, however, had ignored the newcomers, already expecting them, and taken those few seconds to slide away and rise once more. Le Duc turned to where Abraham now approached, crying out sharply and lunging. He would have taken the younger vampire out in the first charge, but Fleurette was too quick. She shoved Abraham ahead, and as he cried out, falling at the unexpected thrust from behind, Fleurette dropped.

Jeanne had not been expecting this. His momentum was gauged to slam him into Abraham full force, and Abraham had been in the doorway. He tried to stop...to fling his arms out and catch himself, but as he moved forward the last foot, his boots met Fleurette where she'd dropped, tripping him and sending him in a long sprawl.

Arms pinwheeling madly, crying out in surprise and sudden fear he careened into the passage beyond the door. There was a loud, whooshing sound as he passed the first alcove, a sharp, empty cry, and Fleurette, who was just rising to her feet, watched in horrified amazement as the huge blades shot out from the alcove...four of them, dicing Le Duc's body into quarters. He flew on past, and the bits of what he had been passed the second alcove, setting off three more blades, one of which caught his head, which had begun to drop down, sending it up again, skittering away.

Fleurette saw his eyes then, hollow and empty, the anger on his lips in no way diminished by the finality of his mis-step. His blade dropped, crashing and grinding, glancing off the others as they passed through the passage, clattering off the wall and setting off the last set of blades. As they slid through the passage, she saw his head a final time, and the blade, as they met. The blade lodged in Le Duc's skull solidly, swinging the remnant of him around and smacking into the wall, cleaving his skull with a soft, wet *shwuk*!

Fleurette wrenched her eyes from the image, twisting back to the room. Abraham was circling slowly to where Montrovant and Gustav were facing off again. Fleurette slid around the opposite side, knowing she was next to useless in a pitched battle with two so old, but that spreading their forces, and Montrovant's attention, changed those odds. As a diversion she was more than adequate.

"You aren't going to get it, dark one," Abraham said softly. His eyes shifted to the side, gaze lighting on the last chest. "There are too many of us, and you have no chance. How does it feel to have everything come down to this? How do you like the idea of your failure brought to you by the hands of the one you decided it was more interesting to have alive and chasing you?"

Montrovant's eyes glittered, and his lips curved into a smile. A momentary shadow passed across his face as he stared out through the doorway to where Le Duc had disappeared. Another ending. Another part of what he had been slipping away.

"Don't flatter yourself," Montrovant replied at last, his eyes intent on Gustav, who circled slowly. The dark one kept pace with his opponent. "I will drink your blood from the Grail this day, boy, and you will be nothing more than the memory you should have been when last we met."

Gustav lunged. Montrovant, ready and just a fraction of a second quicker, slid to one side, grabbing the arm that thrust the dagger to his throat and dragging it past him, tossing his opponent hard to the wall, where he landed with a crash that stunned him for just a second. Montrovant turned then to Abraham, lunging, but at that second, Fleurette dove in from the side, sending a quick kick toward his head.

Montrovant dodged the kick, barely, but it slowed his forward momentum enough that Abraham was able to move safely out of the way and aim a kick of his own, which the dark one did *not* manage to dodge. It connected solidly, and Montrovant rolled away, a flash of shadow, and was suddenly across the room, glaring back, bent slightly where his ribs had absorbed the blow. "It will take a great deal more than that, Abraham, to bring an end to the nightmare I have become to you. Do not make the mistake of believing for even an instant that I won't walk on the ground that covers you when your brief stay here is done."

Gustav was on his feet again, and Montrovant spun so that his back was to the chest. Regardless of the disadvantage it put him at, he wasn't moving away from his goal. His three antagonists moved forward together once more, and he squatted slightly, taking a defensive stance and watching warily. He knew he was faster and stronger than any of them, but he would not underestimate a foe at such a crucial moment. He had done so in the past, and he had paid the price.

Before he could make a move, however, or face another attack, soft laughter floated in from the passageway beyond, and they all froze. Kli Kodesh appeared in the doorway seconds later, a shock of hair held high in his hand, part of Jeanne's scalp still clinging to it.

"It would appear your hotheaded young protégé made a tactical error, Montrovant," the ancient cackled. "Oh, this is too delicious."

He flung the bit of scalp to the side with a shrug and stepped to the center of the room, ignoring them all and turning, taking in the scene with eyes bright. Montrovant had seen the old one in this mood before, and it did not bode well for the events to follow.

"You have led us a long way if your only plan was to end it yourself," Montrovant said at last. "I grow weary of the game."

As he spoke the dark one concentrated. He'd considered every possible scenario, or so he'd believed, for this final moment. He'd known there would be conflict, had known, even, who and what that conflict might entail. He'd underestimated Abraham, but the young one was not the danger. None but Kli Kodesh had ever truly stood in his way.

But it would end. As Kodesh turned to him once more, getting ready to make some inane comment about how entertaining it had all been, or how it would end, Montrovant struck. He lashed out with his mind, focused and powerful, putting every ounce of his will behind that strike, every pent-up frustration, every dream and desire of his long quest.

The effect was one he'd learned from Eugenio long years past, a thing he'd tried, shrugged his shoulders at, and tossed aside, but recently reconsidered. Sometimes the old ways were not wrong. Sometimes there were things one could learn if one paid attention.

There was a crackle of tension in the air, a sudden stab and draining of energy as it took effect, and Montrovant staggered back. He was blinded himself for a few seconds, but the gasps and cries around him told him that, at least in part, he had succeeded. Even Kli Kodesh let out a sudden, keening wail. For once, the old one had not foreseen everything.

Blinking once, Montrovant opened his eyes and glanced about quickly. The others were staggering blindly, fists pressed to their eyes, lost. With a fierce cry of triumph, he turned, slipping to the side of the chest and taking the hasp in his hand firmly, jerking up and out with incredible strength and flinging the wooden lid back with a crash. He only needed a moment. He had no idea how long the blindness would last.

To blind those within range had never seemed an important skill when he was new to the Blood. Eugenio had shaken his head, insisting, telling him over and over that there were no weapons one could do without, that there was an instant in time for each bit of knowledge to prove its usefulness. Cowardly as an attack, this particular bit of learning had finally found its moment.

As he tossed the lid back, he stepped back quickly. A cloud of dust had risen, as if flung, as he pressed the top open, and before he could react it had settled over him. He shook his head in annoyance, stepping closer again, peering inside, his hands tossing the top layers of packing away quickly. He was past the first layer, mostly silk cloth, and pulling packages from the interior, when he noticed that his arms seemed heavier. Blinking, he fought the sudden lethargy, eyes narrowing.

He pulled free a larger package, dragging the silk wrapper from it with a growl. A stone, a simple stone. He pulled free another, and the same thing, this one flat and oblong, but stone. A low cry rose from deep in his chest. He clawed at the box, his knees growing weaker, realizing too late his error in opening the chest so hastily. Cursing, he fought to remain upright, dragging each package free, the stones dropping away to the sides now and his bright, hungry eyes watching in panic as they fell away.

Then he slumped forward, unable to rise, the motion causing another cloud of the odd dust to rise. From far away he heard voices...heard Kli Kodesh.

"Stay back!" the old one barked. The voices were nearing, and Montrovant's fogged brain realized that the blindness had worn off. "Don't go near him until he is perfectly still and I can close that chest, or you'll end up the same way."

Montrovant felt his head crash down into the chest...hard...felt the world slipping away beneath him, and managed only a final curse of frustrated rage as his mind emptied and flowed away from him. His final coherent thought was how much he hated Kli Kodesh's cackling, ancient laughter, as it echoed through his mind and chased him into darkness.

TWENTY

Montrovant awakened slowly, shaking his head to try to clear the odd lethargy that had claimed him. At first he had no recollection of where he was, or what had happened, but as the haze faded and his thoughts returned, he bucked up, trying to rise, eyes wide open very suddenly, twisting from right to left. He could not move. His arms were held tightly, and his legs bound so completely they were held immobile. The most he could do was to writhe, worm-like, on the cold stone where he lay.

"Ah," a cold, rasping voice said softly, "he has rejoined us."

"You!" Montrovant spat. He tried to move again, actually succeeded in sliding an inch or two across the floor toward Kli Kodesh's boot before lying in place and arching, struggling against whatever bound him.

"You will find the bands quite sufficient to contain you," Kodesh said softly. "They worked well enough on young Abraham here that you should have been convinced long ago."

Montrovant shook again, screaming in rage. Helpless.

His gaze shifted about the room, and he realized he was no longer in the vault. It was a large chamber, richly hung with tapestries and luxuriously furnished. There were others, many others, gathered around, but only four stood near him. Kodesh, Gustav, Abraham, and the girl he'd seen, the girl who'd killed Jeanne.

"It was not in that chest," Kodesh said softly. "I never underestimated you after our first meeting, dark one. You would have found it and taken it if I'd made it that easy. Those other treasures were very real, and there were forces within that room that, if you knew their secrets, could undo the world as we know it. The Grail, beyond all that, is special. It is safe. You pulled away the lid, but you did not look beneath the chest, where the second vault's security begins."

"You lie," Montrovant spat, eyes blazing, and arching again from the floor. "You lie again as if it is easier to you than any other speech. If I am a fool, it is for believing you ever had the Grail in the first place."

"I will tell you truly," Kodesh said, laughing with a brittle, harsh tone that removed all trace of humor from the sound, "I have never been able to separate myself from it. You are damned, dark one, but I am doubly cursed. My existence, such as it is, is not mine to end, even should I want to. I am bound in ways you could never understand, and the Grail is very real. You were right to covet it, to seek it. You were wrong to believe you could succeed. I am not the only power standing between you and such a holy relic."

"You will not keep it from me," Montrovant raged.

"You are correct in that, Montrovant," Abraham cut in, stepping forward and leaning close. "We will keep you from it instead. I think you will appreciate what is in store for you; perhaps better than any other, you will see the irony."

He stood aside then, and Montrovant caught sight of a coffin-length wooden box. It was not quite as large as the one in which he'd imprisoned Abraham, but it looked very solid, and there were metal bands along the length of it and across the sides, waiting to be bolted in place.

Montrovant struggled wildly then, and the others did not hesitate longer. Abraham moved to his feet, and Gustav to his shoulders, and he was lifted and carried quickly to the box, writhing in their grip, and lowered inside without ceremony. He tensed his muscles, screaming loudly and tearing the skin, snapping bone, gritting his teeth as he struggled against the binding steel, in vain. The pain cleared his thoughts for a bright moment of agony, and that became the last sight, the image that stuck in his mind; the four of them, staring down at him. Each face was etched in a different expression.

Kli Kodesh, grinning as always, watched and enjoyed the play of emotion over Montrovant's face, and the thought of the dark one's fate. Gustav, eyes still angry, watched sullenly. Abraham, torn between memories of his own shorter imprisonment and near destruction, and a satisfied smile of revenge. The girl—Montrovant didn't even know her name, but she watched him with the only hint of real emotion in the group.

Then Montrovant knew only darkness as the lid was shoved into place, and he struggled harder still, hearing the metal bands wrapped tightly over the wooden lid, and the scraping of the bolts being pressed into place and cinched tight. His mind slipped slowly into that darkness, and he screamed. Over and over, louder, louder still, until it seemed the box, and the world beyond it, must crumble and fall away from the force of his voice alone. There were no answers, and the bolts were tightened quickly and with finality.

Outside the crate, the screams were only soft, muffled echoes, easily forgotten. As Gustav's men completed the securing of the crate, and carted it down to the lower level to be loaded into a wagon, the others turned away, moving to a table near the wall. Kli Kodesh sat at one end, Gustav at the other, and Abraham pulled a chair out for Fleurette to join him along the outer edge.

At first, all were silent, lost in their own thoughts. Then at last Abraham spoke.

"We will leave tomorrow at sunset. I want to get back to Santorini and Rome before too many days and nights pass away. I have a keep to claim, and a lot of questions to get answered before I know how I stand there. I'm not too happy about being chased by Noirceuil, and Lacroix is on his way back there now, as well as Montrovant's men. There will be a lot of questions on all sides, and too few answers."

"They will be happy enough to see you when you bring back both word of our new location, and that crate. I believe there are very deep vaults in the basements of the Vatican. Montrovant will not be searching for any Grails in the near future, and it will be quite the coup for your bishop as well."

Abraham only nodded. "That crate will not see the light of another day, unless the Church falls. If that happens," he added, shrugging, "he will likely be stolen, or burned, along with all the other secrets the Church hides."

Kli Kodesh laughed again then, and there was a bit more of real mirth in the sound. "Now *that* is a show I will not want to miss. I only wish, in a way, that if it were to happen, that Santos would be around to share it. Remind me one night, when I visit you again, to tell you the story of how Montrovant and I met."

Fleurette watched, and listened, her eyes dark. Turning at last, she watched Abraham closely. "I will go with you, because there is no other choice left."

Abraham stiffened. "That is the only reason? I did what I did to keep you from Noirceuil and Lacroix. I did not think of what it would mean until I held you, and realized I would lose the one being in life and death who'd taken a moment to care what happened to me. I am sorry."

She watched him still, not moving. Finally, she spoke again. "I am not sorry. Not yet. I had nothing, and that is why I left it behind so easily. I expected nothing, and was offered this. I will not decide so quickly that I hate it, or you. Too much has happened, and not all of it bad." Her face softened a bit at this. "I wanted adventure, and that you have given me, and plenty."

Gustav rose then, voice devoid of emotion. "I have much to do here. The vaults must be cleaned and repaired before Rome gets it in their head to send someone to investigate security. The artifacts must be re-packed and inventoried. It will take time, but that is never a problem for me."

"You have always guarded your secrets well, Gustav," Kli Kodesh said softly. "Even Santos was not better in that respect, and he was very powerful."

Gustav walked away and did not look back. The others fell silent, splitting off slowly as the dawn approached.